THE INVADERS

Can the strike force of a foreign army invade the United States?

Yes, when its leader is a North Vietnamese colonel who helped write the book on guerrilla warfare—and when his expediter is a black American deserter whose specialty is murder. They both understand terror and the power of fear, and know that each well-placed explosive can perpetuate havoc in a city.

Colonel and deserter are thrust together in Saigon where they form an alliance of cunning and hate. And in their path—through chance whim of the Pentagon—stands one man, a young lieutenant with no field experience. Only he suspects the scope of their plans, and the enormity of their fanaticism.

Set in 1968, the action moves from the back streets of Saigon to the deep jungles of the Ho Chi Minh trail to the drug factories of Marseilles and finally—with ruinous purpose—to the all too vulnerable New York City. The invasion is a success, the war has begun

(Continued on back flap)

by the same author

THE PROBABILITY FACTOR

(Continued from front flap)
—a highly trained unit of terrorists is on the battlefield and opposed only by one determined lieutenant.

The Invaders is a highly plausible novel of fast moving suspense whose story is fresh and whose excitement is gripping.

THE INVADERS

WALTER KEMPLEY

SATURDAY REVIEW PRESS / E. P. DUTTON & CO., INC.
NEW YORK

Published simultaneously in Canada
by Clarke, Irwin & Company Limited, Toronto and Vancouver

ISBN: 0-8415-0393-1
Library of Congress Cataloging in Publication Data
Kempley, Walter.
The invaders.
I. Title.
PZ4.K323In [PS3561.E422] 813'.5'4   75-38704

1898604

for Betty

THE INVADERS

1

The 107-millimeter Chinese rocket shell struck the wooden frame house near an upstairs bedroom window. Sleeping in the bedroom was Heather Potter, age eight. She was killed instantly in her bed. Her parents, Merle and Phyllis Potter, died moments later in the fire that followed the explosion.

By the light of the January dawn four hours later, there was nothing left of the house except the cement block foundation and various lumps of ash and metal, all joined by grotesque ice shapes created by the water from the firemen's hoses.

An official account stated the explosion and fire were caused by two tanks of propane gas used by the Potters to heat their water and cook their food. The story fit the circumstances. Rural houses around Ossining, New York, often used propane, and occasionally, an accident does happen.

But the Potters were, in truth, casualties in a war, the final three fatalities sustained during an invasion of the continental United States by an enemy force.

The charred remnants of their bodies were buried three days later. Neighbors discussed doing something about bottled gas. And then, almost as quickly as the explosion itself, the Potters were forgotten, the end of a chain of events begun four years earlier halfway around the world in Vietnam.

Lieutenant Gerald A. Skilling surveyed his first command: an empty two-room office on the third floor of a building on Rue Pasteur in Saigon. He closed the outer door behind him, leaned against it, and sighed.

His muscles twitched with the fatigue of his flight from Washington. Washington. Thirteen hours earlier. That made it what? Tuesday? Wednesday? Yes. It was midnight Tuesday in Washington. It was 1:00 P.M., Wednesday, February 7, 1968, in Saigon.

He smiled, happy his mind had been able to function enough to place him in time. His face was smooth, boyish. Even the smile didn't wrinkle it. At twenty-six, he looked twenty.

Green carpeting. He sighed again. There were four indentations in the carpet, tracks of a desk that had once stood facing the front door. On the wall, an oyster-colored square was suspended in the middle of an expanse of tired gray paint. Something had hung in that square. A diploma, perhaps.

The carpet showed scuffs and burns of cigarettes that had never reached an ashtray. A waiting room. Waiting for what? For whom?

Skilling removed his cap and ran a hand over his hair. It was short hair, cut close to his scalp to disguise his one cosmetic defect of adulthood, a receding hairline.

He pushed away from the door and walked into the inner office. His office. The green carpeting covered this floor, too, and in the center of the room sat a telephone, foreign looking, black, the line snaking its way to the wall. There were no squares on this wall; nothing had hung in here. Again, four tracks of a desk, and whoever had been in here had his desk almost in the center of the room. Skilling disliked whoever had been here. He would have his desk by the windows.

He looked down on Rue Pasteur. Confusion. The motor scooters, bicycles, and cars reminded him of corpuscles being pumped through an artery. The traffic moved in spurts, as if some giant heart forced it along.

It had been only ten days since he'd been handed this assignment. Assignment, he thought. Impossible goddamned burden is more like it. His eyes had been two of the thousands in the Pentagon that viewed, studied, computed, and rearranged military police affairs. In at nine, off at five. A nice company. Plenty of fringe benefits. He knew nothing of the military police, of guard duty, patrols, arrest procedures. He did know ledgers, office management, requisition requirements. And because he did, he had been chosen. His leadership in budget control had landed him on foreign soil. The army way. But a column of figures is a column of figures in Saigon or in Washington. So be it. Still, why me, he wondered, and he thought back to when he'd first been told.

"We're losing ten men a day in Nam by desertion." Colonel Christopher H. Lancto held up ten pudgy fingers to Skilling. "Ten," he said again. "Now, there's something wrong there."

Skilling had nodded. "Yes, sir. It does seem a high figure."

"I've been given approval to go ahead with a pet project of mine," said Lancto. "A special unit, a small force of men to be based in Saigon, whose only job will be to harass, capture, and generally raise hell with deserters."

"Yes, sir," said Skilling. "It sounds like quite a good approach."

"My idea," continued Lancto, "is to give them a free hand—to a point, of course. If this unit can bust up some of those deserter gangs over there, it'd make the whole bunch of them sweat."

"I would think so, sir." Skilling wasn't at all certain why Lancto was telling him all this. He assumed, at the time, he'd be handling the appropriations.

"Think you can handle it?" asked Lancto.

"Handle it?"

"Yes. I'm putting you in charge."

"Here?"

"No, for God's sake. There. In Saigon. I want a man there to keep things in check."

"I'd be commanding the unit?"

"You'd have complete access to Provost Marshal and Military Intelligence files. There'd be no legwork, so to speak. Too small for that. Strictly a strike force."

Skilling shifted his weight. "Sir, I—"

"Your first command, right?"

"Yes."

"Well, then, congratulations."

"Thank you, sir."

"Now, Skilling, let's just remember what it's all about. Those field men in your command have the notion that we're made of money. All right. I give 'em the fact they're out on the firing line. But if this unit is going to work, there has to be checks and balances. You know what that's all about." Lancto opened a drawer and took out a stack of service records. "These are your men. Take it all with you; get to know them. I'll give you a week or so to clear up things here."

He stood up. Skilling picked up the pile of records and nodded. "I appreciate this opportunity, sir," said the lieutenant. He shook hands with Lancto and went to his desk to study the records of his men.

"Lieutenant Skilling?" A corporal stood in the door of the office in Saigon. Skilling answered from the inner office and hurried out.

The corporal looked down at a sheaf of papers in his hand. "I got some furniture for you, sir. Sign here."

Skilling took the papers from the soldier. He studied them and saw that it was a complete list in triplicate of the furniture being delivered. "I'll sign it when you bring it up," said Skilling.

The corporal shook his head. "I'm supposed to get it signed now, sir. Before I can release it from the truck."

"You bring it up. Then I sign it."

"Well, sir, it's not the way we do it, you see." The corporal stared directly at Skilling.

"Corporal, you bring that furniture up here right now, dammit. Then I'll sign the papers."

The corporal nodded. He reached out for the papers from Skilling, but the lieutenant pulled them back. "I'll keep these. Just get moving."

The corporal disappeared down the steps. Skilling walked to the window in the inner office and looked out. Directly below him was an army truck. Two men were slouched against the side of the truck, waiting. After a moment, the corporal came out. Skilling could see them talking. Then the corporal began waving his arms, and the two other men went to the back of the truck and began unloading a desk.

Skilling studied the list in his hand. That corporal was trying something funny, he thought. Probably he was going to keep some of the furniture in the truck and sell it. Like hell. Skilling heard a knock on the outer door. He glanced out the window, but the three men were still there at the truck. He moved across the floor and looked outside. Another corporal was standing at the door.

"Yes?" said Skilling.

"Lieutenant Skilling?"

"Yes."

"Sir, I'm Corporal Steven Rhinebeck." He smiled. Then he added, "Reporting for duty, sir."

Rhinebeck's bulk nearly filled the outer doorframe. He didn't move, just stood waiting. The smile was large and genuine.

"Corporal Rhinebeck," said Skilling. "Yes. Come in. You're the first one. They're bringing up the furniture now."

Rhinebeck moved into the outer office, and he seemed even larger to Skilling as he approached. Yet, he wasn't frightening. It was his proportions. He was well put together, no part of him more massive than any other. He was like a normal man magnified. Rhinebeck raised his hand to give Skilling a piece of paper dangling there. Skilling took it.

"My orders," said Rhinebeck.

"Just relax, Corporal."

Rhinebeck lowered his eyelids a fraction of an inch, and his whole body became at ease. "Anything I can do?"

"I don't think so. Not yet," replied Skilling.

"Could I ask you, sir? Why are we workin' out of an office downtown?"

"I'll answer all your questions when everyone is here. No sense repeating myself."

"That's true, sir." Rhinebeck moved to a wall and leaned against it. He seemed content to wait. Skilling couldn't help staring at the soldier. Skilling's frame was slight, his muscles stringy and loose. This man's arm seemed to hold more power than Skilling's whole body.

"I'm big, aren't I," said Rhinebeck. He smiled.

Skilling smiled back. "You sure are, Corporal. Sorry for staring."

"That's okay, sir. I'm used to it."

"Did you ever play football?"

"That's always the first question," said Rhinebeck. "And the answer is no. And in answer to your next question—because I didn't want to."

"Okay, Corporal. No more questions."

"That's okay, Lieutenant. I don't mind."

Skilling remembered Rhinebeck as having a good sheet, and he now understood why. Any soldier would think twice before resisting arrest by Corporal Rhinebeck.

The sound of squeaking wheels could be heard in the hallway, and Skilling turned to the doorway to see a soldier pushing the desk into the room on a dolly. "Where do you want this, sir?" asked the mover.

"Over against the wall is fine," said Skilling. "How long do you figure for you to unload?"

"Couple of hours, sir," the soldier answered.

"Okay," said Skilling. "Try and move it along."

"Oh, yes, sir." He pushed the desk over against the wall of the outer office. He lifted one end of the desk and shoved the dolly out from underneath with his foot. He did the same at the other end of the desk, then picked up the dolly, and walked out into the hall.

14

Almost immediately, another soldier came in pushing a filing cabinet. Skilling pointed at the wall, and the man nodded and put the filing cabinet in place.

By 4:00 that afternoon, all the furniture was in the office, and Skilling began to check it against the list. He found two filing cabinets, two lamps, a chair, and a typewriter missing. By this time, the remainder of his unit had joined him and were lounging about the office. Besides Rhinebeck, there was Corporal Larry Cramer, Sergeant Henry Logen, Corporal William Jorgensen, and Corporal Charles Fuller. In addition, Sergeant Archie Holland reported. He was to handle the office chores exclusively, and he was thirty-six, the only man in the room not in his twenties.

The obvious theft being attempted by the movers angered Skilling. It was such penny-ante stealing he felt insulted.

"Corporal Rhinebeck," said Skilling.

"Yes, sir."

"I'd like you to accompany these men down to the truck. We seem to be missing some items."

The trucker corporal spoke up. "You missing some things, sir? You sure?"

Skilling ignored him. "If they're not in the truck, I want you to arrest all three of these men on the spot. Would you like some help?"

"No, sir," said Rhinebeck. "I don't think I need any help." He turned to the three movers. "Come on, men. Let's check that truck again."

Within five minutes, Rhinebeck was back with the missing items. Skilling signed the sheet.

The trucker smiled. "Sorry about that little mix-up, sir."

"You're a small-time hustler," said Skilling. "If I didn't have more important things to do, I'd have your ass. Now, get out."

The trucker started to speak, then shrugged, and turned and walked out of the office. The other two followed him. Skilling was left with his command.

"Come on in the inner office," said Skilling. "I'd like to give you all a rundown of what in hell we're going to be doing. Then, I'm going to sleep."

He sat on the corner of the desk in his office, and the rest of the men stood in front of him. "You can sit where you want," said Skilling. Rhinebeck sat where he was on the floor. The others found chairs and settled in.

"This unit," began Skilling, "is to be totally concerned with deserters. I'll report directly to the Pentagon, and the only book we have to follow is one we write ourselves. I'm going to be honest with you. I don't have any experience in this line of work. But you men do. However, that doesn't mean you can go off on your own. This unit may not have any rules to go by, but the army still does. And, I want you all to know that I go by army rules."

Skilling stood and shifted his eyes from one man to the next. "My orders are to know where every nickel is spent. Since this unit will operate mostly undercover, don't think you won't have to account to me for expenses. I'll give you some freedom. If the situation calls for you spending money, spend it—up to a point. But if there are any big expenses you plan to incur, you'd better check them out with me before you move, or else it'll come out of your pay. Is that clear?"

Cramer crossed his legs. "Okay, sir. We won't spend any money. But can you tell us what in hell we're going to do?"

Skilling realized then how tired he really was. It's going all wrong, he thought. He took a deep breath and held it a moment. Then he said, "The army is having a hell of a time with deserters. The big problem is the gangs. One soldier living with a girl isn't a problem—not a big problem, anyway. We're going after the gangs. You men will infiltrate, work undercover, and we'll do what we can to break up some of those gangs. Then we make sure the other gangs know about it. Make them sweat a little."

"Sir?" It was Sergeant Logen.

"Yes," said Skilling.

"Is this office part of our cover-up? I don't understand. What're we doin' on the Rue Pasteur?"

16

"I guess you could call it a political move," said Skilling. "We'll have access to both the Military Intelligence and the MP files. But we don't want to work out of either place."

"So, we're just an orphan child," said Logen. "No offense, Lieutenant, but we have about as much chance of breaking up a gang as I do of screwin' Joey Heatherton."

Skilling clenched his teeth. "Why is that, Sergeant?"

"I know of three gangs right now. I can pretty much tell you how to find them, but they're not stupid. I mean, maybe they are stupid to desert, but they're not stupid enough to let some cop like me walk in and play toesies with 'em."

"You're saying you don't think we can do the job?"

"I'm saying this, Lieutenant. I'll do any job you assign me. And so will the rest of us. But we're dealing with men who don't give a damn. Every one of them is a goddamn killer. The army made sure of that. Then, there's one other big problem. Look around."

"I don't understand," said Skilling.

"We're all white, for Christ sake," said Logen. "I'd guess eighty percent of every gang is black, and some are all black. They're even more suspicious. Every damn one of them sees himself as some sort of general who is goin' back to the States and get together an army and take over. With them, it's not just havin' a gang here; it's like a rehearsal."

Skilling slid off the desk and walked to the window. He watched the congestion—the bicycles, the motor scooters, the Renault taxis. The exhaust gases hovered like a willowy tunnel over the street.

"To tell you the truth, men," said Skilling, "I'm too damn tired to think. You made some good points, and I see what you mean. So we're going to have to work out an operation where we can do what we've been ordered to do with what we have. And we're going to do it. That's all there is."

Logen spoke softly. "Why don't you go to bed, sir. We'll report back whenever you're ready."

"I'll be in tomorrow morning—sometime. You men can be

17

here at oh-eight-thirty and get this place straightened out. You can also try and come up with any ideas you might have on how we can operate. Sergeant Holland, I expect the phone people to be here fairly early. Make sure everything is working and set up right."

"Yes, sir," said Holland. "But it won't make a hell of a lot of difference. You can't get anybody on these damn phones anyway."

"Takes two hours to call crosstown," said Cramer. "You can walk it faster."

Skilling didn't want to chatter about the Saigon phone system. He felt alone, separate from these men. They'd paid their dues, he felt. He could show them a thing or two about the Pentagon. He could tell them a good restaurant in Washington. But Saigon? A wave of self-pity swept over him. He blinked his eyes and shook himself back. The men were staring at him.

"All right, then," said Skilling. "Dismissed."

"You all right, sir?" asked Logen.

"Yes," said Skilling. He looked down at his wrinkled clothes. He felt the swelling in his stomach as his tired muscles gave way to the pressures of fatigue.

The group moved slowly out of the inner office. Skilling felt he'd muffed his first encounter with his command. Admitting he had no experience had been a mistake. No, he thought, they would have found out, and it would have been worse. Well, I've got to stop thinking about it.

He went directly to his quarters, where he quickly undressed, pulled down the shades, and crawled into bed. He didn't bother to set his alarm. Whenever he woke up, he woke up.

2

It was 4:10 A.M. when Skilling awoke, his body aching and his brain awash with doubts. His first emotion was anger. Why in hell did I have to wake up now? Shit. Then, fear. Christ, I can't do this. I'm a goddamn office manager. These bastards will eat me alive. Then, pity. It's not my fault I was in the Pentagon. It's not fair for them to shove me into a situation like this. Just not fair.

He turned on the light by his bed and went to the bathroom. He didn't look at his face in the bathroom mirror, but he splashed water on it. He felt like he had a hangover—something he'd yet to have from drinking. But a hangover must feel like this.

Back in bed, he switched off the light and lay with his hands under his head. Was he sick? No. Was he sure? No. It could be some tropical thing. Had he drunk any of the water? No. It's not that. He'd been warned about that. Perhaps it was just the air. The smells were horrible. And strange. Things were floating about in the air, foreign things. He had been breathing in some of those foreign things.

He sat up. Christ, stop it, he said to himself. Calm down. You're just tired. Go back to sleep.

He bounced himself flat again and tried to think of pleasant things. But everything pleasant turned out to be 8,000 miles away.

He considered writing his parents. But he immediately negated it. He had his own command, and even if he felt a failure so far, he was proud of the fact that he had even half a dozen men to order about. But whenever he wrote anything to his parents, they always wrote back mentioning how someone he knew in high school was married or engaged or "moving up the ladder" or dead. Christ. He knew barely half the people his parents told him about and cared about none of them.

He often felt like writing that he was pregnant and see if they wrote back that Donna Petersen or Elmer Potter or Florence Dirks had an operation.

What would he do about what the sergeant had said. He was absolutely right. Without one black, they were severely handicapped. He had briefly studied the desertion figures before leaving Washington, and he guessed the sergeant's 80 percent figure could be correct. Well, they'd just have to get along. Or he could write a memo back to Colonel Lancto.

He turned on his side, sliding the pillow under his arm. It had to work. He'd make it work.

He awoke again at 6:30 and decided this time to get up. He felt more refreshed now. Outside, he heard activity. The world was stirring.

Sergeant Holland had arrived at 8:00, fifteen minutes before Skilling. He was busily straightening the outer office, neatly stacking supplies in a cabinet.

"Good morning, Lieutenant," said Holland. He didn't seem surprised to see him.

"Good morning, Sergeant," said Skilling. "How long do you think it'll take you to straighten up in here?"

"Another hour at the most, sir."

"Could you give me a hand?"

"Sure, sir."

Holland put down the supplies and followed Skilling into the inner office. "The first thing," said Skilling, "is to get this damn door fixed. It won't close."

Holland inspected the lock. He opened and closed the door, leaning close to try and see why it didn't catch. "It seems to miss by about a quarter of an inch," said Holland. "We'll have to order a man up here to move it."

"You can't do it yourself?"

"Well, look at it, sir." Skilling walked over and bent down. Holland opened and closed the door. "See. It misses. The lock or this other thing will have to be moved."

"Couldn't we just hit the damn thing with something?"

"I'll try, sir," said Holland.

Holland returned from the outer office carrying a stapler. He cracked the door a few times and then tried closing it. "It didn't move, sir."

"Well, Christ, forget it. I'm not going to order a carpenter. Not yet, at any rate. They'll think I'm putting in bookshelves and a bar. Just forget it."

"Right, sir."

Skilling walked about the room. "Let's put the desk by the window." They both took an end and moved it near the window.

"Do you want to look out, sir?" asked Holland.

"Yes, I think so."

"Then, we'd better turn it the other way."

"No. I want my back to the window so I can turn in my chair and look out. I don't want to face out away from the rest of the office."

"I see, sir." Holland put down his end of the desk and grabbed a swivel chair and moved it behind the desk. "There."

Skilling sat in the swivel chair. He swiveled to look out on Rue Pasteur. "Yes," said Skilling, "this'll do."

"What supplies will you need, sir?"

"The usual, I guess. Pencils and notepaper. We'll have to keep a tight budget, so I want some sort of a ledger kept. I'll okay every expenditure. You know the forms for that, I take it."

"Yes, sir."

"You can keep most of the files out there, but I'd like one file in here. One that locks."

"They all lock. How many drawers do you need?"

"Four should do it."

"Yes, sir."

Holland walked to the outer office. Skilling heard him move a file. "I'll give you a hand."

The two men moved the filing cabinet into the room. "In the corner, I think," said Skilling. They placed the filing cabinet in a back corner.

"Is there a key for this desk?" asked Skilling.

"Should be in the middle drawer, sir."

Skilling opened the drawer and found two keys taped to the front on the inside. "Right." He peeled the two keys off and tried them in the lock. They worked. He pocketed the keys.

"Chairs, sir?"

"Chairs?"

"Where do you want them and how many?"

"Four and anywhere will do."

Holland nodded and began to move the chairs about, counting. "You want me to keep the couch in the outer office?"

Skilling nodded. "And the other chair."

Suddenly, it was done. Skilling sat and surveyed his office. He was open for business.

"Good morning, sir." It was Rhinebeck.

"Good morning, Corporal."

"I thought you were going to sack out, sir."

"Couldn't sleep."

"Is there anything I can do?"

"No. Not yet. I'd like to wait until everyone is here."

"Right, sir."

Rhinebeck moved to the outer office and sat down. He and Skilling were facing one another through the open door. Skilling looked down at his desk, began to make notes.

By 8:45, everyone was waiting in the outer office. Skilling rose and walked to the door. "Come on in."

Sergeant Holland said: "You want me, too, sir?"

"No, Sergeant. You keep at what you're doing."

"Right, sir."

The other five men came in and stood at loose attention.

"Sit down," said Skilling.

Sergeant Logen spoke. "Sir, I've been thinking about our problem."

"Okay," said Skilling. "We'll get to that. First, I'd like to fill you all in on procedure. As I mentioned yesterday, we're all going to have to go by the book. If any expenses are incurred, I want to okay them first. In some cases, I'll do it afterwards, but it'll have to be on the merit of the expense.

"Now, then. Some of you were late this morning," continued the lieutenant. "Don't let that happen again. A lot of eyes are on this unit."

"I think that's all clear, sir," said Sergeant Logen.

"Make damn sure it is," said Skilling. "Now, as to the day-by-day operation. I want a report each day from each one of you. I want to know what you've done, where you've been, what you've spent. It doesn't have to be long. Just make it accurate. Then, each morning about this time, we'll meet in my office. That's when we can go over your progress. Is that clear?"

They all nodded. Sergeant Logen shifted in his seat. "Do you mean we're on our own?" he asked.

"To a point," said Skilling. "If one of you hits something good, we can all work on it. Otherwise, you can pretty much work with your own leads."

Sergeant Logen smiled. "Yes, sir," he said. "I think that's a good idea, sir. I don't know about the rest of you, but I've got some definite leads."

"Let's discuss that," said Skilling. "Any of you know of any gangs operating we can hit fast?"

23

"Most of the deserters are in Cholon, Lieutenant," said Logen. "It used to be a twin city with Saigon, but they both just grew together. Now, it's sort of a section. The Chinese section."

"Why do they go there?"

"Well, sir, in the first place, the Vietnamese and the Chinese don't get along. The Viets hate the Chinese worse than us, I think." The others smiled.

"They're being offered protection in Cholon?" asked Skilling.

"Well, yeah," said Logen. "You can buy protection in Cholon. But you can buy it in Saigon, too. You can buy anything here. Cholon is also damn hard to know, too. I mean a lot of grunts go there for Chinese food, but they stay with the main streets. You get off those streets, and you'd better know where in hell you're going. And there's more back doors in that damn place than dog's got fleas. It's a perfect hiding place. That's it."

"Which makes our job even more important," said Skilling. "If we send a patrol for a gang, we'd better be able to tell them where those back doors are."

"Nobody's been able to yet," said Logen.

"We will," said Skilling.

There was a short silence. "Sir," said Logen, "there's some things you'd better know."

"Go ahead," said Skilling.

"First, this eight-thirty bullshit won't work." Skilling's face flushed, but Logen went on. "If we're going to infiltrate, it's night work. If I even get on the edge of a gang, you won't see me for a week. It's a sure tip-off if I got to report back here every morning to fill out a report."

The other four men were looking at the floor. "We'll do it my way for a while," said Skilling.

"Yes, sir," said Logen.

"You might as well get started," said Skilling. "Go out and see what you can turn up."

"Sir," said Logen, "where can I fill out a clothing allowance?"

24

"Clothing allowance? What for?"

"Well, we'll have to work in civilian clothes. And I'm certain the army doesn't expect us to wear our own clothes while on duty. So, I'd like to request an allowance so we can buy some civilian work clothes. Obviously, sir, the deserters don't wear their uniforms."

Skilling squeezed his pencil. "For today, Sergeant, just go out as you are, and see what you can pick up. Dismissed."

The five men shuffled out. Skilling thought he heard one of them giggle in the outer office. He wished he could slam the door. That bastard Logen had made a complete fool out of him. Goddamn him, I'll transfer his ass if he smarts off again.

3

Eddie Palmer felt a hand on his chest. As he awoke, the sensation of long fingernails skating over his skin made him smile. He kept his eyes closed. He thought to himself, couldn't be no MP, not with hands like that.

"Ong Eddie," a soft voice said.

Ong Eddie. Damn gook talk, he thought. He'd read about it in the small book he'd been issued when he came to Vietnam.

> As befits their ancient culture, the Vietnamese have developed over the centuries an elaborate system of addressing one another to show respect for age or a person's position in the family or one's educational achievements. As a guest in their country, you will not be expected to know these fine differences in forms of address, but you should follow these general rules:
> •Always use *Ong* (*Um;* Mr.), *Ba* (*Bah;* Mrs.), or *Co* (*Ko;* Miss) when you speak to a Vietnamese, no matter how long you have known the person.
> •In writing, the family name comes first, then the middle name, and then the first name. Thus, "John Samuel Johnson" would become "Johnson Samuel John" in a Vietnamese letter or document. In speaking, however, you do not use the family name but only the first name. In this manner, you would say "Mr. John" instead of "Mr. Johnson."
> •If you know it, include a person's title or profession in your greeting. For a noncommissioned officer, the correct form

would be "Mr. Sergeant John," while for a doctor you would say "Mr. Doctor John."

"Ong Eddie," the voice said again.

Ong Eddie, he thought. That's me. Ong AWOL Eddie. Mr. Deserter Eddie.

He opened his eyes. The young Vietnamese girl, Ngo Thi My, was leaning over him, tickling his chest. She was a prostitute, a hootch girl, and Eddie lived with her in an apartment in Cholon. He'd been there for nearly a month.

"Hey, Co My, baby," said Eddie. "What's doin'?"

"It is time I go to work," she said. "You want anything?"

"What's to eat, baby?" He rolled up on one elbow.

"Good stuff. I cook for you. You eat now. Hot. I go. You want me in bed? Got to do fast."

"No, baby, you go to work. Man, you're a weird lady, you know that?"

"No let rice burn. Bad luck. Very bad luck. Good-bye." She turned and started for the door. Eddie rose out of bed, naked, and followed her. She threw the bolt on the door lock, turned, and smiled.

"Oh, oh," she said. "Big one."

"Don't gimme none of that hooker shit, baby. Just go to work. I'll see you later tonight."

"Yes. See you. We smoke skag tonight. Whoopee. Good-bye, Ong Eddie."

She closed the door. Eddie flipped the bolt back in the lock. "So long, Miss Hooker, baby," he said to the door. He turned and tried to decide whether to go back to bed or not. It was already hot, and the bed was wrinkled and uninviting. He walked to the narrow window and looked out.

In the street below, Vietnamese men and women hurried with a smooth flowing motion, and from Eddie's vantage point, they almost appeared to be on roller skates. He checked both ways on the street, not knowing what he might see, but he usually looked out the window regularly. He figured if he ever saw a patrol down there, he'd have a two-minute start. More than enough. Thirty seconds would do.

He padded over to the food My had left for him. He pulled the rice off onto a table beside the burner. He lifted the lid. Plain rice. In another pot, he found something; he didn't know what. But from the smell of it, he guessed it was something made with the sausage My cooked often. He shrugged. Food was food. Dink sausage or a pizza on 125th Street—what the fuck was the difference, he thought.

He heaped a plate full of rice and then scooped the other mixture atop it. He found the sausage and added it as the final layer. The *nuoc mam* sat beside his plate, but he moved it away. My used the salty liquid on everything, but he shuddered at the taste of it. Tastes like fish shit, he thought.

He had learned to use chopsticks well, and he sat in a chair beside the window, still nude, and ate his lunch. He drank a bottle of Ba Muioi Ba, the Vietnamese beer, with his lunch, and he felt quite satisfied when he'd finished. He leaned back and picked his teeth with his fingernail.

He thought about doing the dishes or making up the bed but knew that My wouldn't like it. Then he remembered he'd have to dump out the rice he didn't eat. It was bad luck, My said, to have rice left. Crazy gook hooker.

Can't burn rice; can't leave any. Both bad luck. He looked into the rice bowl and saw that he'd eaten more than he thought. There was only a small portion, so he scooped it into his hand and shoved it in his mouth. So much for luck, baby. Maybe she's a crazy dink, but I ain't about to push anybody's luck, man. Not now. Besides, I always eat my rice.

He thought of his mother in Harlem, a frail woman with sunken eyes that made her cheekbones even more prominent. She looked like a woman Eddie had seen in a book, an Egyptian tomb drawing. Except Egyptian tomb drawings didn't look tired, and she looked tired all the time.

His young sister, thin, bewildered, almost seeming to wonder how the misfortune of birth had placed her in Harlem with a brother who had turned to the street and a mother who had turned to Jesus.

Rice and heat. It was all he'd ever known.

Eddie opened another bottle of Ba Muioi Ba and let part of it spill out of his mouth and down onto his bare chest. Today was going to be a big day for him. If everything went right, by tomorrow he'd be a member of the Skulls, one of the several gangs of deserters in Cholon. It was tough to get on a gang. Everyone was suspicious. But one of the members of the Skulls had known Eddie when they were both in combat. Eddie couldn't remember his real name, but he called himself Mau Mau now.

The Skulls occasionally hijacked an army truck in Saigon for their operating capital. They needed somewhere around $50 a day for their place in Cholon, four rooms on the top floor of a building overlooking a big vegetable market. The leader of the Skulls was a white man, a former sergeant first class named Calahan. There were nine other regular members, and the sergeant kept them supplied with women and drugs. He was thinking about admitting Eddie to the gang, but he was taking his time, making Eddie sweat.

Tonight, they were planning to hijack a truck, and Eddie had been invited along. "We see how you handle yourself, man," Calahan had said.

4

"Hey, Eddie. How you doin', man?" It was Mau Mau.

"Hey, Mau Mau. How's your ass?" Eddie gave a little wave as he stepped into the rooms of the Skulls. Two other members of the gang were lying on mattresses. They didn't react to Eddie entering. He looked at them. They were out of it.

"Draggin', baby. What can I lay on you, man?"

"A beer, man."

Mau Mau gestured, and Eddie helped himself to a cold beer. He sat down. "Where's Calahan?"

Mau Mau shrugged. "Who the fuck knows, man."

"The gig still on?" Eddie asked.

"It better be," said Mau Mau. "We are out of bread. You still livin' with that little gook bird, man?"

"Yeah," said Eddie. "She is good to me."

"Well, you good to her, too, right, man?"

"I give her everythin', man. Everyplace."

They laughed.

Two hours went by before Calahan showed up with three other members of the Skulls.

"Where is everybody," Calahan said.

"I don't know, man," said Mau Mau.

"Shit," said Calahan. "Those bastards know we got a job tonight."

"You got me," said Eddie.

"Yeah, man," said Mau Mau. "Eddie here is worth ten men, right, Eddie?"

"Only in humpin'."

"Shee-it," said Mau Mau, and he pushed Eddie on the shoulder.

"Can the crap," said Calahan. "We need bread. We got to hit a truck tonight. Right away. What's with those two?" He indicated the two men on the mattresses.

"They're spaced out," said Mau Mau.

"It's a hell of a time," said Calahan.

"You gave 'em the dope, man," said Mau Mau.

Calahan's face flushed red. "Get their asses up. We're goin'."

"We better get our pieces," said Mau Mau. "And one for Eddie."

Calahan went to a corner of the room and pushed back a screen. Sitting there were five M-16 rifles and a pile of handguns. "You know how to handle an M-16, Eddie?" asked Calahan.

"Like my own cock, man," said Eddie.

"Give those two .45s," said Calahan, indicating the two men on the mattress. "Let's go."

"Where?" asked another member of the gang.

"We'll scout," said Calahan. "Stick close, and keep those pieces out of sight."

For the first time since he'd deserted, Eddie felt some fear. They were on the street, eight of them, all deserters. They were dressed in civilian clothes and carried not very well concealed weapons. The two men on drugs had to be steered down the street. Eddie thought they might as well be carrying signs that said they were deserters. Anger built up inside him against Calahan. No planning. No papers. They were sitting targets.

They were walking in a small street off Cong Ly. If that bastard gets me caught, thought Eddie, I'll kill him.

Then Calahan spoke. "Get back," he said. "Here comes a truck."

About a block away, an army truck was moving toward them. There was no way of telling if there was anything in the truck, but Calahan was desperate and was going to stop it. They all moved toward a doorway and stepped inside.

One of the men on drugs spoke. "I'll stop it, man," he said. He pulled out his gun and walked to the center of the street.

"Grab the son of a bitch," said Calahan, but it was too late. The truck was bearing down, and the deserter was outlined in the headlights.

He raised his .45 and pointed it at the truck. "Hey, man, stop," he said. Then he stood with both hands forward, as if to halt the oncoming truck with his body.

The truck slowed; then the driver stepped on the gas. The drugged deserter fired his .45, and the noise exploded around them.

"Run," said Calahan, and the gang bolted in both directions out of the doorway.

Eddie didn't move. He watched the truck hit his companion almost straight on. He was lifted into the air and speeded ahead of the truck for an instant and then fell to the street, one leg bent the wrong way. He skidded a short distance before the truck ran over his body.

The truck stopped then. The driver stuck his head out and looked around. Eddie heard him speak to someone else.

"The bastards all ran," he said.

A corporal swung down out of the truck and walked back to the body. The driver followed him. They looked down at the lifeless form.

"Shit, he's dead," said the driver. "What'll we do?"

"We do nothin'," said the other man. "We just drive on."

Eddie stepped out, the M-16 leveled at them. "What you do, man, is start walkin'." He gestured with the rifle. "That way."

They both turned toward him. "You son of a bitch," the driver said.

"I'm gonna drop you both," said Eddie.

The driver started to walk, and the corporal joined him. They walked past Eddie and on down the street. They stopped a little distance away, and Eddie put the rifle to his shoulder and pointed it at them. They turned and moved on to the corner and disappeared from sight. Eddie ran to the truck, jumped in, and threw it into gear. He careened off down the street, heading for Cholon.

Once in Cholon, he stopped the truck. He walked around to the back and lifted a canvas. Inside were boxes, a dozen of them.

A voice behind him spoke. "For sale?" it said.

Eddie whirled. A small Vietnamese was standing there, smiling. He looked at Eddie and then dropped his gaze.

"What'd you have in mind?"

"One moment," he said. Eddie guessed his age at about fifty, but he wasn't certain. The man walked to the truck, boosted himself up and inside. In a moment, he came back.

"Thirty thousand piasters," said the man.

"A hundred thousand," said Eddie.

The man nodded and made a gesture. From out of a building behind him, a dozen men ran to the truck. They began to unload. The older man got down out of the truck and counted out the money for Eddie. By the time he had finished, the truck was unloaded.

"You will take away the truck?" asked the old man.

Eddie nodded. "It's nice doin' business with you." He walked around to the truck and got in the cab. He drove it to the edge of Cholon, pulled it over to the curb, and left it quickly, walking back in the direction of the Skulls' headquarters.

"Hey, Eddie, I thought they got you, man." Mau Mau was smiling.

"No," said Eddie. "They didn't get me. Did everybody make it back?"

"We ain't seen Kink yet," said Mau Mau. "He was the other one on the stuff."

"Goddamn bad luck," said Calahan. "There's gonna be hell

33

to pay, and we're runnin' short of bread."

"It wasn't bad luck," said Eddie. "It was shitty plannin'."

"Fuck you," said Calahan.

"Fuck you," said Eddie. He brought the M-16 from behind his back and fired one shot straight into Calahan's chest. Calahan died with surprise on his face.

Everyone else in the room froze. Eddie turned to them. "I took the truck after you ran off. I got a hundred thousand piasters for it. You want somebody to run this gang, you can follow me. You stay here, and the Man is gonna rack your ass. It's up to you."

"I'm with you, man," said Mau Mau. "I thought about killin' that bastard myself a couple of times."

"Grab a piece," said Eddie. "Nothin' else."

Mau Mau nodded and went behind the screen. He came out with an M-16. "Anybody else?" asked Eddie.

The other three men shrugged. "Why not?" said one. They took the rest of the weapons, and Eddie led them quickly off and back to My's apartment.

5

Sergeant Logen's eyes didn't avert under Lieutenant Skilling's gaze. "You mean to lie in a report, Sergeant?" asked Skilling. "That what you're asking me to do?"

"That's right, sir," said Logen.

Skilling got up and walked to the door between the two offices. Sergeant Holland was busy at work. Skilling closed the door and slid a chair over to keep it closed. He turned back to Logen. "What if the truth comes out?" asked Skilling.

"Who knows the truth. All we know is a deserter is dead with an M-16 slug in him. It was probably some sort of power play, or it could have been a lover's quarrel for all I know. The thing is, whoever shot the bastard is not going to step forward. If he does, we can say we deliberately lied to flush him out."

Skilling sat back down. "Go on," he said.

"Well, sir, it's simple enough. From what I hear, this guy Calahan was the head of a gang. Boom. Calahan is dead, and there's no more gang. At least, I can't find any trace of them. They called themselves the Skulls. All I suggest is, we present the facts and, maybe, bend the truth a bit. There's one dead man, one missing gang. That's what we're supposed to be doing."

"I don't like it. I really don't like it."

"Of course you don't, sir. As long as we both stick to the same story, there's no harm. As I say, we can always cover our tracks by saying we deliberately lied." Logen lit a cigarette.

"I could have you court-martialed for even suggesting this," said the lieutenant.

"Bullshit, sir," said Logen.

Skilling leaped up from his chair. "Goddammit, Sergeant, you're going too far."

"Listen," said Logen, "you want to make this operation work, or do you want to play soldier? It's your choice." Then he added, "Sir."

"What I want, Sergeant, is to run this command without any interference from a smart ass."

Logen shrugged. "All right, Lieutenant, maybe I came on a little strong. I'm sorry. But all we got to show for a week's work is a lot of chits for bar bills and not one concrete goddamn lead. But this can give us a little operating room. The brass will think we're right in there. And who's to say this couldn't have happened? What we're doing by filing this report is buying time."

Skilling sat down. The sergeant was right. Too damn right. "Make out the report," he said quietly.

"Thank you, sir.

"Lieutenant, let me say something. There are at least a hundred ways I could be screwin' the government and the army. I know more black market operators than I do soldiers. I can figure out ways, and make them work, too, to drain off so much money over here it'd make your eyes bug out. But, shit, sir, I'm not. All I want to do is fake a report so we can close down some of those bastards. Now, does that make me Benedict Arnold?"

Skilling nodded. "Make out the report."

"We'll have your colonel back at the Pentagon so excited, he's liable to give us more men. There's nothing like success, sir."

"Damned if you're not right, Sergeant." Skilling looked at his sergeant. Logen's face was broad, and his neck was wide. His entire head and neck had the appearance of being the business end of a bullet, except for the hair. It was long and shaggy. "Sergeant."

"Sir?"

"Do you have any suggestions about the operation of this unit?"

Logen seemed to study Skilling for a brief instant. Then he spoke. "Yes, sir. I think we're scattering our shots too much. We need to show results. Let's concentrate on the strongest leads we have and make some arrests, break up a gang or two. I think it'd mold us into a unit, at least."

"A victory or two?"

"Exactly. We could also hold down expenses that way."

Skilling smiled. "You know how to get to me, don't you, Logen."

"Well, sir, let's just say I understand your problems."

"All right. Do it. But whatever direction we go, I want in."

"You want to go out on the street?"

"Yes."

"Okay, sir. No sweat. You can move with me. But you'd better let your hair start to grow. You look like you could stand inspection."

"I guess I do look pretty army."

"We'll get you a hat, sir."

"Good. What time tomorrow? Ten?"

Logen laughed. "Ten it is, sir." He turned and left the room, leaving the door standing open again.

Skilling felt better than he had any time since he'd arrived in Saigon. He picked up a pen. He started to write. "Dear Folks." They don't even know I'm in Saigon. Won't they be surprised.

6

Eddie propped up another pillow behind his head and began to read. "The easiest rule for you to remember is that a Vietnamese does not appreciate physical contact." He looked down at My, asleep beside him. He put his hand on her stomach, and she stirred. Eddie smiled.

He read. "Do not offer to shake hands unless the Vietnamese does so first. Above all, never touch a Vietnamese on the head, since a widespread belief is that the body's spirit or soul resides there and that a touch violates its harmony.

"The same goes for the shoulders," the book went on. "Many Vietnamese believe that a genie resides on the shoulder. A touch would disturb him and bring the person bad luck. If you should accidentally touch a person's shoulder, you must immediately touch the other shoulder and in that way offset the genie's displeasure. Be careful not to cross your legs so that the soles of your feet point toward a person or a shrine. Do not display emotion in public."

Eddie eased slowly out of bed. My continued with her regular breathing, and Eddie walked to the window. He looked out. Christ, he thought, this is a long way from 125th Street. He held up the book in his hand and continued.

"When you give a gift, hold the present with both hands.

Even when you offer cigarettes to a Vietnamese friend, it should be done in this manner.

"While many of these beliefs may seem odd and out of place in a modern world, they are very real to the Vietnamese. Respect them, and you will gain the firm friendship of the Vietnamese you meet and work with."

Eddie put the book down. He took his clothes from the back of a chair, slipped them on, and then sat in the chair to put on his shoes. When he had finished dressing, he slipped quietly out of the door and walked off briskly down the street.

He had some difficulty in finding the place he'd stopped the truck. The streets were unfamiliar to him in this area of Cholon. But after about half an hour, he found where he'd parked the truck two nights before. He entered the shop where the men had gone. The shop sold curios and souvenirs. A young woman was behind the counter.

"Good morning," she said.

"Good morning," replied Eddie. "I want to see the man who runs this place."

"May I not help you?" she asked.

"I have business with the man," said Eddie. "Would you please get him."

She gave a slight bow and disappeared into a back room. Eddie looked around. Mostly junk stuff. If this guy was in the black market or some kind of racket, this place was a front for him.

The curtain parted to the back room, and the Vietnamese who had bought the goods from Eddie was standing there. His face did not show any sign of recognition. Eddie kept his face still.

"Yes?" said the man. "You wished to see me?"

Eddie bowed his head. "It is nice to see you again," said Eddie.

"Again," said the man. "We have met?"

"Could we talk alone?"

"That is not necessary. What could we have to discuss?"

Show no emotion, Eddie thought. "Stolen goods, hijacking, murder, and money," said Eddie.

The old man spoke sharply. "Tho," he said. Through the curtain stepped a Vietnamese about Eddie's age. He had his hand behind his back.

"Hold it, my friend," said Eddie. "You misunderstand." Eddie reached into his shirt pocket and brought out a pack of cigarettes. He extended the pack with both hands. "May I offer you a cigarette?"

The old man bowed and took one. The girl extended a lighted match, first to the old man and then to Eddie.

The old man puffed and then said, "How do I misunderstand?"

"My name is Eddie Palmer. I am the leader of a group of men. I am a businessman, and I am offering you a business proposition."

The old man flicked his head, and the young Vietnamese returned to the back room. "Please come in."

Eddie bowed. "Thank you." Eddie walked past the old man, who stepped aside, and entered the back room. It was an office, rather plain. There was another door leading out of the room. It was closing as Eddie stepped in. Eddie stood in the middle of the room until the old man had entered and seated himself.

"Sit down, please," said the old man.

"Thank you," said Eddie.

"My name is Duong Van Minh," said the old man.

"I am pleased to meet you, Ong Minh."

"You have been here long?"

"No."

"You do well."

"Thank you."

"Some tea, perhaps?"

"Thank you."

Eddie waited until he was given the familiar green tea. The

girl served it, and Eddie looked directly at her only once. She had brown eyes big enough to swim in, thought Eddie. Maybe he could make more than one deal here.

The old man then spoke. "You came about a business transaction?"

"I wish to organize my men," said Eddie. "I need a place to sell my goods. I don't know your business, and I don't want to know, but I need someone I can go to. I also need someone I can buy from. I want forged papers. I want other quarters for the men and myself. Safe quarters. I come both as a supplier and a customer."

"What is it you have to sell?"

"With a little notice, Ong Minh, I will sell you anything you want. On order."

"It is dangerous work."

"I figure we rent some sort of a warehouse as a dropping-off point. We can settle the money—fair money, Ong Minh—once a week. I sell to you; I buy from you. All at a place some distance from both of us."

"Most interesting, indeed." The old man peered at Eddie, and Eddie held his eyes. "This group of men of which you speak. Are they reliable?"

"I will be responsible for them. They are not reliable. But they will be."

"I will think over your business proposition. Can you return tomorrow?"

"Tomorrow," said Eddie. He stood, bowed, and left the back room. The girl was standing beside the door. Eddie stopped.

"You been workin' here long?"

"All of my life," said the girl. "That is my father."

"Figures," Eddie said, and he walked out onto the street.

When he returned to My's room, she was awake and talking to Mau Mau. "Hey, man, where you been?" asked Mau Mau.

"I been doin' business, man," said Eddie. "Big business."

41

The next morning, Eddie awoke early. He quietly woke Mau Mau. "What you want, man?"

"Get up, man. You gonna protect my flank."

"What you talkin' about, man?"

"Move it, man. We got big business."

Mau Mau followed Eddie back into My's room. She was asleep, and Eddie kept his voice low. "I got your uniform of the day, man." Eddie went to one corner of the room and pulled out a wrapped-up bundle. "Put this on."

Mau Mau unwrapped the bundle. "It's a gook pair of pajamas. Man, you think somebody's gonna take me for a gook. You and me is niggers, man."

Eddie smiled. "You wear that hat. It won't cover your face, but from every direction but the front, you'll look like a gook. Take the stock off an M-16, and put it in that basket over there. Carry the basket in front of your face if somebody looks like they're comin' over to you."

"What am I supposed to do, man?"

"I told you. You're protectin' my flank. I got this hard-nosed old gook I'm goin' to see. I don't trust his ass. He's not gonna turn me in, man, but he might just mess with me to see how good we are, you dig?"

"No, man."

"He's got a black market operation goin'. I'm tryin' to set up a nice deal for us. It'd be good for him, too, but he's got to know whether he's dealin' with pros or not. Listen, you stand by the door. If there's any trouble, I'll give a little whistle. You drop that basket, and you point that M-16."

"I point good, man."

"If things gets too tough, man, you spray, you dig?"

"I dig. I dig." Mau Mau took off his clothes and put on the Vietnamese clothes. The long trousers all but covered his sandaled feet. The tunic buttoned up around his neck. Finally, the cone-shaped straw hat fit down over his head. Eddie had been right. From the back, he looked not unlike a thousand others on

42

the streets of Saigon. The only problem was his height.

"I wished you could scrunch down, man. You're too tall for a gook," said Eddie.

"Shee-it, man, gimma break."

Mau Mau kept about ten paces behind Eddie as he walked along the streets of Cholon. For the first few blocks, Eddie checked Mau Mau. But, eventually, he relaxed somewhat. Mau Mau not only stuck with him, but he seemed to keep an open path between them, sometimes crossing a street to do it. He's a good man, thought Eddie.

Eddie stopped in front of the old man's store to give Mau Mau a chance to come up a bit. Then he walked inside. The girl was there.

"Is Ong Minh here?" asked Eddie.

The girl bowed and gestured with her arm to the back room. Eddie crossed the store and stepped inside. The old man was seated at a table, writing.

"Ah," said the old man. "The American deserter."

"Good morning, Ong Minh."

"You have returned."

"I said I would."

"What is it you seek?"

"An answer."

"So. My answer then is that if you are not out of my shop immediately, I will call the authorities and have you arrested. You have dishonored my name and my house." He struck a small brass cymbal on the table with his index finger. Instantly, the door behind him opened, and two young Vietnamese stepped into the room. They closed the door and stood facing Eddie.

"If my name was worth a shit, man, I'd say you disgraced the hell out of it yourself." Eddie whistled and remained facing the three men.

As they stared, Eddie saw the old man's eyes shift to the door Eddie had just entered. Eddie stepped aside and turned. The

43

young girl walked in with Mau Mau a step behind her, his M-16 pointed at the small of her back.

The six people stood, not moving now.

"It's your move, Ong Minh," said Eddie.

The old man lifted his hand slightly, and the two younger men left through the back door. "May my daughter return to the shop?" he asked.

Eddie made a similar gesture, and Mau Mau lowered his rifle. She stepped back out into the shop, and Mau Mau followed.

"Well done, Ong Eddie," said the old man. "Tea?"

When Eddie left the shop nearly two hours later, he fought to keep from shouting out on the street. He was in business— big business. Minh's operation staggered him. It was worth millions, and Eddie and his gang had become a part of it.

He and the old man had worked out a system. Eddie was to be on call, at any hour, for Minh. Minh could supply false papers, uniforms, whatever was needed for Eddie to roam freely in Saigon. Minh also knew of various cargoes about the area, material that would bring high prices. All Eddie had to furnish was the muscle. Neither was to interfere in the other's operation, and the only thing they would share was profits.

Minh had provided Eddie with new quarters. He had also approved of Eddie's idea about the warehouse. It would be the drop-off point for everything. It was large enough to handle more than one truck, and it had a rear exit.

It only remained for Eddie to start supplying the goods. And their first hijacking was set for late that afternoon.

7

"You look at the eyes, Lieutenant. The pupils. His are the size of a pinhead. He's high." Sergeant Logen and Lieutenant Skilling were having a beer in a bar in Cholon. They were both wearing civilian clothes.

"Shall we take him in?" asked Skilling.

"I suppose we could. But that'd be the end of us around here. Word gets around fast. And all we'd have is one junkie deserter."

Skilling nodded. "Could we follow him?"

"He could be a gang member, Lieutenant. But, usually, they hang together. There'd be two of them or three. No, I'd guess he's probably a loner—living with a hootch girl and high half the time on cheap skag. But listen, Lieutenant, if it'd make you feel any better, I'll call in a couple of MPs. We'll have to let them roust us, too, but it'll give us another report." He smiled at Skilling.

The lieutenant smiled back. "All right, Sergeant. At least I won't have to fake this one."

Logen left the bar and was gone about three minutes. He came back then and sat down beside the lieutenant. "They should be here in a few minutes," he said.

The two MPs came in quickly and efficiently. One moved

toward the bar area while the other kept near the door, on the ready. The lieutenant watched with fascination. He was seeing his first actual arrest.

The inside MP came to them first.

"Papers," he said.

Logen and Skilling handed him their papers. He read them, looked them each in the eyes, and then returned the papers.

Then he moved down to the other man. The deserter hadn't actually noticed the MPs. When he turned, his mouth started to move. Then he put both hands on the MP's chest and shoved. It caught the MP off guard, and he stumbled back, falling over a chair.

The deserter bolted for the door, and the second MP stood in his path. The deserter was committed now, and he ran headlong for freedom. Skilling watched as the MP raised his stick. He brought it down on the deserter's head and stepped aside with the grace of a bullfighter. The deserter took a half step and collapsed on the floor, his face sliding into a table leg.

By then, the fallen MP had reached the downed deserter. He placed a sharp kick into the man's ribs, and the crack could be heard throughout the bar. The lieutenant started to get off his stool, but Logen's hand restrained him. Skilling relaxed.

The two MPs then picked up the man by the shoulders and dragged him out of the bar. It was all over in less than two minutes.

The Vietnamese bartender had stood motionless the entire time. When they all heard the sound of a jeep driving off, they let out a collective sigh.

"Jesus, Sergeant," said Skilling. "Was that really necessary?"

"No," said Logen.

"I guess you get sadistic men in the MPs no matter how hard you try," said the lieutenant.

Logen turned slowly and stared at the lieutenant. Then he continued on around and put his elbows on the bar, facing the door. "Sir, what can I tell you? Those men aren't your normal, everyday Americans. On the other hand, this is—" He stopped

46

and put his hand on the lieutenant's arm. "Come on. Quickly."

The sergeant got up, and Skilling followed him. He went out onto the street and took a quick left and began walking.

Skilling caught up. "What is it?"

"See the tall Vietnamese ahead of us—the one in the black pajamas?"

"Yes."

"He's as black as his pajamas."

"Another deserter?"

"Hell, yes, Lieutenant. But this one is different. That's no junkie. He's up to something, and he's sure as hell a member of a gang."

"Why?"

"I think he's riding shotgun for that man ahead of him. See?"

Skilling noticed another black walking about five paces in front of their man. "I see him."

"We'd better split up, sir. Two of us are too much. Either drop back or cross over. Move away from me somehow."

"Right."

Skilling took a half right and crossed over to stop in front of a fruit vendor's stand. Then he slowly began to follow again, keeping behind and to the right of Logen.

They came to a corner. The two men ahead turned left, and Logen was almost to the corner when the two men appeared again. They had turned left, made a U-turn, and were heading out to the right. Logen quickly moved on, cutting almost directly in front of them. He continued on up the street. Skilling acted quickly. He turned right, about fifteen feet ahead of his quarry. He walked casually, looking about, but he didn't wait for them to catch him.

About halfway down the block, he stopped at a shop. Strings of brass bells hung in the doorway. Wicker baskets piled atop one another afforded Skilling the turn he needed. He looked back down the street just as the black dressed in the Vietnamese clothes turned into a doorway.

The lieutenant found he was holding his breath. He relaxed

and continued to look at the goods in front of him.

He was considering what next to do when a voice behind him said, "Lookin' to buy a basket, Lieutenant?" Logen had circled the block and come up behind him.

"Logen, this is hellish work."

"Did you get a make on the house?"

"See the three-wheeled bicycle with the wood piled on it?" Logen nodded. "That's it."

"Good work, sir. Now, this is more like it. I'll go round up some more of the men. We'll check out the building."

"Can't we just raid it?"

"Which room? They sure as hell have another way out in case of emergencies. And, besides, we don't know how many of them there are or how well armed they are."

"Okay, Sergeant. You flushed them; we'll play it your way. I'll go get some help."

He started off down the street. Logen called after him. "Sir. Not that way. Back the way I came."

Skilling stopped. He nodded at Logen and turned around and headed out of sight.

When the lieutenant returned later with Corporal Rhinebeck, the sergeant was gone.

"No offense, sir," said Rhinebeck, "but are you sure this is the right street?"

It was a good point, and Skilling looked around. "Yes. Yes, I'm sure. There was a bike parked in front of the house, but it's gone now."

"Which one, sir?"

"See the shop with those big bales in front of it?"

"Yes, sir."

"It's the next one down."

"The kind of brown one?"

"Yes."

"Okay, sir. I've got it."

"You wait here. I'll try and find out what happened to Logen."

48

"Don't worry about it, sir. He can handle himself."

The lieutenant looked around. "I'll make a phone call at that bar over there on that corner."

"Got it, sir."

Skilling turned and walked toward the bar. He found a phone and put a call into Sergeant Holland. Holland reported no word from Logen. Skilling gave Holland the number and location of the bar and then ordered a beer.

About half an hour had gone by when Skilling saw Logen walking casually down the street. He breathed a sigh of relief. It wouldn't do to have one of his men killed by a deserter. He watched Logen talk to Rhinebeck. Then Logen and Rhinebeck both turned and walked toward the lieutenant.

"It's all set, Lieutenant. We got lucky." He turned to the bartender. "Ba Muoi Ba," he said.

"How'd we get lucky?"

"About twenty minutes after you left, four blacks came out. Deserters sure as hell. They were packing guns, too. They stood there for a minute, and then this other black comes out with a Vietnamese girl. He talks to her for a minute; then they take off."

"Did you follow them?"

"I followed her. I figured it was her place they were using. And I knew I could tail her without any trouble. She's a prostitute by the name of Ngo Thi My. Now all we have to do is get a party ready for them. We don't even have to call for help."

"What do you have in mind?"

"I figure either they're all gone or most of them are. If we go up and wait for them in her place, we can pick them off as them come back. Simple."

"Not quite so simple," said Skilling. "What if they all come back at once. It's the shoot-out at the O.K. hootch girl's."

"We could take that chance, sir."

"Rhinebeck, call Holland and have Cramer, Jorgensen, and Fuller get here as fast as their ass will carry them," said Skilling. "And tell them to bring weapons. We're going on a little raid."

49

Logen bribed the shopkeeper in the building to tell them the prostitute's apartment. It was on the third floor, and they quietly climbed the stairs, each man carrying an M-16 rifle. They arrived at her door, and all the men looked at the lieutenant. It was quiet inside the apartment. He waved Cramer, Rhinebeck, and Fuller to the left of the door. He, Logen, and Jorgensen stood a little to the right.

"Let's take it," whispered Skilling.

Skilling reached up and knocked. Then he stepped back away from the door. The men listened. There was no sound from the apartment. Skilling knocked again. Nothing.

Logen smiled. "Try the door, sir."

The others smiled, too. Skilling shrugged and reached for the knob. He turned it and pushed. The door swung open. Before it had reached forty-five degrees, Logen had leaped into the apartment, his gun at ready. Cramer ran in behind him and took up another position. Then Skilling came in, and the rest followed.

"Shut that door," said Skilling. Fuller pushed it closed.

The men moved to another door to their left. This time Logen opened it and ran in with one motion. It was an empty bedroom.

"Nothing," said Logen.

Skilling moved cautiously to the window and looked out. "Here's your escape route, Sergeant. It's an easy jump to the next roof."

"All right," said Logen. "All we've got to do now is wait. How about it, Lieutenant?"

Skilling nodded. "We wait."

They were there nearly eight hours, but their only arrest that day was Ngo Thi My, a Vietnamese prostitute.

8

"Eddie," said Mau Mau. "I gotta hand it to you. This is a fuckin' palace."

The quarters provided by Minh were, indeed, a palace compared with the usual hideaways of American deserters. There were two floors with an exit to the roof. The top floor, actually the fifth floor of a building, had three rather large rooms. The fourth was divided into seven smaller rooms. There was a bathroom on each floor.

"We'd better sleep on the top floor," said Eddie. "If there's ever any trouble, we can just scoot the fuck out on the roof."

"Cool," said Turk, one member of the gang.

Mouse, another, smiled. "We needs some tail up here, man. I ain't screwed nobody in the past month without Apache Joe sittin' there watchin'."

Apache Joe smiled. "Shit, man, when I seen how bad you screw, I stopped watchin' the first night."

"We got some talkin' to do first," said Eddie.

"Talk, man," said Mau Mau.

"You all are shit, man," said Eddie. "You are sittin' on a million dollars, and you're smokin' skag and screwin'."

"Yeah, man," said Turk. "But if I had a fuckin' million dollars, all I'd do with it is buy skag and cooze."

"Whatcha gonna do when this war is over, man?" asked Eddie.

"This war never gonna be over, man," said Apache Joe.

"Man, whatcha tryin' to say, Eddie?" asked Mau Mau.

"I am sayin' this. I got us a deal to make big money. But we got to watch our ass. We got to get together a gang that is the best there is. If we play it right, we can all go back home with new papers and a few thousand in our pants. In the meanwhile, we can live high off the hog, man."

"I like the last part, man," said Mouse.

"I'm gonna lay it on you straight, man," said Eddie. "Startin' now, we got new rules. You remember Calahan. Well, he didn't follow the new rules."

The others stirred a little uncomfortably. They all remembered how Eddie had coolly killed their onetime leader. They knew he would cheerfully do the same to them.

"I don't likes rules, man," said Apache Joe. "That's why I got the fuck out of that mother army, man. But talk, man. I'll listen."

"I figure we can do about five thousand dollars a week. There is five of us. We divide by six. I get two shares; everybody else gets one. Dig?"

"Keep talkin', big daddy," said Turk.

"We're gonna plan every job. I'll do that. But this whole thing is gonna be organized. No mistakes. Out of the five big ones comes our expenses. Whatever's left over, we split the way I said. You can have all the ass you want. Skag, no. I don't want no operation fucked up by some hophead nigger. You get two days off a week. If you wanna go outa your mind them two days, that's your problem. But when we work, we work. Dig?"

"Man, you sound just like my captain," said Apache Joe. "You're a drag."

"That's the last thing I gotta say," said Eddie. "Mau Mau, is you in?"

Mau Mau nodded. "I do, darlin'," he said.

"Then, you is my second in command. When I'm not here, Mau Mau is in charge. You get extra for that, Mau Mau. It comes out of expenses. The rest of you has got to say right now where you stand. Because if you don't want to do as big daddy say, you get out now."

"How much you figure we can pocket, man?" Mouse asked.

Eddie shrugged. "Maybe five, six hundred a week."

"Oh, shit," said Mouse. "That's more'n I made in a year in 'Bama. You got yourself a nigger."

"Turk?"

"As longs I don't have to call you sir, Eddie. I mean, that makes my ass ache to call somebody sir."

"You can call me Governor Wallace long as you follow orders," said Eddie.

"You got me, brother," said Turk.

"Me?" said Apache Joe. "I'll give it a try."

"No try. In or out," said Eddie.

"In," said Apache Joe.

"That's good," said Eddie. "Apache, you was in ordnance, so Mau Mau tells me."

"That's right, man."

"I want you to fix those M-16s. They're too big. Too noisy. Can you do it?"

"I can damn near make a pistol out of 'em," said Apache Joe. "Silencers is gonna take time."

"Just tell me what you need," said Eddie.

"I'll draw it out on a piece of paper," said Apache Joe.

"That's good. You just cut yourself a little bit bigger slice of the pie if you keep those pieces of ours in runnin' order."

"I like pie, man," said Apache Joe. "I'll start workin' on 'em right now."

"Not now," said Eddie. "We're gonna need 'em tonight. We got business."

At 6:10 that evening, posing as MPs, Eddie and his gang stopped and hijacked a medical supply truck carrying nearly $50,000 worth of various drugs. The old Vietnamese had told Eddie of the truck.

The truck was taken to the drop-off point, unloaded, and then

53

dumped in another section of Saigon. The entire operation took a total of only an hour and forty-five minutes.

At 8:30, five prostitutes showed up at Eddie's new headquarters, and the party lasted until nearly 2:00 in the morning.

Everyone agreed that Eddie was a genius. And as Eddie said, "Man, we're gonna kick the shit outa this town."

9

It was a way station on the Ho Chi Minh Trail, a patch of stubby ground chopped away from the road into the jungle, carved inward to protect and hide it from the sky. Perhaps a hundred men were there, some heading south, others north to Hanoi. There were mostly soldiers. Then, there were the men with their bicycles and the A-frames built to fit their backs and bicycles and used to cram with supplies desperately needed in the South. Finally, there were a dozen trucks. All these, silent, hidden.

The station was called, simply, Ba. Number three. It was commanded by Sergeant Nguyen Van Hung, a thirty-two-year-old man who had been in the army since his sixteenth birthday. It was his job to check in each man who arrived at Ba each day and to give him further orders on where he should be the following day.

It was 4:00 P.M., now, the beginning of the day for men on the Ho Chi Minh Trail. By 5:00, Ba would be empty of travelers. By 6:00 the next morning, it would be full again. There would be new faces, new men. But, again, it would be soldiers and men of the bicycle brigade.

Ba contained food and spare parts. In addition, there were a small ammunition cache and a few barrels of gasoline. Trucks were being used more and more these days as action stepped up in the South.

Ba was 1,350 feet up on the crest of a small mountain. Its elevation protected it during the rains, and when many other way stations were bogged down in mud, Ba drained fairly dry.

Sergeant Hung was nervous today. His commander, Colonel Ngo Duc Linh, had slept the day at Ba. Colonel Linh terrified Sergeant Hung. Linh had been with General Giap in their victory over the French at Dien Bien Phu in 1954. A formidable man, a dedicated soldier was Colonel Linh. He was stationed in Hanoi, but part of his duty was to supply and command a portion of the trail. He did it from a room in the capital, but often, as now, he traveled his length of the trail, checking, inspecting, ordering changes. Colonel Linh had arrived from the south in the early morning and had gone directly to sleep. Sergeant Hung knew he must soon speak to Linh. He must awaken soon. Ba was stirring.

Colonel Linh was, at that moment, already awake. He heard the sounds around him. A sniffling. A quiet cough. Spitting. Each sound muffled, made by men who moved and lived and fought in silence. The wrong sound in the jungle meant death.

It was a difficult life in the jungle, and Colonel Linh felt a wave of relief to know he was headed back to Hanoi. He had spent years in the jungle, killing and hiding. Now he went out only when he felt he was becoming too remote. Foolish, perhaps, but his superiors seemed to understand.

The cover of darkness was fast approaching, and Linh knew he must be moving soon. He felt for his notebook and pulled it from inside his shirt. In the notebook, carefully folded, was a letter. There was just enough light to read it. He knew it by heart, but it helped to see the tiny, delicate scrawl of his wife. Her handwriting had been so like her.

He read.

My darling husband. And so the struggle goes on. You are so near in miles, I feel, but since I can only wonder where you are

56

exactly, you may as well be on the other side of the world. I am sorry to sound depressed. I am foolish. I think it is the enemy planes. They move so quickly, and you cannot prepare yourself. Suddenly, there is an explosion, and they are overhead. But I needn't tell you of American airplanes, my husband. I am a foolish woman to talk of such things. Hanoi has risen wonderfully to the bombings. I am proud of our people, as you must be.

Enough of the war. I saw Nhu at the market. He sends you his best. He is working repairing bomb damage. He seems to be getting along with his one arm. He says he feels lucky.

The girl next to me at the factory has become pregnant. I admire her. To be pregnant at a time like this would frighten me, I think. How can she know the future? How can she

Colonel Linh folded up the letter. It was all he had left of his wife. Their apartment and belongings had been completely obliterated by an American bomb aimed at the Hanoi power plant. His wife was found with this letter clutched in her hand. Perhaps she had known in that mini-fraction of time before her death that she was doomed, and she had grabbed at something. At anything.

Linh looked up in the sky, wondering if he, too, would die with this letter in his hand. A cursed letter? He shut his eyes to relax. In a moment, he opened them and calmly replaced the letter in the notebook. He carefully adjusted it so no piece of it stuck out past the pages of the notebook. The letter was nearly a year old now, and the paper was beginning to weaken.

He forced his mind onto the present. He became aware again of the jungle, of the dampness in the ground. He was aware, too, of the soreness of his body. He twisted the muscles of his face, curling the corners of his mouth up and down. Now he rubbed his biceps, made the blood speed up through his veins. His frame was small. His wife used to call him the perfect Vietnamese. His muscles, however, seemed stretched too thinly for his bones. The skin on his face, too, was pulled tightly on his skull, and it left him nearly wrinkle-free, even at forty-six.

The colonel now rolled up on an elbow and then to a sitting

position. He rubbed the small of his back. Was the ground damper this year than last? It seemed so. But he knew better. At his age, it was difficult sleeping on the ground. During twenty-five years, his body had absorbed too much from the dirt. He was saturated with jungle dampness.

He remembered his wedding night. He had come in that same day from over five months in the jungle, and his back had been infected by the bites of leeches. He had left blood on the silken sheets of his wedding bed. He remembered wondering if he was some sort of subhuman creature who shouldn't be sleeping in a bed with a civilized woman. His wife had cried the next morning when she saw the sheets and had bathed his back and rubbed it with salve.

How he hated Americans. They had taken her away, the only joy he had ever known, the only civilized moment he had ever experienced. In speaking to other soldiers, he repeated the accepted line: Don't hate Americans; hate only American soldiers. But he hated all Americans. He wanted them all to feel pain, the pain he felt on his wife's death. The pain he still felt. He hoped they would, one day, live through the horror of death exploding about, coming from somewhere unknown. Death always came from somewhere unknown. The sky, the horizon, the trees beyond. Always somewhere innocent, restful. Could there be anything more pure than the sky? And yet the sky had taken his wife. He ached for revenge. And if all went well, he would one day have it.

A leafy jungle growth to his left moved and his aide, Lieutenant Trunon Van Tri, stepped up and stood over him.

"You slept well, sir?" asked Tri.

"Yes."

"Do you wish to speak with Sergeant Hung?"

"Yes."

"Shall I bring him to you?"

"No." Linh stood slowly, brushing off his clothes. "I will go to him."

"He is there," said Lieutenant Tri, gesturing, "by the gasoline barrels."

Linh and the lieutenant walked toward Sergeant Hung. The soldier had seen them coming and continued to work but straightened as they neared. He stood at full attention by the time Linh came up to him.

"Ba runs well, Sergeant Hung?" Linh asked.

"Yes, sir," said Hung.

"That is good," said Linh. "All goes well all along the Ho Chi Minh Trail. The war goes well."

"That is good," replied the sergeant.

"Supplies are plentiful," continued Linh. "If you need gasoline or weapons, speak now."

"I need nothing, Colonel." He shifted his weight. The colonel made him most nervous.

"Then keep up your good work here. It will not be long now. The supplies are moving south. That corrupt government can't last much longer. But, you and I, Anh Hung, will fight on for twenty years." The sergeant stood, rooted to the spot. Linh felt the ache of his sleep travel up his back. "But it will not be necessary to fight that long, of course. Victory should come any day. Any day."

"Yes, sir," the sergeant said.

"That will be all," Linh said softly. Sergeant Hung gave a small bow of the head and backed away from Linh. Hung had been stunned by the famous warrior calling him *Anh*. Brother. Only a close friend or a colleague of equal rank would call him *Anh*. He quickly turned to the business at hand, calling for the men and trucks to speed up their movements.

Linh watched Ba clear. Soon, only the men stationed there were left. He nodded his readiness to depart and climbed into the front seat of an ancient Renault. Lieutenant Tri stationed himself behind the wheel. The rear seats of the car had been removed to clear it out for cargo. Sergeant Hung called for his men to stand at attention until Linh's car was out of sight.

Throughout the night, he and his men worked with renewed vigor.

Linh had welcomed the softness of the car seats, but they became harder each kilometer they traveled. They would be in Hanoi by morning. Linh shoved all his discomforts and pain to a far corner of his brain. He thought of the men heading south to kill and disrupt. How many times he had traveled the same trail over the past years. Now, he headed north in darkness, back to his desk, his empty life. What was left of his life? Only work. And memories. And hate.

He had seen pictures of American cities, American factories. How vulnerable they looked, how easy to destroy. How long had it been since he'd killed one of the enemy? Over a year. He thought back to the moment. It had meant nothing. There had been no sweet taste of victory in the killing. Linh remembered staring at the dead body. The soldier had been young, too young to be married. There had been no wife to grieve for him. His parents, certainly, had buried their faces in sorrow. But it was not the same. Parents and children understood death, knew it would some day part them. But when one loves a chosen mate, he imagines it will continue forever. Death is unexpected, unwarranted.

He wanted his enemy to hurt as he hurt. He wished them pain and suffering and the endless torment of despair. But wishes meant only more agony for him. His enemy lived beyond his reach. He was alone in the jungle.

Still. There was the plan.

"Lieutenant."

"Sir."

"I have watched your career, and it pleases me," said Linh.

"Thank you, Colonel." Lieutenant Tri moved in his seat.

"It resembles my own," said the colonel. "Perhaps that is what struck me about it. You rose from the ranks. I was educated in the military ways by the French. Still, I often think that had little to do with any success I have had."

"You are a dedicated soldier, sir," said Tri.

"Yes." The Renault bounced in a hole and creaked in agony. Linh put his hand on the dashboard to steady himself. "Lieutenant Tri," continued the colonel, "what do you see in the future?"

"The future, sir?"

"Yes. What are your ambitions?"

"I am happy only to serve."

"Come, Lieutenant. I know better."

Tri turned briefly to look at Linh's face. The colonel kept his head turned forward toward the road. "I have ambitions," said Tri. He paused.

"You need not be afraid to speak," said Linh.

"I am not afraid, Colonel."

"You are cautious, then."

"Yes. Perhaps."

"Tell me of your ambitions."

Tri again looked at the colonel, and this time, Linh was turned in the seat, looking directly at him. Tri turned back quickly to watch the road. He spoke slowly, pausing between each word. "I want to do more," he said.

"Yes?"

"Sir, I remember seeing a boxing match when I was younger. The men were two Thais, one young and unpolished, the other older and experienced. The older man demolished the younger one. When the young one would try to punch with his fist, the older man would kick him. When the younger man tried to kick, the older man smashed his face with a fist. No matter what the young man did, the experienced fighter caught him unawares, hit him from a direction he least expected. I feel, often, like that young fighter. I want to hit out and destroy the enemy, but I keep getting hit from where I least expect it."

"It is a frustrating experience, Lieutenant."

"More than that," said Tri. "I sometimes think it can destroy me. That, of course, is what the enemy expects to happen. And knowing that makes it even more painful."

"I am going to speak to you of a plan I have," said Linh. "You know me well enough to realize I am not given to flights of fancy. Know only that I am deadly serious. All I ask from you now is a promise to never break the confidence I am placing in you."

"Sir, I assure you that—"

Linh interrupted him with a wave of his hand. "Enough. It had to be said." There was silence for a moment. Then Linh spoke again. "I propose, Lieutenant, to take a force of men to the United States. Once there, we will rain down as much destruction as is possible on the Americans and their war plants. I will make them feel the ache of war." Linh's hands rubbed his legs. He turned in his seat. "That is my plan."

Lieutenant Tri's mouth opened slightly as the colonel spoke. He shut it.

Linh continued. "Perhaps you think twenty years of war has scrambled my brains, Lieutenant. And so it has, at least a portion of it. But I am still a soldier. And as a soldier, I tell you my plan can work."

"But surely you'll be immediately captured," said Tri.

"Each raid will be more difficult," said Linh. "However, it is my surmise that the initial raids can be carried out with no difficulty."

"What will it do to the war here? It would mean an invasion of our country."

"It will change the war. Like your two boxers, the sparring will be over. We will stand toe to toe with the enemy, each with his hands on the other's throat. When one dies, the contest will end."

"We cannot hope to defeat the United States."

"The United States will defeat itself. Many Americans are already tired of their leader's war against us. If we can hurt them enough, they will cry out for peace."

"Or an atomic attack."

62

Linh shrugged. "Either way, the contest will end."

"It seems so overwhelming."

"Lieutenant, I learned about war by being in war. Schools teach old lessons. We have proven here that ten men, properly placed and timed, can be worth a hundred of the enemy. Three men at the right turn in the road can close down a hundred miles."

"That is true, sir. But the United States. It is—so far."

"Again, Lieutenant, it is in knowing your war. One false passport in this operation is worth ten of World War II's attack landing craft."

"You have an actual plan?"

"I do."

Tri was silent for several minutes. Linh leaned back in his seat and relaxed. It was such an utter relief to finally speak openly of his plan. He knew Tri would join him. Everything is tumbling about in his head, thought Linh. But finally, he will say yes. Hearing himself say these thoughts out loud washed him with confidence. For the first time, he knew he could actually do what for so long he had only wished.

Tri cleared his throat. "Sir," he said, "if you say it can be done, I believe you. I am honored to serve with you now, and I am honored you have asked me to serve with you in your attack."

"I am happy," said Linh. "I know you will serve well in the future, as you have served well in the past."

"What is our next step, sir?"

"Our next step, Lieutenant, is to return to Hanoi safely. Patience."

10

"Turn on the tape recorder," said Skilling.

Logen nodded and pushed the two buttons on the Sony recorder. He placed the microphone on Skilling's desk a foot or so from Ngo Thi My, the young prostitute. She had barely moved since she had been brought in. Only her eyes shifted toward a noise or a movement by one of the men. Now, she stared at the microphone in front of her as though it was the head of a poisonous snake.

"Don't be frightened," said Skilling. She shifted her eyes to him. "Tell me your name."

She spoke almost inaudibly. "Ngo Thi My."

"You'll have to speak up," said Logen.

"Ngo Thi My," she said, louder.

"And where do you live?" asked Skilling.

"I live at twenty-three Cong Ky," she replied.

"What do you do for a living?" continued Skilling.

"I hootch girl."

"A prostitute?"

"I guess. I fuck for money."

Skilling sighed. "Jesus," he said.

"It's the only word she knows, Lieutenant," said Logen.

"I know. I know." Skilling moved to the desk and sat on the

corner, facing the microphone and My. "All right, My, what can you tell us about the men in your apartment?"

"Eddie live with me. He good to me. Others only been there two days. Sleep on floor and shit like that."

"Can you tell me about Eddie?" asked Skilling. "Do you know his last name?"

"No. No know his last name. Only Eddie."

"Did the others call him anything besides Eddie?"

"Man."

"Man?"

"Hey, Eddie, man. You goin' out, man. They always call each other man."

"Anything else?"

She shrugged. "No," she said. "They talk a lot. More than hootch girls. All the time talk."

"About what?"

"About fuck. About money. All the time how they make money. About army."

"Were they deserters?"

"I don't know. What is deserter?"

"Were they army men who ran away from the army?"

"Oh, sure. They all run away. They hide all the time. Plenty scared of getting caught. Except Eddie. He not scared."

"Why not?"

"He just not scared. Him and me, we sleep together. Noise come in night. I jump. I scared. I look at Eddie. His eyes open. He listen. He wait. But he not scared."

"How long has Eddie been with you?"

"One month. We meet at Dragon Lady. That bar where I fuck. I ask him to come live with me. He do. I am happy. Big deal to have U.S. person living with you. Other hootch girls no like unless they have somebody. I very happy with Eddie."

"Do you think he will come back?"

"He no come back. He no show up at Dragon Lady. Eddie gone."

65

"Do you have any idea where he might have gone?"

"If I know, I go there. My sad. No more Eddie."

"Did he ever mention how he got his money?"

"I give him money."

"That was his only money?"

My put a finger to her lip and looked up toward the ceiling. "He come home with money one night. He say he rip off somebody."

Skilling continued. "Let's get back to the others. Do you remember their names?"

"No."

"Anything about them?"

"One squeeze titty when Eddie not look. I not tell."

"Why not?"

"He ask Eddie if he fuck me. Eddie say no. He say when gang have girl it for everybody in gang. Eddie say he want to die. Man not say any more. But he squeeze me. I not know why Eddie care. I fuck friend of Eddie. I no care."

"Did he mention the name of the gang?"

"Sure." She tapped her head with her knuckles. "Skulls."

"Is there anything else you can recall?"

"Eddie eat lot of rice. He say his mother cook rice like me."

"Did he mention where he lived?"

"Sure. New York. He say he take me there after war over. Now we not go, I guess. Shit, man."

Skilling nodded, and Logen punched the tape recorder, stopping it. "All right, My. You can go now."

"Okay. You see Eddie, you tell him I wait. A little bit."

She stood. She was barely five feet tall and slight. Logen moved the chair holding the door closed, and My walked with liquid grace out of the office. Skilling plopped in his chair. "Christ, what a depressing war this is," he said. "How old is she?"

Logen shrugged. "Late teens, I guess."

Skilling swiveled his chair to look out the window. "We're

destroying this place. A teen-ager. 'I fuck for money.' "

"Don't let it get you, sir."

"Oh, Christ, no. Why should I care about some gook. She's only a human being."

There was an uncomfortable silence for a moment. Then Logen said, "Well, we know what happened to the Skulls, anyway."

Skilling turned back. He closed his eyelids and sighed. Then he opened them and said, "Yeah. I guess Eddie, whoever he is, has taken over. But where are they now?"

"They'll turn up. They always do. They probably moved to new quarters."

"Sergeant, put somebody on finding out the last name of this esteemed gentleman. I know there are a lot of deserters. But this one is black, his name is Edward, and he comes from New York. We should be able to narrow the field."

"Right, sir."

"I want to know that bastard's name."

"I'll put somebody on it first thing in the morning."

"What time is it?"

Logen looked at his watch. "It's a little after four, sir."

"Okay. I'll see you tomorrow."

"You leaving, sir?"

"I'm going to go get drunk, Sergeant."

11

When Eddie walked into Duong Van Minh's shop, his daughter was waiting on a customer. She signaled with her eyes, and Eddie stepped into the back room. The room was empty, but almost immediately, the back door opened, and Minh entered. They both bowed to one another. Minh was carrying a small case, and he put it on the otherwise barren desk.

"I have our week's business," said the old man.

"Good," said Eddie.

"It has been a profitable week for both of us."

"I figured."

"You would like to see?"

"Yeah," said Eddie. "Not every week, maybe, but I'd like to see."

The old man smiled and bowed. He opened the case and removed a ledger. He turned it facing Eddie. "For your convenience, I have translated the portions that may interest you."

Eddie looked down at the neat column of figures and the smallish handwriting detailing each hijacking. At the bottom of the column of figures was the total of over 1 million piasters.

Now Eddie smiled. "That's about four thousand dollars."

"Indeed," said the old Vietnamese.

"But the expenses seem high, Ong Minh."

"But as you can see, you needed many things. In the future, your expenses can be held in check."

"Yeah." Eddie knew his expenses had been high the first week. He'd spent lavishly on food and women, and he'd ordered a rather large cache of arms and ammunition. "Well, it looks okay. Not a bad beginning."

"How would you like to add another three hundred thousand piasters?"

"Keep talkin'."

"You must understand, Ong Eddie, that our relationship has caused some ill feelings. Where I was once a rather small businessman, due to your efforts, I am expanding. To expand, one needs room. Is that not so?"

"That's so."

"A man stands in the way of my expansion. Of our expansion, Ong Eddie."

"Then you're about to expand—all over the place."

"Thank you. Perhaps you can make it look like a raid by the VC," said the old man.

"No, man. You miss the point. We want everybody else in your line of work to know who did it."

"I see. You may be right."

"It works. You wanna know how those big dudes in the U.S. keep everybody in line? They kill a few people. Not all the time. Just every once in a while. The dudes, they act surprised, and they send flowers to the funeral. And they're always out of town. But everybody knows who did it."

"And the others are afraid."

"Yeah. There's only one problem. Are we buckin' a gang?"

"Yes."

"Then that puts your life on the line unless we get all of 'em."

"The gang will not strike back against me. They are only being paid by him. I shall put them all on my payroll."

"Yeah. That's smart. Any family?"

"Two sons."

"We better take them, too."

"It is in your hands."

"One final thing. You better have a good alibi. Be somewhere when it happens."

"Tomorrow night I am taking my daughter to the *cai luong.*"

"What's that?"

"The theater. It is like a singing play."

"That's cool, man. Tomorrow night it is, then. What time is this play?"

"Eight o'clock."

"Too late. I may need the light. You go to the play, but go to an early dinner beforehand. You get me?"

He nodded. "My daughter and I will be at dinner from six o'clock on."

"That's good enough. Now, who am I killin'?"

The old man reached into the case and removed a piece of paper. "This is his name and address. Do you know the place?"

Eddie read. "It's not far from here, right?"

"Yes. It is a place where they sell and repair motor scooters."

"Yeah. Now, who's gonna finger this dude?"

"I do not understand."

"How am I gonna know which one, man? It's bad business to go and kill everybody in the place."

"My daughter knows him and his sons. But I do not wish her to be involved."

"Just let her come with me now and point 'em out."

The old man nodded. His hand reached under the desk. The back door opened, and a young man stepped out. The two spoke, and the young man stepped past Eddie into the store. Then the daughter appeared. They, too, spoke in Vietnamese. Then the old man said, "She will show you."

"There's a café across the street. Will you buy me tea?" she said.

"My pleasure," said Eddie. He turned to the old man. "There's only one thing left, Ong Minh. The bread. The money."

Again, the old man reached into his case. He removed a paper sack and put it on the desk. "This is everything, including the extra three hundred thousand piasters. Do you wish to count it?"

Eddie smiled. "If I can't trust you, Ong Minh, who can I trust?"

The old man bowed his head. Eddie picked up the sack. He turned to the girl. "If we're gonna have tea, I'd better know your name."

His chair scraped as the old man stood. "My daughter, Duong Thi Mai."

"Co Mai," said Eddie.

She smiled, and Eddie took her arm and led her onto the street.

The street outside was glutted with traffic, both human and machine. Eddie had false papers in his pocket and felt enough at ease on the street to be just jostled about, to become part of the activity. Mai didn't speak and seemed intent on threading her way toward their destination. Eddie dropped behind her and watched her walk. He wondered if he should try something with her, but he decided against it. No good to fool around at the office, he'd always heard. Don't ball any chick you got to work with, he thought. If you ball good, you work bad. If you work good, you ball bad. Right on.

Eddie sniffed. For a brief moment, he felt as though he were walking on a New York City street. But then the smells penetrated his consciousness. That's not New York smells, man. Nothin' in New York smells that bad. Unless it was Blind Joe's Pool Hall.

"We will sit here," said the Vietnamese girl. Eddie nodded. He watched the girl sit and marveled at how gracefully she did it. She was a real piece, Eddie thought. Those eyes and that hair. But what he liked most about her was what he liked most about all the Vietnamese girls. They were girls. Real girls. Girl girls.

"You wanna beer?" asked Eddie.

"We may be here some time. I will have tea, thank you."

She pulled her chair around a bit toward Eddie for the best view, and Eddie signaled to a waiter. "Tea and a Ba Muioi Ba," he said. Then, to her, "You want somethin' to eat?"

"No, thank you," she said.

"That's all," Eddie said to the waiter. The man turned toward the counter and left.

"There," she said. "There is one son."

Eddie turned and saw a man in his middle twenties, walking out pushing a motor scooter. Another Vietnamese walked behind him, probably the owner of the scooter. "Okay," said Eddie. "I got him. The one with the scooter." She nodded.

Eddie stared at his face. He tried to disregard the man's clothing. Only the face. And he wondered about the man, what he would think if he knew his executioner was sitting across the street, watching him. He felt like going to the man and telling him to have a good time tonight because it was his last night on earth. Eddie looked at the girl, who had her eyes averted downward. This may be my last night on earth, thought Eddie. Who the fuck knows?

"You know why we're here?" asked Eddie.

"Yes," she said.

"Everything?"

"Yes."

The waiter arrived with the tea and beer. Eddie was silent while he put it out on the table. He paid the waiter and gave him an extra 200 piasters. The waiter glanced at the girl, then bowed and left. The man across the street had turned back into the garage now as the Vietnamese drove off on his scooter.

"That's one," said Eddie.

"He is the eldest," said the girl. "His name is—"

Eddie interrupted. "I don't want to know his name."

She nodded. "I understand," she said.

"No you don't," said Eddie. "I just don't want to think about too many things, that's all. His name isn't important. Only the face. That's all."

She turned to her tea, sipping tiny portions at a time.

"You got a boyfriend, Co Mai?"

"No."

Eddie took a swig of beer. When he looked at her again, she was watching the garage. "Somebody else?"

"I think the father is there in the garage, but I cannot tell. It is too dark."

Eddie saw the figure of someone moving in the back of the garage. He couldn't distinguish any features. "Okay. Just keep watching."

They sat in silence for a few moments. Then she said, "Do you have someone, Ong Eddie?"

"A girl?"

"Yes."

"I used to but not anymore."

"Does someone wait for you in the United States?"

"Nothin' for me in the United States. Anything you want there, you buy, you dig? And I don't mean like just buy a girl. I mean you got to buy everything."

"I do not understand."

"I live in Harlem in New York. That's trouble. Rats and garbage and outa-their-head junkies. First you buy out of Harlem. You move to a better place. See? Then you buy a nice car. When you get a nice place to live and a nice car, then you get the girl. But you got to start buyin' her, too. She want a better house and a better car. Man, it's just one big buy."

"I see," she said.

"Maybe," said Eddie.

"It is the same here. Without money, there is no life. There is only the street and death."

"You're not doin' so bad," said Eddie.

"My father is a merchant. Years ago, we would have lived well. But now, he must do better. Expenses are high. There are many mouths to feed just for my father to stay in business."

"Yeah. War is hell."

They sat there for nearly an hour before Eddie finally was able to get a clear look at the older man. Then the younger son came out into the light, and Eddie had marked his targets.

"I'll walk you back to your father's place," said Eddie.

"Thank you," she said.

The two of them again threaded their way through the seemingly mindless traffic. In front of the store, Eddie bowed. "I'll see you again," he said.

"Thank you for the tea," she said.

"I enjoyed it," said Eddie. "It was nice to talk to a girl."

She bowed and turned into the store. Eddie made his way back to their headquarters to map out plans for the murder of three men.

Mau Mau, Turk, and Apache Joe were drinking beer when Eddie walked into their headquarters.

"Hey, man," said Mau Mau.

"It's payday," said Eddie. He raised the paper sack he'd been carrying since he'd left the old man's place.

"Cool," said Apache Joe. "Lay it on me."

Eddie sat at a table and dumped the money on it. Turk whistled.

"Shee-it, man. Look at all that bread," he said.

Eddie started to count the pile. He removed 300,000 piasters and set it aside. The rest he divided into six equal piles. There was nearly $700 for each man and double for Eddie.

"Come to the Man," said Eddie. Turk, Apache Joe, and Mau Mau all took their money. "Where's Mouse?"

"He's upstairs," said Apache Joe. "He and some hootch girl are ballin'."

"I'll keep his pile," said Eddie. He pocketed his money.

"Hey, Eddie," said Turk. "There is another pile there, man."

"Yeah," said Eddie. "That's bonus money. We got a little job to do for it."

"We gettin' paid in advance?" asked Mau Mau.

"For this, we are, man," said Eddie. "There's over a thousand there, man. All we got to do is shoot three bullets for it. That's about four hundred bucks a bullet, man."

"Dig," said Mau Mau.

Apache Joe smiled. "Who we gonna kill, Eddie?"

"I don't know the names," said Eddie. "But they're nothin' but gooks."

"Shee-it," said Turk. "I'll shoot 'em for a dollar a gook if you throw in a piece of ass."

"Yeah, man. And that's another whole dollar," said Mau Mau, laughing. Then he turned to Eddie. "When we do this little killin', boss man?"

"Tomorrow night. Apache Joe, you got those silencers ready yet?"

"They're cool, man," said Apache Joe.

"They work?"

"Hey, man, sure they work. This ain't no dumb nigger you talkin' to."

"Dig," said Eddie. "I'll tell you about it tomorrow. It's cool. But meanwhile, we are gonna talk about our money. You all want to carry that bread around?"

"What you got in mind, man?" asked Mau Mau.

"I figure we should put the money away. I don't mean so we can't get at it. But it's bullshit if we get stopped carryin' a load like that. Even if our fake papers pass, they are gonna ask a lot of questions."

"That's heap smart shit, man," said Apache Joe. "Where you figure we can stash the cash?"

"I ain't goin' to no bank, man," said Turk. "Them bastards'll steal from you quicker than anybody."

"You right, Turk," said Eddie. "I figure we can get a cashbox for each of us. Solid and fireproof, man, but nothin' so big we can't run with it if we have to. Dig?"

"Yeah, man," said Mau Mau. "We can all keep our own key, right?"

"Right," said Eddie. "I am gonna donate fifty thousand pias-

75

ters to petty cash, too. Now, dig. That's for emergencies and cooze."

"That's what cooze is for," said Mau Mau. "Emergencies."

"Right, man," said Eddie. "We see how it works. If you wanna buy smokes or clothes or anything your ass desires, you pay for it. But if you're bringin' a bird up here to ball and everybody gets their gun for fun, you take it outa petty cash."

"Oh, darlin'," said Turk. "You is the best mother I ever had."

"You better believe," said Eddie. "Apache Joe, you hook me up a silencer on one of those M-16s. I wanna test it. Other than that, it's party time, man. Just be ready to move by tomorrow afternoon."

By 10:00 that evening, everyone was drunk but Eddie. It wasn't that he didn't want to join in, but he felt he had to test the gun. He left without them even knowing he was gone. He had the M-16 wrapped in paper under his arm. It was short now, barely longer than a pistol. And the silencer fit neatly on the end of the barrel.

Eddie walked for two blocks, keeping in the shadows. He was without papers. Then he came to a large building. It was built of stone, and there was a large expanse of the material facing the street. Eddie crossed the street, moved back into a niche between two shops, and unwrapped the gun. He put it on semiautomatic and pulled the trigger. There was a quiet *pfft* noise. A piece of rock exploded from the building across the street. Eddie smiled. Beautiful, he thought. That Apache Joe knows his ass.

He moved it to automatic and pulled the trigger a quick squeeze. Spanging rocks and dust appeared on the wall. The quietness of the weapon in Eddie's hands was almost eerie. Man, thought Eddie, that fuckin' army don't know shit about weapons. But this is a piece. This is a real piece.

When he returned to headquarters, the big room was empty. Only the debris of a party remained. Eddie assumed they had all gone to their rooms with a hootch girl or had passed out in bed. He moved some of the litter from a table and sat and slowly

76

cleaned the gun he had just used. It took him nearly thirty minutes as he lingered over the task. When he'd finished, he placed the M-16 carefully in the closet, put away the gun oil and rag, and locked the door.

Eddie thought about how he would kill the men tomorrow. Then he closed his mind to it and decided to get some sleep. He'd fake it tomorrow. Yeah, he liked that. Whatever happens, happens. He fell asleep almost at once.

Eddie arrived at the café with Mau Mau about 4:30. It was insurance in case their marks left early. But they were all there, Eddie noticed. And at about 5:15, a truck pulled up at the garage full of new motor scooters.

At 5:30, Mouse and Turk came into the café and sat down at another table. Apache Joe was to stay outside and down the street. At 6:00, Eddie and Mau Mau paid their check, left the café, and turned up the street, stopping after they had gone about fifty feet. They then crossed over to the garage side and waited.

At 6:10, Mouse and Turk came out of the café. At that moment, they all converged on the garage.

The truck of motor scooters was nearly unloaded when they walked in. Apache Joe stayed outside, his modified M-16 out and ready but hidden behind a small sign advertising Champion spark plugs. He casually leaned on the sign and waited.

Inside, Eddie quickly unwrapped his gun. The truck driver saw him first and started to run. Both Eddie and Mau Mau fired at once, and the man took one running step and then pitched forward onto his face.

The three other men were near the rear of the garage. The father, more than the sons, seemed to sense what was about to happen. He picked up a wrench and started for them.

The sons put their hands in the air. Eddie shot the sons first. They were caught in the chest and were knocked backward into a line of motor scooters.

Then someone spoke. "Look at that old bastard comin' for

you, Eddie," said Mau Mau. "The old son of a bitch has got guts."

"Yeah," said Eddie. "See?" And he finished the clip in his M-16, aiming for the old man's stomach.

"Neat, man," said Turk.

"I didn't even pull no trigger," said Mouse. "Shee-it."

"You pull it now, Mouse," said Eddie. "I want a lot of bullets in those bastards. Make sure they're dead."

"Okay, man," said Mouse. He walked from corpse to corpse, letting go a short burst into each one at point-blank range. "That enough, Eddie?"

"If they ain't dead yet, they never gonna be," said Mau Mau.

"That's enough," said Eddie. "Now lets load up these scooters. We might as well make a few extra bucks."

Mouse, Turk, and Mau Mau started to push the scooters into the truck. Eddie went out to Apache Joe. "It's all done, man. You made some good pieces. Real good."

"I told you I do good work," said Apache Joe.

"Right on. We gonna load up those scooters. You stay here until I pull out with the truck." Apache Joe nodded. Eddie returned to the garage to help with the loading. In twenty minutes, the truck was full.

"Shee-it," said Mouse. "Killin' is a lot easier than stealin'."

Eddie smiled. "You didn't do so bad, Mouse. You made about five hundred today. You gonna be a rich dude."

"I be so rich, I am gonna have to be white," said Mouse. He laughed, turned, and picked up his M-16 and fired around the room, sending oil cans flying.

"I like to see a man who enjoys his work," said Eddie. "Now you all split. I'm gonna drive this load to the drop-off point. I'll be back when I can."

"Right, man," said Mau Mau. "I'm feelin' so good I just might celebrate again."

"Cool," said Eddie. "Pick me up a hootch girl. Killin' gives me a real good hard."

78

12

"How long you been on the loose, man?" A young, pimply-faced youth at the bar turned and spoke.

"Who's on the loose," said Lieutenant Skilling.

"You. You're always lookin' over your shoulder. Shit, man, it's all right. I'm a deserter, too."

Skilling smiled. "You got me. I been gone from the good old army about two months now. How about you?"

"The same. Little over two months. You wanna beer?"

"Don't mind if I do. I'm a little short of bread."

The young man signaled the bartender and held up a beer bottle and two fingers. "How you makin' it? Your bread, I mean." The young man picked at his face with his right index finger.

"I've been stealin' what I can. Mostly out of trucks and things like that."

"Christ, you're gonna starve. Where you live?"

"I'm stayin' with a hootch girl, so I guess I won't starve. She gives me money. Not much, but a little."

"I'm with the Zappers."

"The Zappers?"

"A gang, you know what I mean. We all live together, and we keep us a couple of girls."

The bartender sat two beers in front of Skilling and his companion. Skilling lifted his beer. "Thanks for the beer. My name's Jerry."

"Mine's Bert. Where you from?"

"Iowa."

"I'm from Mississippi."

"That's funny. You don't have an accent."

"Well, I wasn't raised there. I was originally from upstate New York. Place called Pine Plains."

Skilling shrugged. "Don't know it."

"It's a small town. My old man was a trucker. He got a job with this trucker in Mississippi when I was in my last year of high school, and we moved down."

Skilling drank his beer. He wanted to get his man off high school days and onto the Zappers. He felt good, Lieutenant Skilling did. He'd been coming to this bar in Cholon every night for the past week. He'd noticed the kid sitting at the bar on a couple of occasions and had deliberately taken a stool beside him tonight.

"You the leader of the Zappers?" asked Skilling.

"Me? Well, no. Not exactly. I only been with 'em for about two weeks. But I been thinkin' of formin' my own gang. It's the only way to operate."

"Yeah. It makes sense. But expenses would be high for a whole gang."

"It's how you organize, man. You know how much money there is in Saigon? Millions. And it's just waitin' there." Bert took a swig of beer, recklessly and with as much dash as he could muster.

"Yeah," said Skilling. "But I'm not gettin' any of it. And I don't figure to. You're different. You got into a gang. You're even thinkin' of forming your own." Skilling turned to Bert. "Say. If you put that gang together, how about me being a part of it?"

Bert looked serious. "Well, maybe."

They drank for a minute. Skilling wondering how he could force his new contact into revealing more than he already had. He decided on a plan. "Listen," he said. "I wish I could buy you a beer, but, well, I don't have the bread."

"Don't worry about it," said Bert.

"Nah," said Skilling. "You buy me a beer; I buy you one. I need a few bucks. Gimme an hour, I'll have a few."

"Whatcha gonna do?" Bert turned, interested.

"I'll go back and get an automatic I got stashed. Then I'm goin' out an relieve somebody of their money."

"You gonna pull a stickup?"

"Hold it down, man," said Skilling. "Yeah. Only I like to call it a loan from a friend."

Bert grinned. "I'll come along with ya."

"You finish your beer. I'll go get my gun. I'll only be a minute. My place isn't far from here."

Skilling turned and hurried out of the bar before his new-found friend could move to go with him. He had only four blocks to walk to a small shop that sold feather flowers and ceramic pots. Skilling had realized an office on Rue Pasteur was too distant, too inconvenient. He had rented a room behind the pottery shop in Cholon as a meeting point for his unit. Skilling hadn't been to his official office in six days.

It was a small room that contained a bed, a table and chair, and a chest of drawers. Each man had extra clothing there. There was also a locked chest containing $100 in Military Payment Certificates, two carbines, a .45 automatic, and ammunition. In the far corner of the room was a hot plate and a small refrigerator. Next to it was a curtain that hid the toilet and washbasin. There were no windows.

Skilling took out the .45 and a clip of ammunition. He took $30 in MPCs and stuffed it in his pocket. He slipped the gun into his belt under his shirt. Finally, he took a note pad from the chest and wrote "Cheap Charlie's" and signed it.

The note pad was the unit's means of communication. If

something was written on it, anyone else checking into the room was to drop what he was doing and rendezvous. It meant that someone had a hot lead and could use help. Skilling had given orders for everyone in the unit to check into the pottery shop twice a day if possible.

Skilling then dropped his identification into the chest and locked it. That done, he sat on the bed for another ten minutes. He'd have to give himself some time so his drinking companion at Cheap Charlie's wouldn't be suspicious.

When he arrived back at the bar, Skilling was relieved to find Bert still there.

"Hey, Bert."

Bert turned. "Hi, Jerry."

Skilling signaled the bartender. "This round is on me," said Skilling.

Bert smiled. "You come into some money?"

"Yeah. Not much, but enough for a few rounds. Thirty bucks in script."

Bert leaned over. "What happened, man?"

Skilling unbuttoned his shirt enough to reveal the butt of the .45 to Bert. "Me and my friend here walked up to some dumb-ass grunt, and the first thing you know, he wanted to gimme all his money. So, shit, I took it. It's the neighborly thing to do."

"Son of a bitch," said Bert. "If that ain't the truth. It's only neighborly."

"So how you want to spend it?"

"It's your money, man."

"Christ, Bert, I don't give a shit about the money, and you're the first white person I talked to in over a month. I want to celebrate."

"Wanna buy some skag?"

"Nah," said Skilling. "I said I wanna celebrate, not go outa my mind. Listen. Bullshit on this beer. Let's order some of the good stuff. You like bourbon?"

"Sippin' whiskey. Yeah."

"Okay." Skilling ordered two Jack Daniel's for them, and they sat and talked. Skilling ordered another and then one more. Bert was very quickly getting drunk. Skilling, on the other hand, was completely sober. He had been taught what to do by Sergeant Logen.

"Always order a Coke chaser," Logen had said. "Then, sip the whiskey, hold it in your mouth, and take a sip of the Coke. When you're sipping the Coke, let the whiskey drain outa your mouth into the Coke. Unless your man is watchin' the level of your Coke, there's no sweat. It's a trick I learned from a B-girl in Chicago."

It was working admirably for Skilling. After their second drink, Skilling noticed Fuller and Jorgensen lounging near the end of the bar. They had received his message.

"Listen, Bert," said Skilling, talking thickly. "We got about eighteen bucks left. What say we get laid."

"Shit, yeah," said Bert.

"My hootch girl is workin'," said Skilling. "How about yours?"

"Mine?"

"You said the Zappers had a couple of girls."

"Oh, yeah."

"Well, let's go give one of 'em the eighteen dollars and have ourselves a time. Whatta ya say?"

"Shit, yeah."

The two men lurched off the barstools and staggered out the door. Skilling didn't look back. He knew his two men would be following them. Skilling tried to hurry Bert along as much as he could. He didn't want the young deserter passing out before they reached the headquarters of the Zappers. "Let's move it, Bert," he said. "I ain't got no fuckin' ID."

They walked three blocks. Then Bert said, "That's it." He nodded toward a two-story building. On the street level was a plumbing shop. Stairs to the side of the shop led to the second floor. "Come on," said Bert.

83

He climbed the stairs to a small hallway. There were five doors down the hall, and Bert headed for one near the back. At the door, he rapped.

A voice from inside asked, "Yeah?"

"It's me, Bert. And I'm drunker'n hell."

Skilling heard a bolt being thrown on the door. It opened. A man was standing there holding an M-16. "Who's your friend, Bert?"

"This is Jerry," said Bert. "Him and me been drinkin'."

Skilling leaned against the doorframe, grinning as drunkenly as he could. Shielded by his body, he slipped an MPC dollar bill into a crack in the doorframe as a marker. The man glanced down the hall. "Get inside," he said. "Both of you."

Skilling and Bert stumbled into the room. There were three men and a hootch girl. Two of the men were playing cards. The third was by himself in a corner smoking a cigarette. Skilling looked at the man's eyes and decided the cigarette was laced with skag.

The man with the gun threw the bolt on the door. He seemed to relax a bit then but kept the M-16 pointed at Skilling. "All right, Bert, you stupid shit. What'd you bring us? An MP?"

Bert swayed. "Oh, no, man. Jerry, he's all right. I seen him lotsa times at Cheap Charlie's. He's on the loose just like the rest of us."

Skilling grinned. "Me an MP? Christ, man."

"Put your hands up, dig? Let's have a look."

Skilling slowly put up his hands. The man kept the M-16 steady and patted Skilling with the flat of his left hand. He found the .45 and pulled it out. He put it in Skilling's stomach and said, "Bang."

Skilling smiled. "Don't mess around, man. That thing's loaded."

The armed man continued to pat Skilling while holding the gun. "Where's your papers?" he asked.

"I got no papers," said Skilling.

"What outfit you with?"

"I was at Cu Chi with the Twenty-fifth Infantry. But, shit, the VC wanted to live there, too. So I figured I'd let 'em."

The man lowered his gun. "Look. Bert ain't no prize package, right Bert? I mean, why you think somebody'd wanna drink with you, Bert?"

"Quit kiddin'," said Bert. "Come on. Me and Jerry want to have a little fun, that's all."

"That's a Zapper hootch girl, Bert. We can't have every son of a bitch off the street stickin' her. Man, we liable to get a disease."

"He didn't mean no harm," said Skilling. "We were just havin' some whiskey, and we decided we wanted to get laid."

Bert smiled. "Yeah, Jerry here says to me he wants to get laid. I bought him a beer, see, and he didn't have no money to buy me one, so he goes out on the street, and he holds up a grunt, for Christ sake, and takes thirty dollars off him. And then he pops for all the drinks. Hey, that's a good buddy."

"Okay, Bert. Your buddy can stay for a while. But if anything happens, it's your ass in a sling, Bert. You dig?"

"He's all right," said Bert, almost whining.

The man with the gun slapped the table. "Hey, listen. Bert wants to get laid. His buddy here has got hot rocks. We got nothin' to do. Let's make a party out of it."

"Yeah," said Bert. "Jerry, give 'em the eighteen dollars. We'll kick in money, right, buddy?"

Skilling reached into his pocket and brought out the money and tossed it on the table. He didn't like the man's tone of voice, but he had to continue to act drunk.

"Hey, baby. Come over here." The man waved at the hootch girl with the gun. "Here's eighteen dollars, how about that?"

"That's okay," she said.

"Well, earn it."

"What you want me to do?" she asked.

"Hey, dummy Bert. Whatta you think she should do for eighteen lousy MPC dollars?"

"We'll just take her in the other room and—"

85

The man interrupted him. "Bullshit, man. She stays right here. And you, too. Come on, Bert. Take off your clothes. You, too, man," he said to Skilling.

"Ah, come on," said Bert.

The man leveled the M-16 at Bert and said, "Take 'em off, Bert. Now." He turned the gun toward Skilling. "Off," he said.

Bert slowly started to remove his clothes. The splotches on his face seemed to be glowing red. He started to speak, but he shut his mouth and undressed. Skilling knew he had better undress, too. And he did.

"Good, man," said the gunman. The other two had put up their cards and were watching and grinning. "Now, you undress your girlie friend, Bert. Come on. Move."

Bert and Skilling walked to the hootch girl. She barely reached to Skilling's chin, and she stood passively while the two undressed her. Then they all stood there completely nude.

"Ain't that a picture," said one of the cardplayers.

"Well, you just gonna stand there?" asked the gunman. "Two studs like you just gonna stand there. Come on. Let's see some action." Neither Bert nor Skilling moved. The man shouted. "Let's see some action."

"Come on, boys," said the hootch girl. "How about an old roll in the hay? Okay? I help."

She reached out for them as the door behind Skilling splintered. He saw only the expression of astonishment on the face of the cardplayer. He started to turn and heard Corporal Jorgensen say, "Don't try it."

The man with the gun fired. Skilling saw Jorgensen pull back out of the doorway. He turned to see the gunman on the floor, pointing the M-16 toward the door. The two cardplayers were racing to a bureau.

Skilling moved. He grabbed the .45 from the table and pulled back on it, slipping a shell into the chamber. He fired once at the man with the M-16, and the bullet caught him in the neck, nearly severing his head from his body.

He turned toward the two cardplayers. One was drawing an AK-47, the Russian-built automatic rifle, out of a long drawer.

"Drop the gun," screamed Skilling.

The cardplayer started to turn, and an explosion erupted in Skilling's ear. Jorgensen was firing. The bullets slammed the man into the bureau, and he bounced off and onto his knees and hung there for an instant. Then he collapsed.

Bert was standing with his arms straight up in the air. The hootch girl had grabbed onto Bert and was screaming. The other cardplayer was yelling, "Don't shoot me."

The man on drugs was still seated, shaking his head vigorously, and holding his arms in front of his face.

Skilling's arm relaxed, and he let the gun fall to his side. He turned. Jorgensen and Fuller were there. Behind them was Sergeant Logen.

Sergeant Logen grinned. "You're outa uniform, Lieutenant," he said.

Skilling felt as though he had to sit down. His knees suddenly seemed too weak to support his weight. He walked to a chair and fell into it. "Holy Christ," he said.

Sergeant Logen motioned to Jorgensen and Fuller. "Get 'em all out of here. Have a wagon come and pick 'em up."

"How about the hootch girl?" asked Fuller.

"Take her along, too."

"Okay, lady. Get dressed," he said. "You, too," he said to Bert.

They dressed quickly, and Jorgensen and Fuller led them out of the room. Skilling took deep breaths, trying to erase the dizzy feeling in his head.

Logen went over to the two corpses and inspected them. From the one, he looked up and said, "That was good shootin', Lieutenant."

Skilling's mouth was dry. He moved his lips, trying to work up saliva. "Just a lucky shot."

Logen was now standing over him. "You'll get over it, sir."

Skilling shook his head. "I don't think so."

"Sir, I think you better get dressed. Some MPs will be here pretty soon."

Skilling looked down at his naked body for the first time. "Jesus," he said. "I forgot."

He stood and quickly pulled on his clothes. He took one more large breath, and let it out slowly. He released the hammer on his .45 and stuck it into his belt again.

"Ready, Lieutenant?"

"The drinks are on me," Skilling said.

Logen grinned. "You know somethin', Lieutenant," he said, "you're turnin' into a pretty good cop."

13

Skilling felt his head. It was tender to the touch, as though pressure might cave it in. His mouth was coated with the residue of the night before. Two thumbs seemed to be pressing down on his eyes. He moved a hand. It was caught in his sheet, so he dropped it. How many drinks had he had?

Not quite enough to erase the picture in his mind of blood pumping onto the floor from the neck of the man he had shot. But his anguish pushed the picture to one side of his mind. At least, his hangover served some purpose.

He finally forced himself from bed and into the shower. He stood in the shower for almost ten minutes, letting the water wash away the stink of three bars from the night before. When he stepped out of the shower, he felt better. Well enough to go back to sleep. But he knew he couldn't.

He dressed slowly. Finally, he left his quarters and caught a cab to the Rue Pasteur office. Before he went up, however, he had a large breakfast.

When he walked in to greet Sergeant Holland, he felt almost alive. Sergeant Holland looked up. "Logen is trying to reach you, sir," said Holland.

"Is he? Okay. Where is he now?"

"He said he'd be at this number for a while." He handed

Skilling a piece of notepaper with a telephone number on it. Skilling took it and walked back into his office. He picked up the phone and dialed. He waited. He knew the number. It was a public telephone near their Cholon place. It clicked. Finally, it rang.

"Lieutenant Skilling?" said Logen over the phone.

"Yes. What is it, Logen?"

"Well, I'm worried, sir. I thought I ought to tell you. It's Rhinebeck. He hasn't surfaced in a week now, and this morning I heard some news that I don't like. Can you come over here?"

"I'll be right there," said Skilling and hung up. He shrugged and left. He hadn't even had a chance to sit down.

Logen was waiting for him in their room behind the pottery shop. Cramer was there, too, lazily cleaning a gun. When Skilling entered, he saw they were both tight and worried.

"Anything?" asked Skilling.

Logen shook his head. "We think he's infiltrated this gang, but the gang may know about him, and if they do—"

Skilling interrupted. "Slowly, Logen. Give it all to me from the beginning."

Logen sighed and sat down. Cramer slapped the gun back together and waited for the sergeant to begin talking. "First, I think we've identified the leader of the gang who was staying with that hootch girl. The Eddie from New York."

"Okay," said Skilling. "But—"

"You said start from the beginning, sir," said Logen, breaking in. Skilling nodded and moved to sit on the bed beside Cramer.

Cramer picked up a small piece of paper. "He's Corporal Edward Palmer, 984-41-19. Stationed at Dau Tieng. Went AWOL in Saigon," he read.

"Okay, we know his name," said Skilling.

"His picture is coming by mail," said Cramer. "That might be of some use."

90

"What about Rhinebeck?" asked Skilling.

Logen seemed to hesitate. Then he spoke. "I think Rhinebeck is with this Eddie Palmer."

"Yeah?" Skilling sat forward. "Good. Good."

"Maybe," said Logen. "About two weeks ago, four dinks were murdered at a garage in Cholon. It was like a gang murder in the old days in Chicago. A truckload of scooters was taken, but from the way the bodies were riddled, I'd say it was meant to be a warning. The CID tells me that the owner of the garage had a black market operation going. Now his territory has been taken over by someone else; the CID doesn't know who yet."

"Okay," said Skilling.

"The killings were done by a black gang," continued Logen.

"Eddie Palmer?" asked Skilling.

"No way of knowing," answered Logen. "But let's suppose it was. Then, last night, a black gang hijacked two truckloads of PX goods. We got some witnesses, and they said the gang was all black except for one man. He was white. And the witnesses kept saying he was a big man. Big tall and big wide."

"Rhinebeck," said Skilling. "He's worked himself in."

Logen nodded. "He's worked himself in, or else they're using him as a decoy to draw fire. One witness said he thought one of the black men was pointing a gun at the white man. The witness said the white man carried a handgun, and he's the one who stopped the trucks."

"If there'd been any shooting, Rhinebeck would have caught it first," said Cramer.

"Maybe they were just testing him," said Skilling. "He had a gun."

"And you're assuming it was loaded," said Logen. "I tell you, Lieutenant, I don't like the way it smells."

"Damn that Eddie Palmer," said Skilling. "The son of a bitch is smart. If Rhinebeck can't get out, he's no danger to them, even if they know he's an MP. And they can use him in their operations to draw fire."

"So, what do you think, Lieutenant?" asked Logen.

"Pull everybody off what they're doing, and let's get out on the streets. Maybe we can find somebody who's seen Rhinebeck. Once you've seen him, you don't forget him."

"Where do we start?" asked Cramer.

"Let's start with that hootch girl," said Skilling. "Pull her in again."

"I'll get her," said Cramer.

"You'd better carry a piece," said Logen. "You want some help?"

"I figured to go on the roof next door and take a peek in, first," said Cramer.

"That's my boy," said Logen.

Cramer unlocked the chest and took out the .45. Skilling turned his eyes away from it. Cramer stuck a clip in the gun, shoved it in his pocket and left.

"Rhinebeck had better be all right," said Skilling. "I'll kill that Eddie myself."

Jorgensen and Fuller arrived after about ten minutes. Logen filled them in on Rhinebeck.

"It's a hell of a problem, Lieutenant," said Fuller. "It's fairly simple to latch onto a gang at random, you know? But to find one particular gang in the whole of Cholon is tough. There must be hundreds of deserters in here."

"I know," said Skilling. "But we've got to try. Anybody got any Viet sources they maybe can squeeze?"

Jorgensen shrugged. "Hell, Lieutenant, you can only squeeze them so much. The deserters are payin' them a hell of a lot more than we can."

The door suddenly burst open. It was Cramer. "Grab some guns. I think we got a break."

"Let's move," said Skilling. "You can fill us in while we walk."

They half walked, half jogged toward the prostitute's apartment. "I got up on the roof next to the apartment," said Cramer. "I looked in, and there must be three or four in there."

"Was Rhinebeck there?" asked Skilling.

"I didn't see him. As soon as I saw there was somebody there, I ducked out and came back. I don't even know if it's the gang we want. She could just be entertaining the troops."

"Either way," said Logen, "we should nab somebody."

"I only hope it's Eddie," said Skilling.

They hurried along, moving pedestrians out of the way. As they neared the building, Skilling said, "Cramer and Fuller, get to that roof, and sit tight. If you hear any shooting, do what you can."

The two men peeled off. "You wanna wait until they get in position, Lieutenant?"

"No," said Skilling. "They're going up. If we flush anyone, they'll meet them coming down."

Skilling, Logen, and Jorgensen moved quietly up to Ngo Thi My's door. Skilling reached over quietly and tried the door. It moved. He looked at both of the other men, nodded, and threw open the door, running into the room. He stumbled and fell over the bodies of Corporal Rhinebeck and Ngo Thi My.

14

"I can understand your feelings, Lieutenant," said Lieutenant Colonel John Champa, head of the military police in Saigon. "But you're workin' outside my command."

"I know that, sir," said Skilling. "But we've always tried to cooperate with you."

"I appreciate that, Lieutenant," said Champa. "But you got to understand the whole situation. Your unit was set up against my recommendation. I think it's a lousy idea, and I think it's been proven now that the whole thing should be scrapped. Bottom line, Lieutenant. I'm not going to help you because I want you and your men out of my command."

"Goddammit, there's a man dead."

"That's unfortunate. But those deserters are tough."

"Then, you're not going to do anything?"

"No."

"You lousy son of a bitch."

Champa stood, his face hard. "How'd you like a court-martial, Lieutenant?"

Skilling stared at him. "How'd you like a report back to the Pentagon, word for word, of what you just said."

Champa picked up a letter opener and turned it over and over in his hand. Finally, he said, "Get out."

Skilling turned and walked out of his office without another word.

Logen was waiting outside. "He wouldn't help," said Logen.

"No. Nothing. He told me he wanted to see our unit broken up. That lousy bastard."

"That figures. Want to try CID?"

"Not now."

"Okay, Lieutenant. You know, we can find Eddie if we work at it."

"The problem is, what's going to happen to us? When my report gets back to the Pentagon, they just might scrap the whole unit."

"Then, we better get off our hump," said Logen. "Let's hit as many gangs as we can and hard. Fuller's got a line on one. So's Jorgensen. Let's hit 'em."

Skilling smiled and put his hand on the sergeant's shoulder. "You sound like a cheerleader, Sergeant," he said quietly. "And I can sure use one."

The next week, Skilling worked harder than he thought possible. He survived on barely four hours of sleep a night, and he almost always ate on the run.

Jorgensen's lead proved to be the best, and the entire group came down on a gang of nine deserters. They not only got the gang, but they captured ten weapons of various types, a dozen hand grenades, nearly a kilo of marijuana, and several ounces of heroin.

They gained a bit of a reputation on that raid because an on-duty MP was with the gang and turned out to be the leader. Skilling couldn't have been happier. He wanted to go in to Lieutenant Colonel Champa and spit in his face. Instead, in his report back to the Pentagon, he credited Champa for help in staging the raid.

They also gave themselves a name that week. The Hom Qua Gang. Whenever anyone asked Lieutenant Skilling when he wanted something done, he'd say, "Hom qua." Yesterday.

In two weeks, they were ready to move in on the gang Fuller had on the hook. And all the time, each man kept looking for Eddie.

The picture of Eddie arrived, and Skilling had several copies made. They circulated the picture, had one stuck up on the wall in their Cholon room.

It was fifteen days after their first meeting that Champa summoned Skilling to his office. The top cop of Saigon was holding a piece of paper.

"This is from the Joint Chiefs," he said. "You want to read it, or you want me to summarize?"

"Summarize," said Skilling.

"It's commending me for cooperating with you," he said. "What in hell are you doing, Lieutenant?"

"Well sir," said Skilling, "when we busted that gang with one of your MPs as the leader, I didn't see any point in rubbing your face in it. So I said you had turned the difficult assignment over to me because you knew one of your men was crooked. I may think you're a horse's ass, but I'm not out to ruin you."

His face reddened. "You got a smart mouth, Lieutenant," he said. "But goddamn if you don't have some brains. All right. If that's all it is, I thank you. The paper work alone would ruin me if I had to explain it from scratch."

"That's okay, sir."

"That'll be all, Lieutenant."

"Yes, sir." Skilling turned to leave. He was almost at the door when Champa spoke again.

"You're circulating a picture. Why?"

Skilling stopped. "It's an Eddie Palmer. I'm pretty sure he's the one who killed my man."

"All right. I'll see what I can do," Champa said.

Skilling smiled. "Thank you, sir."

Champa called after him. "Next time you visit, if there is a next time, watch your mouth."

"Yes, sir," Skilling called back.

96

Sergeant Logen was dozing when Skilling entered their Cholon room. He woke up immediately. "Just resting my eyes," he said.

"You're entitled," said the lieutenant. "And I've got some good news. Champa has promised to see what he can do about tracking down our Eddie."

"That's good, sir. Every little bit helps."

"He's got a lot of men out there."

"Well, as I say, every little bit helps."

The days became weeks. Neither the Hom Quas nor the Saigon MPs could trace Eddie. But Skilling's work improved; his knowledge broadened. Fear surrounded the Hom Quas now. Every deserter gang in Cholon knew of them, knew they would kill if necessary, knew they were hunting relentlessly.

In two months, 168 deserters were arrested as a direct result of the Hom Quas. Two more men were added to Skilling's command, both black, a Sergeant Floyd Payne and a Corporal Earl Childs.

Lieutenant Skilling had tried to double his operation but had been refused. In fact, he'd been given a mild reprimand for being somewhat over his budget. He was able to bring monetary problems under control by suggesting to Sergeant Logen that some of his black market contacts might give them a better rate of exchange on their operating money. Logen raised their budget by 30 percent by laying the money off on his contacts.

Still, no Eddie. Lieutenant Skilling knew he was out there. He knew the best-operated gang in Cholon was Eddie's group. They struck hard and fast and effectively. They dealt in smuggling, hijacking, drug peddling, and murder.

Skilling and Logen tried to retrace Rhinebeck's steps. Somehow he had penetrated. But they were never able to find out exactly how or where or even exactly when.

Skilling put a prostitute from the Dragon Lady on payroll. She had an American baby nearly a year old and was most willing to cooperate. He closed down his room behind the pottery shop and set up headquarters in the girl's apartment. He paid the rent, which was about the same, and the unit operated out of there. It was a three-room apartment; Skilling and his men used one of the rooms, and the girl used the other two.

The girl gave him what information she heard as a prostitute. She also served in the role of a girl friend if one of the Hom Quas brought a deserter up to the apartment. The deserter seldom was suspicious of a man living with a hootch girl.

But, still, no Eddie.

"Look, sir," said Logen one day, "you got to get off this Eddie character. We'll find him one day. But if we don't, you shouldn't give yourself an ulcer over him."

"Did you ever have a small piece of glass in your finger? You can feel it, but you can't see it?" asked Skilling. "That's the way Eddie is with me. I forget about him for a day or so, and then, bam, something reminds me of him again. Then I start digging again. Don't worry, Sergeant. I know you're right."

Then, suddenly, they had a lead. A deserter was wounded in a hijacking. He turned up at a civilian doctor's suffering from severe loss of blood. He had lost consciousness, and the doctor had notified the MPs. The deserter was transferred to a military prison hospital unit, where he was identified as Private Duane Lange.

Private Lange had deserted nearly eighteen months before. The thing that drew Skilling to him was that he had held a modified M-16 on the Vietnamese doctor before he had passed out. It had a silencer and was the type used by an assassination team. Skilling knew he was a member of one of the most organized deserter gangs, perhaps Eddie's.

Skilling had him set up in a ward next to one of his new men, Corporal Childs. Childs was bandaged, given a cover story about his supposed capture, and told to see what he could find out. Then Skilling waited.

"Hey, man, you awake?" Childs turned in his bed and smiled at the man.

"What the fuck's this place?"

"Oh, that's good, man."

"What is this? I mean it, man."

"You really don't know, man?" asked Childs.

"No."

"You're in the can, daddy. Behind the big slammin' door."

"Oh, man, no."

"Well, it all in how you look at it, man. Big daddy doctor, he say you lucky to be still among us mortals, dig? I heard him say that very thing. You a deserter?"

"Why?"

"Well, if you ain't, then you about the only one in here. I am just tellin' you, as my captain use to say, welcome aboard."

The man turned away and didn't speak. Then he said, "I hurt."

"I reckon you do," said Childs. "You lost so much blood when they dragged you in here yesterday I thought you was white."

The man didn't move, and Childs saw that he had fallen asleep again. Childs relaxed in his bed. It had been a beginning.

Later the same day, they talked again. "My name's Childs," said the undercover man. "What's yours?"

"They call me Mouse," said the wounded man. "You and me are in the jailhouse?"

"That's right. I'm here for twenty years at hard. You, too, I reckon."

"Where's the guards?"

"Outside. They keep this place locked up, man. You're not thinkin' of bustin' out, man. You can't even stand."

"Not yet."

"What happened to you, man?"

"I got me a bullet."

"Me, I got beat up. They worked me over good with them billy clubs, man. Broke a couple of things."

"Why?"

"Tell you the truth, man, I sold some skag to an MP. Shee-it. So he says I'm under arrest, and I says good-bye, Charlie. But he had two of his rotten friends waitin' at the end of this little alley, and they just naturally all but beat me to death. How about you, Mouse?"

"I caught one durin' a truck hijackin'," he said. "I knew I was in trouble, man, so I lit out for a gook doctor. But I guess I passed out, and here I am."

"You workin' alone?"

"No, man."

"Well, why didn't your brothers help you?"

"Our boss-man Eddie, he say if you catch a bullet, you got to sweat it out, man. Like they woulda dragged my bleedin' ass back to our digs and put a patch on me, and that'd be that. Eddie say no doctor. That the rules, man. So I hauled ass."

"This Eddie sound like a bad cat."

"He is a mean mother. But we're livin' high off the hog, that's for sure. But I ain't about to die for no gang."

"No way, man. Everybody always askin' you to die. The United States askin' you to die. Those chicken officers askin' you to die. Shee-it, there's a lot of folk sure playin' fast and loose with my ass."

"Dig, man."

Childs reached his hand under his pillow and pushed a button. Lieutenant Skilling, in uniform, was waiting at the call box. He straightened the MP armband and walked down the hall toward the ward.

Once inside, he walked directly to Childs. "All right, soldier," said Skilling. "The doctor tells me you're well enough after your accident to talk a bit."

"Accident?" said Childs. "Shee-it. Man, I catch you alone some time, daddy, we see who have the accident."

"Tough, are you?" said Skilling. "Maybe you are tough. But you're kinda stupid, selling skag to an MP lieutenant."

"I is a dumb nigger, jack."

"I want to talk to you, Childs. We know you're just a small-time pusher. And we're not after your kind. I could talk to the military court and have your sentence cut way down if you could give me a few names."

"Oh, sure, sir. I'll give you names. Hows about Willie Mays. Then there's Rosey Grier. That's a nice name."

Skilling showed annoyance and came around to stand over Childs. "Don't give me any smart-ass talk, you black bastard. Where'd you get that skag?"

"I grew it, man, in a window box. I is a poppy grower."

Skilling leaned over to almost touch his face. He spoke through clenched teeth. "You know what twenty years of hard labor means, black boy? That's hard labor. None of that civil rights shit in prison, big mouth. Just hard labor, bad food, no pussy, and if you keep up with the smart mouth, you're liable to have other accidents. You get me?"

"Oh, Lieutenant," said Childs, "you is scarin' me somethin' awful. I'm liable to turn white overnight."

Mouse giggled. Skilling wheeled on him. "What's funny?"

"Nothin', man," said Mouse. "I got a bullet in my funny bone. I can't help it."

Childs roared with laughter. Skilling looked down at them both. "A couple of smart asses. Real smart asses. We'll see how smart you are when you get out of here." He turned and walked toward the door.

Childs called after him. "See you in twenty years, darlin'."

Then Skilling was gone. He almost jumped for joy in the hall. Childs had played the scene wonderfully. Eddie, thought Skilling, your days are numbered.

The two men talked the next day, and about four o'clock, Childs was taken out of the ward for X rays. Once out of sight of Mouse, he met Skilling and gave him a rundown.

"I think we got our gang," said Childs. "The leader's name is Eddie, and this Mouse talks about capturing an MP."

"Okay," said Skilling. "Slowly. Everything he said."

Childs talked and mentioned the names of the gang members, their past exploits, some of their future plans. He had a great deal of information, all of it totally useless as far as locating the gang.

"That's okay," said Skilling. "Just keep pressing him. He'll tell you where they hole up."

But for the next two days, Mouse opened up about almost everything except the location of Eddie's headquarters. He was always evasive about their hideout, although he described the interior. At the end of the day, Childs would be taken from the room on some excuse or other, and he would meet Skilling or Logen in the hallway.

Then, the fifth day, Mouse mentioned the view from the windows of their hideout. He talked about watching a couple through a window across the street. He discovered it was a prostitute who kept the room, and she would, from time to time, have men in there. Mouse had amused himself by watching. And in his conversation, he mentioned the name of the building: the Shanghai Continental.

It was late Thursday afternoon before Childs was able to reach Skilling with the news. Skilling and Logen immediately went to the hotel, a four-story white stone building. Unfortunately, it was on a corner. Eddie's hideout could be in any one of three directions. The fourth side butted up against a taller building.

Skilling decided to put everyone on it. He had Childs removed from the hospital, and that evening the Hom Quas had dinner together at a restaurant across the street from the Continental.

"We could scout the hootch girls working there," said Logen between bites of food. "If necessary, we can go up with them. If you can see her room from the hideout, you can see the hideout from her room."

"It's a possibility," said Skilling. "We'd better find out how many girls are working the place first. My budget couldn't stand it if it was over two girls."

"I might kick in a little on that kind of an operation," said Logen, smiling.

"Childs," said Skilling, "he gave you the impression he looked down into the window?"

"That's right, sir," replied Childs.

"So that eliminates the building we're in. It's three stories. It's got to be one of the two on either side of the Continental."

"We can stake out the buildings," said Logen.

"I don't want that bastard slipping through our fingers again," said Skilling. "You've all got your pictures of Eddie?" The group nodded. "Okay, when we finish dinner, let's see if we can't get a lead from one of the shopkeepers in the buildings. Logen, you take a man and work the building on the far side of the street. Childs, you come with me, and we'll ask around at the building on the same side. The rest of you hang back enough so it won't look like a crowd but stay close enough in case we have to move fast."

They finished their dinners quickly. All the men were caught up in the hunt, and the fervor of Skilling had rubbed off a little on all of them. And none of them had forgotten Rhinebeck.

The first man Skilling talked to, a Vietnamese rice dealer, nodded his head when he saw Eddie's picture. "Yes," he said. "Upstairs. He live."

It was that easy.

Skilling thanked the man, and he and Childs went out to collect the rest of the Hom Quas. In ten minutes, they were grouped around the corner.

"The first man I asked," said Skilling. "Christ. The first man."

"Now what, sir?" asked Logen.

"That's a good question. As much as I hate to say it, I think we should call in some help from Champa. Those bastards up there are killers."

"I agree, sir," said Logen. "It's still our bust."

"Okay. Then, we'll take shifts watching the building. I'll go talk to Champa and see if he's got any suggestions. Our only worry is that the rice dealer might mention to Eddie that someone showed him his picture. Otherwise, they don't have any reason to get out."

"Childs, get around there now, and keep an eye on the rice dealer," said Logen. "But keep out of sight."

Childs nodded. "Right."

"Someone will relieve you in a couple of hours," said Skilling.

"That's okay, sir," said Childs. "I been flat on my ass for over a week." He moved on around the corner and out of sight.

"Set up some kind of schedule, Logen," said Skilling. "I'll put in a call to Colonel Champa."

"It's almost nine, sir," said Logen.

"I'll try him at home," Skilling said. "He's always on call anyway."

Before Skilling could leave, Childs ran back around the corner. "I saw him," said Childs. "I saw all of 'em."

"They came out?" asked Skilling.

"Why didn't you follow them?" asked Logen.

"You didn't tell me to, Sergeant," said Childs. "Besides, this Eddie comes out right across the street from where I'm standin'. I was lookin' for a place to settle. And he looks me straight in the eye. I mean, straight, man. I figure if he saw my face again this evenin', it'd blow everything."

Skilling nodded. "I think you're right, Childs. Good work. Let them go on about their business. We know they're in there. Tomorrow, I'll get Champa to hustle up a helicopter. We'll take a look at the building from up above. We'll sew that bastard up tight. Was that rice dealer still there?"

"No, sir," said Childs. "He split, I guess."

"Okay. Then let's all go home and get a good night's sleep. Everybody report into the Rue Pasteur office first thing tomorrow. Champa's office is on Pasteur, and I'll check back in with

104

you after I've seen him." Skilling clapped his hands together. "Goddamn. I think we're gonna nail that bastard."

But when the Hom Quas and a score of MPs struck the following day, they found empty quarters. At the very moment of the attack, Eddie Palmer, Mau Mau, Turk, and Apache Joe were over fifty kilometers from Saigon, heading toward the rain forests of Cambodia, their mouths gagged, their hands tied behind their backs. They were prisoners of North Vietnamese Colonel Ngo Duc Linh.

15

Once Colonel Linh had revealed his plan to Lieutenant Tri, the entire operation seemed to flow smoothly. Linh found that the time he'd once spent hating and daydreaming of inflicting hurt on the enemy was now spent in careful scrutiny of his plan.

A dozen men were recruited to assist Linh. A bombed-out village in Laos, now abandoned, was set up as headquarters. Only one building remained upright, but various bunkers had been built by the villagers. Four of those were in good-enough shape for habitation. One was under the still-erect house. The village was near enough to the Ho Chi Minh Trail, a five-hour walk, and yet remote enough to remain deserted. Linh's only worry was the Montagnards, the mountain people who were friendly or dangerous depending on who was paying them. They were the only ones who might stumble on the village and disrupt Linh's plans.

He was careful not to change anything in the village in case an overflight might reveal his presence there. Food and various other supplies were all stored in one of the bunkers. Two of the bunkers were used for sleeping. The fourth bunker, the one under the house, was used by Colonel Linh for living and working.

The men were all regular Vietnamese troops who had served

under Linh at one time or another. Each had been approached first by Lieutenant Tri. He felt them out and then, if they seemed willing, brought them to the colonel, who swore them to silence and then explained the broad scope of his plan. It was a credit to Colonel Linh that in picking the twelve men, Lieutenant Tri had to interview only twenty-three. Colonel Linh had made certain that every man chosen had lost someone because of American bombing.

Once the men had been picked, Colonel Linh engineered their "deaths." The men's papers and indentification were put on soldiers already dead. It took some time before each man was "killed" because Linh took care in finding bodies that were similar in size and age. And the bodies also had to be sufficiently burned or mutilated so that no positive identification could be made.

The entire process took two months. Lieutenant Tri and Colonel Linh remained "alive" during this time. Linh had to keep his contacts in Hanoi to supply the men and to continue carrying out his overall strategy.

The men, meanwhile, studied English, learned what they could about the nomenclature of the United States, and kept fit by exercising.

It was during this time of training that Linh realized a definite weakness in his plan. The United States was so vast, so foreign that to be successful, Linh needed some Americans to join him in the force. He felt that the Americans would best serve him if they were part of the unit, not merely prisoners. It was then Linh decided to capture some American deserters. For their services, he could offer them passage back to the United States and money. From what he'd heard about the deserters, some of them might willingly join him. Either way, he needed information about the United States from people who lived there.

Colonel Linh led the expedition to Saigon. He had been born in the village of Vung Tau, 150 kilometers from Saigon. He knew the dialect of the South, and Lieutenant Tri and any of his men would immediately be spotted as Northerners if they went on their own.

So it was that Linh, Tri, and four men left the Laotian village on a Friday night, headed for Saigon. Linh had reported that he and Lieutenant Tri were off on one of his regular inspection trips of the Ho Chi Minh Trail. The timing would be difficult because Linh didn't know how long they would have to be in Saigon. Lieutenant Tri and the men were to wait a few miles outside Saigon, in VC territory, while Linh went on in, disguised as a farmer and carrying the necessary false papers.

It was the most difficult phase of Linh's plan to date, but the fact that they were moving forward at all buoyed the spirits of everyone in the troop.

Night after night, Lieutenant Tri pushed the tiny Renault car along the Ho Chi Minh Trail, through Laos and on into Cambodia. Once inside South Vietnam, they traveled by foot, keeping to the rain forests and trying to avoid contact with anyone.

Tri and his men set up a small encampment just fifteen kilometers from the outskirts of Saigon. They were safe in the area because government troops never penetrated it, and the Americans were busy in other areas. The VC claimed the territory as their own but only occasionally made a show of strength there.

At the camp, Linh slept for a quick two hours until daylight. He then changed into the clothes of a peasant, mounted the bicycle they'd brought lashed atop their Renault, strapped on a heavy bundle of betel nuts, and began peddling toward Saigon down Highway One.

By 9:30, he was in Cholon. Linh was familiar with Saigon from his youth. During World War II, he had been sent from Saigon to France to be made an officer by the French, who jointly ruled Vietnam with the Japanese. And when the Japanese occupation collapsed after their surrender to the United States, Linh joined the Vietminh. Led by Ho Chi Minh, they took control of Vietnam in August of 1945.

It was in September of 1945 that Linh began to hate the

United States. Ho Chi Minh had proclaimed Vietnam a demo-
cratic replublic and appealed to the United States for support
against the French. But the United States failed to reply. It was
then the French army returned to Vietnam and launched a
campaign to reconquer the country.

In 1946, Ho Chi Minh called upon the people to expel the
French. Colonel Linh had been in a war ever since.

For the next few years, they battled the French army. And
again the United States was an enemy. They were helping the
French invaders. In 1954, the Vietminh defeated the French at
Dien Bien Phu, and Colonel Linh had thought his fighting was
ended. But a Geneva agreement divided the country in half.
Linh remained in the North with Ho Chi Minh and began the
fight again. He was then nearly thirty years old and had been
fighting for almost half his life.

And Linh was now back in Saigon for the first time since the
late 1940s. The size and activity of Saigon amazed him. What
had once been the Paris of the East was now a city gone mad
with congestion and construction.

Linh didn't try to hide his surprise or shock. He knew a simple
peasant from the outlying districts must feel the same kind of
awe and even fear upon visiting Saigon. So he rode his bike,
staring and shaking his head at the confusion. He became one
of a million.

Linh knew of several contacts in Saigon, Communists working undercover. But he had determined to spend his first day
merely wandering about, listening and scouting. By noon, he
felt his scouting was a waste of time and decided to reach one
of the Communist contacts without any further delay.

The man was large by Vietnamese standards, heavy, and slow
moving. His name was Ho Duc Soh, and his position was one
of a respected merchant of Cholon. He dealt in all manner of
food stuffs: rice, fruit, and vegetables. However, he was also the
final destination for an even wider range of smuggled goods
coming south on the Ho Chi Minh Trail.

Linh had difficulty speaking to the man because he ignored Linh, taking him for a peasant. After a wait of about ten minutes, Soh spoke to Linh. "Do you wish to buy or sell?" he asked.

"I wish to speak to Ho Duc Soh," said Linh.

"I am Ho Duc Soh."

"It is not necessary to know my name," said Linh. "Know only that my business is not betel nuts, as yours is not rice."

"I sell many things besides rice; that is true."

"So true, Ong Soh. Only this week, you received merchandise designed to blow open the belly, not to feed it. One case contained twelve mortars, caliber sixty millimeters, made by the People's Republic of China and bearing the numbers—"

"Please come back into my office," said Soh. He showed fear in his face for but a moment. Then he regained his composure. But he hurried Linh out of his shop and into a back room. There he stood, waiting. "What is it you want?"

"I seek information," said Linh. "Then I will leave."

"What information?"

"I wish to know of the American deserters who live in Cholon."

"What exactly do you wish to know? They are all about. Many hundreds of them."

Linh did not wish to reveal any part of his plan to this man. He proceeded cautiously. "Can they be bought?"

"Many will kill for money. All will steal and rob. Yes, they can be easily bought."

"How could I contact some of them. I do not want the soldier who is on drugs. I do not want men who feel they were forced to flee their army. I want men who hate. Those who will kill for money."

Soh was frightened of the man speaking to him. There was death in his eyes. He wondered for a moment if he was about to meet his death. But he felt safe in his shop. And he had always been a loyal Communist. But he must hurry this man along on his mission, whatever it was. "There are many men living with prostitutes. They would not suit you. They live on the money made by the girls. You seek one of the gangs. There are several known to me. All will kill. All have the hate you seek."

"Where can I find these gangs?" asked Linh.

Soh told Linh of a gang. "I do not know where they live. I only know they work with Duong Van Minh, a merchant not far from here. They have made Minh one of the most powerful black market operators in Cholon."

"Thank you, Ong Soh. I will trouble you no more."

"No more?"

"Never." Linh picked up his betel nuts and left. Soh breathed a sigh to calm his nervousness and did his best to put the entire incident totally out of his mind.

Linh watched the shop of Duong Van Minh until nearly night-fall. He then made his way quickly out of Saigon and slept the night a few meters off a road. The next morning, he returned to Cholon to again take up a vigil at the Vietnamese merchant's shop. It was about 2:00 in the afternoon when Linh saw a black man enter the shop. He did so with conviction, not pausing to study the merchandise. When he left a few minutes later, Linh followed. The black man led him to a five-story building. He went inside, and no one came out again until after dark. Linh was now hidden between buildings to avoid being questioned.

It was about 10:00 when Linh saw the black man come out with three others. They were dressed in uniforms and strode quickly away.

In three hours, the three others returned. They were laughing and joking with one another. In another forty-five minutes, the black man he had first seen returned. He went inside, and Linh surmised they had been out performing some function for Duong Van Minh. Linh then crossed over to the building and crept inside.

He was on the third floor when he heard their laughter. He continued on up the stairs until he was halfway between the fourth and fifth floors. There he crouched and could hear the noise of the men, only occasionally making out a word. Satisfied he had found their hideout, he went back to the street and spent the night behind the garage of the Continental Hotel.

Early next morning, he started his journey back to Lieutenant Tri and his men. He had spotted his target. Now all that remained was to capture it. At noon, he rejoined his unit. He told them of his work and then spent the remainder of the day working out a plan with Lieutenant Tri.

The following day, he ordered his men to get what rest they could during the day. He, too, lay on the spongy softness of the earth, trying to sleep and preparing himself for the night.

About midday, Linh roused his men. They were ready to move. Linh approached a farmer on the road and bought the supply of chickens the man was taking to market. Each of his men took some of the chickens, and they set out on the highway for Saigon.

They had no difficulty reaching the inner city. They spent the remainder of the daylight hours in a market near the Continental Hotel. Linh actually sold the chickens but kept the large basket of betel nuts. Buried inside the basket were five AK-47s.

When darkness came, Linh led his men to where he had spent the night, a narrow alleyway behind the hotel garage. There he distributed the guns, and he left them to watch for the black men to emerge.

It wasn't quite 9:00 when he saw them come out. He signaled his men and moved to fall in behind the black deserters. The black men were walking leisurely, sure of themselves. Linh watched them turn a corner. If they continued on in the direction they were headed, it would be perfect. Linh waved to his men and started to circle the block to move in ahead of the deserters.

The street they were running down was dark, and Linh no longer tried to conceal the AK-47 he was carrying. He could hear the feet of his men behind him. At the corner, he turned to his right and ran to take up a position where the deserters would have to pass.

He reached the corner and looked around. The deserters were perhaps twenty paces away, still moving slowly. Linh whispered to Tri, who had just run up. "Cross over the street. When they reach midpoint, we'll move. Watch me."

Tri took two men and ran to a position across the narrow street. Linh heard a baby crying in a room above him and hoped they would not have to shoot.

The first of the deserters passed him. Then they all passed him, and Linh signaled Tri. The deserters had no time even to draw their weapons. They were surrounded by the black barrels of the AK-47s.

Linh moved his men quickly. They disarmed the deserters, gagged them, and tied their hands tightly behind their backs. Then Linh started his tortuous way out of Cholon. It took them the rest of the night, hiding and dodging. Dawn was breaking as they reached the safety of the forests outside Saigon.

16

Mau Mau started to swear when the gags were taken off, but Eddie cut in with a sharp, "Cool it, man." Mau Mau shut up and stared.

Eddie saw the older one watching him and then turn away to speak to another man. He knew he'd made a mistake. The old man now knew he was the leader. Well, Eddie thought, it's not too bad a mistake.

Two of the Vietnamese came over to Eddie and jerked him bodily onto his feet and shoved him over toward the older Vietnamese. Eddie winced with pain. The tight bonds on his wrists had made his arms numb up to his elbows.

"Cut his bonds," said the older Vietnamese in English. Eddie felt a knife slash through the ropes. He tried to move his arms around, and the pain shot up to his shoulders. But he held his face expressionless. He moved his arms slowly, easing them into position. He fought crying out, making some sort of noise to ease the strain. The man before him watched. "It is painful?" he asked.

"No," said Eddie.

"You are an American deserter," said the man. "I am Colonel Ngo Duc Linh."

"I am Edward Palmer, 984-41-19, a corporal, on a three-day pass in Saigon. There's a big mistake."

"You work with Duong Van Minh. You steal, rob, smuggle, and kill for money."

"All right," said Eddie. "Let's have it. What's goin' on? We're in VC territory. We'll all be in trouble if we don't move."

"On the contrary," said Linh. "I am a colonel in the North Vietnamese army."

Eddie's eyebrows flicked up in spite of himself. "North?"

"We have many miles to go," said Linh. "I am going to offer you a proposition. If you accept, you will be under my command. If you choose not to accept, you'll be free to return to Cholon."

Like hell, Eddie thought. We'd make about ten feet if I don't go along with this dude. "What's your proposition," said Eddie.

"I need the services of an American," said Linh. "At this point, I need only tell you that you would be paid well. But it would require, perhaps, killing some of your own people in the United States."

"What's paid well?"

"One million dollars."

Eddie stared into Linh's eyes. "One million?"

"Delivered in the United States."

"Don't shuck me, man," said Eddie. Linh stared. "Don't try and fool me," Eddie translated.

"I do not fool you."

"Keep talkin'."

"I need information and intelligence from you," continued Linh. "All I require is obedience and the performance of certain tasks, which I will elaborate upon later. That is all I will say."

"How about them?" Eddie jerked his head toward his three men.

"They are your decision," said Linh. "If you think they would be helpful, they can accompany us. Otherwise—"

Otherwise a bullet, thought Eddie. "They can be helpful," said Eddie.

"It is your choice," said Linh. "But I will tolerate no trouble from them."

Eddie now rubbed his arms, trying to make his blood move. "You need an American," said Eddie. "And you're gonna pay him one million. Interesting."

"Do not try and figure out my plan or your future," replied Linh. "I have told you all I am going to. If you do not care to participate, I will return to Saigon and capture more deserters. Perhaps one of your men would do the work."

"My men do what I say they do," said Eddie. "They're good men, but they're my men. Don't try anything with them."

Linh looked into Eddie's brown eyes. An incredible stroke of luck to capture him, he thought. The man is ruthless, unafraid, and sure of himself. He will do well. He will also agree, thought Linh. Then he said, "The stakes are high."

"All right, Ong Linh," said Eddie. "We're in the action."

Linh nodded and turned to Tri. "Feed everyone, and we will then move on."

Eddie spoke to Tri. "A knife," he said. Tri looked at Linh, and Linh nodded. Tri handed Eddie the knife, and he walked to his men sitting on the ground. He cut their ropes.

Mau Mau whispered. "What's goin' on, man?"

Eddie spoke softly. "Man, I don't know, but those are North Viets. The one's a colonel, and he's offerin' us some action in a gig. I don't know what in hell it is, but you look at that dude's eyes, and you know he ain't no man to fool with."

"You mean we're workin' for North Nam?" asked Apache Joe.

"You got it, baby," said Eddie. "Just play it cool, or our brains is gonna be dumped all over this here jungle. Who knows. He's talkin' big loot. Maybe he's just lookin' to do a little honest smugglin' of dope. And he needed some professionals."

"Well, shee-it, man," said Mau Mau, "if there's bread involved, I don't care where it comes from. But I can't spend no North Vietnam money nowhere except North Vietnam."

"He is talkin' American bread, man," said Eddie. "And he is talkin' big."

Mau Mau smiled. "You can look at it this way, daddy. It ain't every nigger served in the North Viet army."

They were given a small ration of rice, and each American ate it gratefully. Eddie noticed there were always two men on guard. One watched the landscape and the sky, and the other watched Eddie and his men.

They traveled all night and, because they were moving under heavy jungle cover, most of the next day. They stopped only once to eat another ration of rice.

It was difficult for Eddie to measure how far they'd come when they reached a small clearing and uncovered a battered car from behind a lean-to of jungle growth.

After a short rest, Linh ordered Eddie and his three companions into the back of the car. His soldiers sat on the hood and fenders. Linh rode inside, and Tri drove. For the next several nights, the pattern was the same. Driving by night and resting by day. Eddie saw hundreds of men and trucks pass them during the night, and he surmised he was on a branch of the Ho Chi Minh Trail. He also felt Linh seemed to be keeping him and his men under cover.

By this time, Eddie and his men were constantly sick. They were forced to drink the water along the route, and each of them was suffering from severe dysentery.

But Linh pressed on. One morning, they continued to travel after sunup. About 10:00, Tri pulled the car over into the jungle, and everyone unloaded.

"I will leave you here," said Linh to Eddie. Eddie nodded, the pain in his stomach forcing him to bend a trifle at the waist. "You have a few kilometers to walk. Then you will be given medication. In two days, you should all be well again."

Linh then climbed into the car and pulled it back out onto the trail. Lieutenant Tri went to Linh and spoke briefly with him. Eddie noted that Tri took some papers out of his pocket and handed them to Linh. Then Linh drove on out of sight.

Tri now signaled for everyone to start walking. Eddie spoke to his men. "We got to walk now," he said. "But where we're goin', there's some medicine. So keep up, man."

It was about five hours of torturous travel before they arrived at what appeared to Eddie to be the ruins of a village. From out of a bunker, some other men appeared. Tri spoke to them, and one man hurried into the only remaining hut. In a moment, he was back, carrying a small box. Tri took a tablet from the box for each deserter. They were told to take the tablet and rest. Each did. Eddie slept fifteen hours.

Linh had been correct. By the third day, Eddie and his men were fit again. The medication, taken twice a day, had cured their dysentery. But they all felt weak. It was nearly six days before they regained their strength.

Eddie quickly decided to sit it out in the village. He knew Linh had gone on to continue to work out his plan, whatever it was. Also, Tri watched him closely. There were twelve men who were always armed. Eddie figured he might be able to take over the camp, but not without losses, and he really couldn't see any advantage to it. It was days back to Saigon and mostly through enemy territory. So he waited.

The Vietnamese in the camp either stood guard on the perimeter or worked inside the hut. They were learning English there and seemed to be studying various maps. But Eddie and his men were kept out of the hut, so he could only guess at what was going on. The English lessons led him to believe that the operation, whatever it was, would take place inside Saigon itself.

After a week and a half, Linh returned. He nodded briefly to Eddie and then went with Tri into the hut. They spoke for nearly two hours. Then Tri came for Eddie.

"The colonel wishes to speak to you," said Tri.

Eddie nodded and walked to the hut.

"Sit down," said Linh.

Eddie pulled a handmade wooden chair into position and sat facing Linh. He didn't speak.

118

Linh continued. "Lieutenant Tri has told me you and your men have been most cooperative. I expected as much. You would wait out a situation until you had the facts. That is good. It is the mark of a leader, I think. What was your position in the army?"

"Corporal," said Eddie.

Linh nodded. "Perhaps that was their mistake. You do not like to take orders, do you?"

"Not unless there's a reason," said Eddie.

Linh took out a map and started to unfold it. "I am now going to reveal part of my plan to you. I suppose you have surmised I may be a smuggler. Or you may even think I am planning a strike against an American base."

"Both crossed my mind," said Eddie.

Linh had now finished unfolding the map and ran his hand across it to smooth it flat. Eddie saw it was a map of the United States. "Here is my target," said Linh, pointing.

"The U.S.?" Eddie said, smiling.

Linh ignored Eddie's amused face. "You will have a say in the picking of cities and targets. This is your country. Where is your home?"

"I'm from New York," said Eddie.

"Excellent," said Linh. "We will go into the exact targets at a later date."

"Look, man—" started Eddie.

Linh interrupted. "Hear me out," he said. "My force will leave from Saigon. We will eventually arrive in your country posing as South Vietnamese businessmen, sellers of brass objects. The crates of brass will include well-disguised mortars and shells. Once inside the United States, we will proceed to various target points. When we are in place, we will attack and destroy those targets. Then we will fade out of sight to attack and destroy again." Linh leaned back.

"Financing," said Eddie.

"Drugs," said Linh. "I will need the help of you and your men

119

on this. Let me say only that I have a feasible plan for obtaining drugs. Enough drugs to finance my plan and make you rich."

"The army, not to mention the police."

"Consider an arms plant in the United States," said Linh. "There is an explosion. Would your authorities suspect a mortar shell? I think not. Consider a gasoline depot. Again, would your authorities dream that a foreign force had attacked it? Even if they did, are there enough men to cover every arms plant, gasoline depot, power station in the United States? Again, I think not."

"You want me to be part of this?"

"I need your knowledge. Correct knowledge. I also need to be able to turn my back on you, Ong Eddie. To do that, you must be a part of this team, not a captive of it."

"I dig," said Eddie. "So how you gonna keep me in line?"

"I will pay after each attack," said Linh. "I am also assuming that since you kill your countrymen without hesitation in Saigon, you will do the same in the United States. As I once told you, these are big stakes—for both of us."

"Where's it all end up for me? That's what I need to know right now."

"You will be rich. You will have a false identity. With care, you could stay in the United States and live well for your entire life. Or you could pick a country of your choice and go there to spend your one million American dollars. That is up to you."

Eddie tipped backward a bit in his chair. He rocked briefly, then sat forward. "Okay, Ong Linh. You got yourself a real partner. I'm in. All the way. All I'm askin' at this point is to know every damned detail of this plan of yours. I'll do it, but I want to make sure it works."

"I agree with you, Ong Eddie. I do not wish to make a foolish mistake from lack of knowledge. Ask what you wish."

"First, how about you and your men. Is someone gonna come lookin' for you?"

"We are all dead, officially."

"That's why you took Tri's papers?" Linh nodded. "And the men?"

"Everyone is dead. My government will not be looking for us. We only have to worry about the mountain people in this area. If they see us, they might reveal our presence. That is why we keep a careful watch and stay out of sight."

"When do we start?"

"We can begin the actual operation a week from tomorrow. A large shipment of raw drugs is being sent south on the Ho Chi Minh Trail. I expect it to go no farther than this village. That is your task, Ong Partner Eddie."

"That's cuttin' it pretty close, isn't it?"

"If it is too soon, there will be other shipments."

Eddie shrugged. "What the hell," he said. "Might as well get started. Ain't makin' no money here."

"Good."

"Then, once we get the stuff, what?"

"We cannot have it processed in this area. It would become known. I have made arrangements to have it shipped to Marseilles."

"It's processed in France, and then we smuggle it into the States, right?" Linh nodded. "Then what?"

"New York, your home, is the drug market of the world. Surely you can find a buyer for it."

"I dig. Okay. Almost any candy store in Harlem handles junk. But we're dealin' with big stuff here, right?"

"Many kilos."

"How do we lay it off?"

"You will solve that problem, Ong Eddie. Of that I am certain."

"If I don't solve it, I don't get paid. Right?"

"Correct."

"Man, I'll solve it. Okay, just tell me the rest of the plan, step by step. I'll interrupt if I got questions."

Linh talked quietly and steadily for the next hour. When Eddie left the shelter, he was convinced of two things. One, Linh was hovering on the edge of sanity. A fanatic. Two, Linh's plan would work. It had holes, but nothing that couldn't be fixed. If all went well, he said to himself, Eddie Palmer, 984-41-19, is going to be one rich nigger.

17

"The shipment is being sent on bicycles," said Linh. "There will be ten men, all armed. They will travel down to here." He pointed to near the demilitarized zone. Eddie nodded. "From there," continued Linh, "they move along Laos, into Cambodia, and on down into Saigon, where the drugs are to be flown out for processing."

"How much exactly are we talkin' about?" asked Eddie.

"Over one hundred kilos. About two hundred fifty pounds."

"Christ."

"The material is a morphine base. The laboratory will turn it into an equal weight of heroin."

"Why don't we hit the factory?"

"It is some distance. Where, I do not know."

"Could we process it?"

"I am told the work can be done in any kitchen. However, it requires acid, and the fumes are rather poisonous. I am not a chemist, are you?"

"Okay, we do it your way. Marseilles. I think you're right about not doin' anything with it here. If we start processin' it, the drug dudes we took it off are gonna know."

Linh nodded. "I have made arrangements to put it on a ship going directly to Marseilles. The cargo will already have been inspected, so our pickup will be made about here." Linh pointed to a spot off the coast of Cambodia in the Gulf of Siam.

"He does the pickup and sails on with our stuff."

"Lieutenant Tri will be a member of his crew, as will another of my men. When the drugs reach Marseilles, the captain will be paid. Lieutenant Tri will then rent a small villa in the hills of Marseilles and wait for our arrival."

"Our arrival?"

"Once Lieutenant Tri has notified me he is ready, we will all fly to Marseilles. Then we will make arrangements to process the drugs. Once processed, the material will go on to the United States."

"Sounds good. Now all we gotta do is heist the goods."

"I have two men preparing to move along the trail with the drugs. You will have to pick a spot somewhere near the Cambodian border to hijack the material. The two men will move on ahead of the drugs and join you so they can identify the drug carriers. We want all of the shipment."

"Very neat. When do we move out?"

"Three days from now."

"Who you sendin' with us?"

Linh smiled. "Again, Lieutenant Tri. He will stay with you until the drugs are taken. He will then go join the ship, and you will move on toward the Cambodian coast. With five of my men."

"Five of your men. And they all know the country?"

"They are somewhat familiar with it. Enough to get you through."

"We're gonna have to get us a boat to get the stuff out to the ship."

"I trust you will use your ingenuity in that respect. The captain will drop anchor just off here." Linh put his index finger on a spot between Ile de Phu Quoc and the coast of Cambodia. "He will report some engine trouble and will stay there a day for repairs. During that time, you must reach him somehow."

"Then, that's it. It's a good plan, Ong Linh. I can't see any real problems. How far ahead of the drugs will we be?"

"Two days. You will move somewhat slower, since you may have to take some care on the trail. There are not many black men who have ever traveled it."

"Just one more thing, Ong Linh. Who's in charge of this operation?"

"Lieutenant Tri will lead the party to a point you choose for the hijacking. Once there, the operation becomes yours."

Eddie stood up. "I got to hand it to you, man. When we get to the States, we can be in the big time. You can come back to Nam rich and famous."

Linh looked up at Eddie and spoke softly. "I do not think I will ever leave the United States."

They hadn't walked fifty yards, and already the village was obscured by jungle growth. There were nine of them, Lieutenant Tri and four men and Eddie and his three. They pushed hard for many days. The heat and the jungle began to oppress them all. Eddie's men were becoming more and more hostile.

"Hey, man," said Apache Joe, "this is bullshit, you know. The army was never this bad, man."

"At least you got somethin' to eat beside rice, man," Turk said. "I got rice comin' outa my ears, man. I ain't no gook. I gotta eat somethin' beside rice."

Eddie nodded. "Hey, man, I know it's tough. But we're talkin' about a million big ones."

"I ain't seen a nickel since I left Cholon," said Mau Mau. "I ain't been laid. I ain't been drunk."

Eddie mimicked him. "I ain't been laid. I ain't been drunk."

"Look, Eddie," said Mau Mau, "we can take these gooks. We can get our pieces back and blow out their guts. That one dink is carryin' our weapons. All we gotta do is grab him and start shootin'. We could be back at our pad in a week, livin' high off the hog again."

"Listen, you dumb bastard," said Eddie. "In the first place, we ain't got a chance out here in this fuckin' jungle without them gooks. But supposin' we did make it back, and we set up operations again. Then what? We live high off the hog, sure. But for how long, man? For how long? Them piasters we had is shit outside Nam. You can't spend 'em in Shanghai or Hong Kong. Nowhere. And the MPC is shit, too. You gonna trade back in your MPC for real money when the war is over? No, man. That shit was all right if there wasn't any other way. But this here is a way out, man. It's real money, and it's a trip back to the States."

"Hey, man," said Mau Mau. "Don't get all riled up. All we're sayin', boss-man, is it ain't no fun no more."

Eddie nodded and grinned. "We pull off this gig, I promise you we have some fun, man. Okay?"

"Okay, man," said Mau Mau. "That's all we lookin' for. Right, Apache Joe? Turk?"

"Yeah, man," said Turk. "And somethin' to eat besides rice."

"Dig," said Eddie.

After days of hard travel, they were finally there. "This is as far as we can go safely," said Lieutenant Tri.

"Then, we'll do the job here," said Eddie. "Nice turn in the trail. We can pop 'em off right there. It all look good to me."

They set up camp about twenty yards off the trail. One of the Vietnamese was always on watch, waiting for their comrades who were preceding the drug caravan. It was late in the second day when they were spotted. They were pedaling hard.

Lieutenant Tri waited until they turned the crook in the trail, and then he hailed them. There was some discussion, and Lieutenant Tri hurried to Eddie.

"They are only minutes behind," said Tri. "We must act quickly."

"Don't get excited, man," said Eddie. "Just pass out the weapons, and we'll have at it."

Lieutenant Tri gave an order, and one of the men brought the modified M-16s over to Eddie. "Hey, Apache Joe," said Eddie, "give these a quick once-over."

Apache Joe picked up one of the guns. Eddie saw Lieutenant Tri stand out of the line of fire, and the other Vietnamese held their weapons at the ready. Apache Joe quickly checked the gun, fired a single shot into the jungle, and then went on to the next one.

Mau Mau came up behind Eddie. "You sure you don't wanna kill a few gooks?" said Mau Mau.

"You gonna kill a few gooks, man," Eddie replied. "But not these."

Apache Joe finished checking all the weapons. "They're ready to go," he said.

"Everybody get a piece," said Eddie. "We'll all work this side of the trail. I'll let you know which gook to pop. We may have to let some go through, you dig? Don't fire till I give you the nod."

"Right, baby," said Turk.

"Soon as you pop him, we drag the bike and the body out of the way. I don't want nothin' showing for the next man comin' along. So don't go blowin' 'em to pieces, dig? You do, you got to clean up the mess."

"What if there's more than one of 'em?" asked Mau Mau.

"We don't want no witnesses," said Eddie. "This jungle's big enough to bury a whole lot of folks."

Eddie's men positioned themselves a few feet off the trail, crouching behind the growth. Eddie stationed one of Tri's men down the trail in case anyone was coming up and into their spot. The two cyclists waited up the trail. Lieutenant Tri stayed in Eddie's line of sight. Eddie stood a few feet behind Mau Mau, the first man in his line.

They waited about twenty minutes. Then Tri held up his hand and nodded. "Okay, Mau Mau. Here comes one. You take him."

The cyclist, his head bowed, was pushing hard. A dirty band around his forehead glistened with sweat. Eddie could hear the whooshing of his breath as he gasped the moist air into his lungs.

When he was directly in front of Mau Mau, Eddie heard the *pfft, pfft* of two shots. The bullets caught him in the chest cavity, and he was knocked over on the trail. Mau Mau stepped out over him, but the man didn't move.

"Let's go," said Eddie.

They picked up the man and carried him back into the jungle. The bicycle was pushed back and dropped on top of the body.

In just over thirty minutes, there were eleven bodies in the jungle. The extra corpse had been collected when a man had come unexpectedly around the curve in the trail as they were killing one of the couriers. In another hour, all the bodies were buried in a collective grave about fifty yards off the trail.

The bicycles were dumped in the jungle except for the two Tri and his man were to ride to Saigon. The drugs were split up between Eddie and his men and the five soldiers going south with them. Everyone moved efficiently and quietly. By the time Tri was ready to leave, there was no trace of the violence.

As Tri mounted the bicycle, Eddie strode over. He lifted his M-16. "We're keepin' these, man," he said.

Tri nodded. "Just be there in four days. My men will guide you, but you are in command. If you run into a bad situation, you will have to get everyone out."

"I dig. Have a good pedal, man."

Tri nodded and shoved off. Eddie signaled, and his party pushed off into the jungle.

Eddie wanted to put some space between the hijack point and his party, and they walked several hours without stop. When they were in sight of the Mekong River, Eddie halted the band.

"Hey," he called to one of the Vietnamese, "is it safe to stay here?"

"Safe, yes," the man said. "No closer to river. We cross river, all is safe. Many people on river."

"Okay. Then, let's stay here. We'll cross the river fresh to-morrow."

They crossed the Mekong in the first light of dawn. Eddie split the group into two parties. He sent one party across with their weapons lashed to a log. They drifted with the current but reached the other side without incident. Then they spaced themselves along the river to cover the crossing of the drugs.

The drugs, too, were lashed to a floating log. Eddie and the others then pushed off. They, too, floated downstream but were able to reach the opposite bank without being spotted. They split up the drugs again and quickly started pushing their way through the jungle for the Gulf of Siam.

Eddie could smell the sea long before he could see it. It was their fourth day on the trail, and it had been rugged going. They were all tired and hot, and most of them were suffering from small cuts and wounds made by jungle plants.

Cuts didn't heal easily in the jungle, and the open wounds attracted a variety of crawling and flying insects. Leeches, too, were plentiful, and every man in the group suffered from the bite of the bloodsuckers.

Linh's men led Eddie to the exact rendezvous, a few kilometers from a small Cambodian village near the Vietnam border. It was in the village that Eddie had to obtain a boat, and because they had moved slower than anticipated, there wasn't much time. The ship was to anchor that evening and fire a small rocket at hour intervals throughout the night until they were contacted.

Eddie sent two Vietnamese on ahead to scout the village. It would be dark in five hours. He left the other three Vietnamese to guard the drugs. He and his three men then followed behind the two scouts.

Eddie watched while the two Vietnamese went into the village and started to talk. There were several small fishing boats in an inlet. The village itself spread like a crescent moon around the end of the inlet. Eddie counted twenty-three people and, from the number of huts, guessed that to be about half the population.

The Vietnamese and the Cambodian fishermen were arguing.

There was a great deal of arm waving, and even from a distance, Eddie could tell that his comrades were not having any luck.

"Mau Mau," said Eddie.

"Yeah, man."

"You and Turk cut over behind that village. They ain't gonna let us have no boat. We're gonna have to take it."

"What're we gonna do?"

"Just space out, man, and don't let anybody through. If somebody tries to run, cut 'em down. Otherwise, just herd 'em back into the village. No shootin' unless you have to, dig?"

"I dig. Come on, Turk."

The two worked their way behind the village. Eddie sent Apache Joe out a few hundred yards so he would be about halfway between Eddie and Mau Mau. They loosely encircled the native settlement.

The two men sent to the village came back to report to Eddie. "They no want to rent boat. They get very angry," said the one.

"Do they have guns?"

"Some. Not many, but maybe more hidden."

"How many you figure are in the village?" asked Eddie.

"Fifty, maybe."

"Okay. You stick with me. We got to have one of those boats."

Eddie stood and started to walk toward the village, his M-16 hooked on his belt at the small of his back. He walked casually. He saw the others walking toward the village. About a hundred yards away, a villager spotted him and began shouting. Other men ran out, and they pointed at Eddie and the two men beside him. Then someone saw Mau Mau and Turk coming from the other side.

Several of the villagers ran into their huts, and they returned carrying rifles. Eddie could see they were old bolt-action guns. One M-16 could match the firepower of ten of those, thought Eddie. One of the villagers pointed a rifle at Eddie, and he raised his hands and kept walking.

130

When Eddie raised his hands, the villager lowered his rifle a bit but kept it at the ready. Eddie was now fifty yards away. Someone in the village shouted.

"What'd he say?" asked Eddie of the Vietnamese.

"He say for us to stop."

Eddie stopped. He signaled to the others and shouted, "Okay, hold it right there."

The villager shouted again. The Vietnamese said, "He tell us to go away."

Eddie nodded. "Tell them there is big money if we can use a boat."

The Vietnamese shouted to the village. Suddenly, the man with the gun fired, and it kicked up dirt a few feet to Eddie's left.

Eddie shouted. "Mau Mau, Turk, Apache. Frag 'em, man." Eddie stood and watched as the tightly knit group of men started to fall. There were screams now, and they turned away from Eddie. From this distance, there was no noise at all from the modified M-16s.

Eddie swung his weapon around and up and started to run toward the village. He could hear the two men running behind him. He fired once as an older man came running out of the end hut in the village. The man was knocked backward into the hut.

Two villagers were firing now in Mau Mau's direction. Eddie cut them down with a burst. By the time Eddie reached the spot where the men had grouped, the fight was over. One man was holding a rifle. He threw it down as Eddie ran up, fear twisting his face. A shattered leg bent back under him, but the pain seemed to be overcome by his terror of the sudden attack.

Mau Mau ran up. "Some son of a bitch damn near killed me," he said. "Shee-it."

Eddie laughed. "It was him, man," said Eddie, pointing at the wounded man with his M-16. He pulled the trigger and put a bullet in his head. "Round up everybody that's alive," he said. "Don't let nobody get away."

They found forty-three others in the huts. The raid had eliminated nearly all the adult males in the village. Several older people were in the group, and the rest were women and children.

"Now what, man?" asked Turk.

"Take those three," Eddie indicated three men who had survived the fight. "Get 'em to tell you how one of those boats works."

One of the Vietnamese spoke. "I talk to them."

"Okay," said Eddie. "Your friend can go back and get the junk. Bring it here. Come on."

The other Vietnamese turned and trotted off to where the drugs had been left.

The remaining Vietnamese started to talk to the three villagers. Eddie didn't bother to listen to the chattering. Several of the women were on the ground, cradling the heads of their dead husbands in their laps. They were crying and wailing. Eddie looked at the group of Cambodians. Almost everyone in the group was crying.

"Christ, what a noise," he said. "Load up a full clip. We gotta shut 'em up."

"Hey, man," said Apache Joe, "we gonna kill everybody?"

"You know it, baby," said Eddie. "These gooks may not talk our language, but they talk. You dig?"

"Look, man," said Apache Joe, "can't we keep out a couple of the young ones? We gotta long wait."

"You thinkin' of ass now, man?" asked Eddie.

Mau Mau laughed. "He always thinkin' of ass."

"Kill 'em all," said Eddie.

Turk joined in. "Hey, man, we can kill the girls when we're through with 'em. How about it, man? Hey, it's been a long time in the jungle, dig?"

Eddie checked his watch. "All right. Shit. We got about four hours before the first flare. Pick out what you want. But listen, man. Don't go gettin' attached to 'em. They gotta die before we split."

"Right on, man," said Mau Mau. "I'll take me that young one over there."

"Hold it," said Eddie. "Let's let the gooks tell us how to run them boats before you go humpin' their women."

The four black deserters waited. The villagers kept in a group, weeping and comforting one another. Then the Vietnamese reported back to Eddie.

"Boat easy," he said. "Big one have motor. Just start up and steer. They not use much. Too far to go for fuel."

"Let 'em show you how to start it. Then make sure it's workin'. Then kill 'em."

The Vietnamese bowed his head slightly and turned away. Eddie watched while the four men went to the boat. He heard the motor kick over. Then it stopped. Then there was a loud burst of gunfire.

The villagers started to scream again, and they looked as though they might all try to run. "They're gonna stampede," said Eddie. "If you want a piece of tail, you better get it fast. I'm gonna start shootin'."

Mau Mau, Turk, and Apache Joe each grabbed a woman from the group. They dragged them to the edge of the group. "Hey, Eddie. Watch 'em, will you man?"

"I'll watch 'em."

"You sure you don't want one?"

"Well, shit. Pull out another one. Maybe those gooks we got with us wanna get a little."

Mau Mau grabbed another young villager and dragged her off with the others. An older woman, evidently her mother, grabbed onto Mau Mau's leg, screaming at him. Mau Mau shot her. Then he turned and began to fire into the crowd.

They started to break away, then, running in all directions. In less than a minute, there were thirty-nine more corpses.

"Just like a shootin' gallery, man," said Turk.

"Put the girls in a hut," said Eddie. "One of you stay with 'em. We'll load up the stuff on the boat when they get here with it."

133

By the time the drugs were loaded on the boat, they still had two and a half hours before their first contact with the ship.

"Okay, man," said Eddie. "I'll keep an eye out. You cats go ahead."

Mau Mau, Turk, and Apache Joe went to the hut with the women. They signaled for the Vietnamese to join them. Three did, but the other two went near the water and squatted down to look out to sea.

Eddie moved to higher ground, cleared a spot for himself, and relaxed, watching the village and the clear, watery horizon until it became dim in the growing darkness. Nearly three hours passed by.

From the village, he could hear an occasional scream and occasional laugh.

Then Eddie spotted the ship, a dark shape on a black sea. He moved quickly down toward the village. "Hey, let's go," he shouted. "The ship's out there. Come on, come on. Move it."

No one appeared as Eddie shouted. Then he saw the figures of the two Vietnamese who had gone to sit on the beach. Eddie shouted. "Over here."

The two men ran over, and the three of them hurried toward the hut. Mau Mau stumbled out of the native house as Eddie arrived.

"Hey, man," said Mau Mau, "wha's all the shoutin' about."

"You're drunk," said Eddie. "Damn."

"Man, we found some of that native stuff. We have a few, you know?"

Eddie stepped by Mau Mau and into the hut. One lamp flickered in a corner of the one-room dwelling. Apache Joe and Turk were crouched against poles supporting the roof. The three Vietnamese were asleep on the ground. Three nude girls were also unconscious on the ground.

"What's happenin', man?" asked Turk.

Eddie whirled on Mau Mau. "Where's the other girl?"

"Other girl?" asked Mau Mau, shaking his head. "Man, they're all in there."

"Damn your black soul," said Eddie. "Gimme that piece." He grabbed Mau Mau's M-16 and stepped just inside the doorway. He killed the three girls on the ground. "I oughta kill all you bastards. You screw up this gig, man, you're all dead."

Mau Mau shook his head again, trying to clear away his drunkenness. "Man, we're ready for anything, man. Hey, we okay, man."

"Sober up," shouted Eddie. "Walk in the fuckin' water or somethin'. But sober up. And when you do, you better find that missin' gook, you dig? If she get away, I am gonna take it unkindly."

Mau Mau walked to Turk and Apache Joe to help them to their feet. Eddie turned and walked toward the boat with the two sober Vietnamese. He could hear Mau Mau behind him, screaming at Turk and Apache Joe.

Eddie fired up the motor just as the first signal light was shot off. It gave him a perfect fix on the boat, and he gestured for one of the Vietnamese to haul up the anchor. Then they slowly glided out into the inky darkness.

A light cut across the water and held the boat in its glare. Eddie shouted. "Cut the light, Tri."

The light went out instantly, and Eddie squeezed his eyes to try and regain his night vision. A spot of white danced about in his eyes, but it faded, slowly. Then he opened his lids and peered ahead. He saw the hulk of the ship straight in front of them. He cut the engine, and the boat drifted bow on into the ship and bounced sideways to float parallel against it.

"Tri," said Eddie, "send some men over to unload."

The heavily loaded freighter sat low in the water. Several sailors leaped over the railing onto the deck of Eddie's boat. They quickly passed the cargo up to their shipmates.

Tri leaned over the railing. "Any trouble?"

"No," said Eddie. "No trouble. How about you?"

"All goes well."

"Okay. That's it, then. Good luck."

The sailors scrambled back onto the deck of the freighter.

Eddie started his motor and wheeled the boat out and away, back toward the village. He heard the diesel motors of the ship start, and he turned to see the freighter churn up a silver trail as it headed out into the gulf.

Eddie held the boat straight for the shore. He ran it aground, shut the motor off, and leaped off the bow into foot-deep water. He could smell the stench of the dead. Mau Mau ran up.

"Hey, man, we can't find her. Shit, I'm sorry. I don't remember her leavin'. We looked all over hell. But we keep lookin', and we find her sure in the morning."

"Pack up," Eddie said coldly. "We're haulin' ass." Mau Mau started to speak. "Now, baby."

Eddie kept the troop moving on into the night. The undergrowth was nearly impassable in the dark, but Eddie wanted to put some distance between them and the village. If the girl did get away, a helicopter could bring Cambodian troops quickly and with deadly results. It made Eddie feel a little better to hear his men being sick in the jungle. But all of them were too ashamed and afraid to ask Eddie to stop. Near dawn, Eddie stopped. He figured they'd made nearly eight miles. Enough. Everyone fell to the ground exhausted.

Eddie listened to the heavy breathing around him. He waited until dawn. He studied their camp in the light and decided they were safe from aerial observation. With that, he turned on his side and went immediately to sleep.

18

"This is goin' to interest you, I think, Lieutenant," said Sergeant Logen.

"What is it?" asked Skilling.

"It's an official note of protest from the Cambodian government to the Republic of Vietnam and to the United States Army, Vietnam."

"It's not about the Hom Quas, I hope."

"No. It's about some black Americans."

Skilling looked up at Logen standing before his desk. It was a Saturday morning, a time when Logen and Skilling tried to clear up desk work at the Rue Pasteur office. "Let me see," said Skilling.

Logen handed the lieutenant the report. It had come through the normal channels of the Provost Marshal's office, one of the many sent out each week. Skilling read quickly. "It just could be our boy," he said. "Christ. Imagine wiping out an entire village. That sounds like our Eddie."

"That's what I thought. There aren't too many black Americans out in the jungles. And that accounts for why we can't find him in Saigon."

"He's out playing Tarzan, and we turned over every rock in the place," said Skilling. "It has to be some sort of smuggling operation."

"Absolutely," said Logen.

"You figure drugs?"

"What else is worth it?"

Skilling tapped the report with his right index finger. "They must have needed a boat to get out to a ship."

"It makes sense. Carry the drugs to the coast, have the ship lay off the coast, and you take a boat out and transfer them. No customs worries at all until you reach port."

"What do you know about drug smuggling in this fair country, Sergeant?"

"Most of it's done by air charter. The factories for processing are mainly in Hong Kong and Thailand. It's run by just about everybody who's tryin' to make a buck, French and the Corsicans mostly. But now Americans are getting into it more and more."

"If it's Eddie, how do you think he fits?"

"Knowing him, he probably hijacked it. He took over a load before it was put on a plane, or maybe the stuff came down the Ho Chi Minh Trail. With all the fighting going on now, it's a little dangerous to be flying around in a chartered plane."

"Where would they be taking the stuff on a ship?"

"Hong Kong. New York. Who knows?"

"I know it's that bastard." Skilling pointed to the report. "Look here. The survivor says that the men who killed the villagers shot with guns that didn't make any noise."

"I guess we can figure it's Eddie. But it still doesn't do us a hell of a lot of good."

"It does me some good. I know the bastard is still around. And I tell you, Sergeant, I'm gonna nail his ass some day."

"Someday, maybe. But this report is more than a week old. He could be anywhere by now."

"If he's in drugs, he has to surface. You've got friends all over. Suppose you put out the word. Have them keep their eyes open."

"Keep their eyes open for what? If they can nail a shipment

138

of drugs, they'll do it. They don't need any word from me."

"How about informers?"

"I don't have any outside Saigon."

"Dammit, then let's make it official. I'll draft a letter saying we have reason to suspect Eddie Palmer of being heavily into drug trafficking. We'll send his photo and his MO out to everybody. Maybe somebody'll get off their ass if they hear anything."

"It's a waste of paper, Lieutenant." Logen looked at the officer. "But what the hell. Wasting paper is the army way." He smiled.

Skilling turned to look out on the street below. "Suppose we go along with your theory that he was meeting a ship. Why don't we check ship departures from Saigon the week prior to this raid."

"Might turn up something. If the ship left from Saigon."

"Then, do it," said Skilling.

Logen found thirty-five ships had left that week. He checked into their registry and found a hot lead. One ship going to Marseilles was captained by a Chinese nationalist who had a record for smuggling and was known throughout the area as a man who would do almost anything for money. The ship was a small vessel registered in Hong Kong. Its cargo was raw rubber.

"We're just supposing, Lieutenant," said Logen, "okay?"

"Suppose away," said Skilling. The two men were lunching on *pho,* a noodle soup sold from carts in the street.

"Suppose our friend hijacked a load of drugs headed for processing in Thailand. Supposing he made arrangements somehow for it to leave the country on a ship headed for Marseilles, captained by a very shady type with a record as long as our book of rules."

"How would he know about the shipment?"

"I don't know."

"Go on."

"He hijacks the drugs, makes arrangements for the ship to pull up off Cambodia. He drops the stuff on the ship, and off it goes to the drug capital of Europe."

"He'd go along, no doubt."

"He would unless it isn't his operation. He could just be the muscle."

"Right."

"The drugs would be processed in Marseilles and shipped on to the United States along the usual smuggling routes."

"Our boy might be the one to pull it off. We're supposing an awful lot, but it's a direction. Now, if we're supposing, let's suppose he did hijack a load of drugs. Then, somebody in Saigon was waiting for those drugs. Can't we nose around a little here and see if we can turn up one angry drug peddler?"

"I already have," said Logen. "There were three deserters killed in Cholon this week. The talk is that it's some sort of gang war between two drug operators in town."

"The deserters were the enforcers?"

"Right. One faction is accusing the other of hijacking. And it's gettin' very ugly."

"Did you hear how much is involved?" asked the lieutenant.

"A big one," said Logen. "Over a hundred kilos."

"My God," said Skilling. "If that's our man and he can pull it off, he's a millionaire."

"Like ten times. What do you think?"

"Has that ship reached Marseilles yet?"

"Fortunately, no. It's an old tub. Slow."

"Is there anyone who owes you a favor in Marseilles?"

"Well, there's a civilian we picked up in a standard bust a few months ago. He was in Saigon from France. Caught him with a broad, puffing marijuana. I slipped him out the back door."

"Want to use up your favor?"

"Might as well."

"Get him to meet the ship when it lands. Can he handle it?"

"Hell, yes. He's in the import-export business."

140

"Meaning?"

"He's CIA, for Christ sake."

Skilling laughed. "You do have a favor coming. All right, if he can just be in port when it docks. He doesn't have to move on it, just observe. Send him our picture of Eddie."

"Will do."

The sergeant had little trouble with his Marseilles contact, a Russell Nimz. Nimz promised to check out the crew of the ship quietly.

There was a long-distance call from Marseilles early one morning for Sergeant Logen. The voice of Nimz came in loud and clear. "You hit the jackpot, Sergeant," said Nimz. "I may even get a promotion out of it myself."

"Fill me in," said Logen.

"Two Vietnamese took off over a hundred kilos. I sat there and watched the bastards do it. Imagine. It all looks so easy."

"Any Americans?"

"No sign of them. But the Vietnamese rented a villa in the hills outside Marseilles. I've got them under observation. Maybe your friend is planning to join them at the villa."

"What are you going to do?" asked the sergeant.

"I'll keep 'em under watch," said the CIA man. "Maybe I can break up an entire ring."

"You're not going to move on them, is that right?"

"No way. And unless something happens, I won't until they move the stuff to a factory. If I can find a factory, I'm a hero. The French police have turned up only six in twenty years of trying."

"Will you keep me informed?"

"You know it, Sergeant. And thanks."

"Thank you, Nimz. When will you bring the French in on this?"

"I'll have to play it by ear. The bust doesn't mean a damn thing to us except that the junk will sure as hell end up in the States. So if we can follow the whole operation through, we could nab everybody on both continents. It's just one hell of a good break for everybody concerned."

"Okay. Thanks for the call."

"Right. And keep in touch."

Sergeant Logen hung up and filled in Lieutenant Skilling.

"Damn," said Skilling. "I'm happy we exposed a drug ring. But I sure wish our boy had been on that ship."

"Hang in there, sir. He may turn up yet."

Three days later, Nimz put in an urgent call to Logen. Both Logen and Skilling were in Cholon working undercover, and it took almost five hours before Skilling received the message. Logen hadn't turned up yet, so the lieutenant put a call back in to Nimz.

"Mr. Nimz," said Skilling. "I'm calling for Sergeant Logen. This is Lieutenant Skilling. He's on an assignment. What can I do for you?"

"Christ, Lieutenant, what in hell took you so long to call?"

"We operate undercover," said Skilling. "What is it?"

"I made your boy, the black one you sent a picture of," said Nimz.

"In Marseilles?" Skilling's voice shook.

"Right. At the villa. He and three other blacks and three Vietnamese. They're all holed up there."

"What are you going to do?"

"I'm still sitting tight. It's workin' out great. We're in on the ground floor of a big one."

Skilling made a quick decision. "I'm coming to Marseilles. Would you mind if I looked over your shoulder?"

"Nope," said Nimz, "as long as you don't interfere. I'm grateful you tipped us off, but this isn't your territory."

"All I want is to see Eddie Palmer in the can," said Skilling. "I don't care who does it. But I know how he operates."

"Okay, Lieutenant. Lemme know when you're comin' in. I'll meet you."

The lieutenant hung up and started to work. His skill at following the rules paid off for him now. If someone knows the rules, he can break them with ease. And Skilling broke about four to get himself a seat on an army transport plane leaving early the next morning for Marseilles. He left word at both of their offices for Logen, who still hadn't checked in. He packed a small bag and took a taxi to Bien Hoa Air Base, where his KC-135 would depart for Marseilles.

Logen called him about an hour before the plane was to take off. "Good luck, sir," he said.

"Thanks, Logen. I don't know exactly what I'm going to do, but I'd like to be there for the kill."

"Just keep a cool head, sir. And stay as long as you want. I can cover for you here."

"Since I made out my own orders," said Skilling, "I just may take a few extra days. Thanks, Sergeant."

The plane flight was uneventful. When he landed at Marseilles, he hurried from the military area over to the civilian depot for customs inspection.

But he never went through customs. When the official saw his name, he waved over a small man, beefy and balding. The man held out his hand. Skilling took it. "I'm Nimz, Lieutenant. You didn't waste any time."

"I've got a personal score to settle with Eddie Palmer," said Skilling. "Thanks for meeting me."

"No problem. Come on. You're checked through." Nimz led Skilling out to a waiting car. The lieutenant listened with pleasure to the French language. It was like music after the choppy, singsong speech of the Vietnamese.

Nimz talked as he drove. "All of them came in on Air France," he said. "I'll give you their names, but I'm certain they're false. They haven't moved out of the villa yet, except the men from the ship stocked it pretty well with food. I suppose they're planning their next move."

"What would be their next move?"

143

"They've got to find a factory."

"Will that be tough?"

"It'll take time."

"What's your plan?"

"Their villa is located near the bottom of a long hill in a deep woodland," said the CIA man. "I've got two men on the road at the top of the hill. They're under constant watch. We'll just sit and wait."

"How is it they rented a villa?"

Nimz gestured with a free hand. "Marseilles is surrounded by woods. In those woods are about thirty thousand villas. I would guess most of the factories operating in Marseilles are in those villas. It's just a good spot, protected and isolated, yet convenient to one of the busiest ports in Europe."

"Well," said Skilling, "I haven't time to sit and wait with you. But I'd sure like to take a look at our quarry."

"I'm on my way there now." Nimz wheeled the small Renault up a rather narrow road, heading away from the dock area and toward the woodlands ahead.

Suddenly, a voice crackled over a radio. "Hello, Audubon, this is a birdwatcher."

Nimz uncovered a walkie-talkie resting on the floor beneath his seat. He pushed a button and spoke. "Hello, birdwatcher, this is Audubon. Go ahead."

The voice crackled on again. "I've spotted three birds flying."

"Right," said Nimz into the radio. "What kind of birds?"

"Two dink birds and one black bird."

"Right," said Nimz. "One of you stay with them to see where they land. The other keep an eye on their nest."

"Out," said the speaker.

"Well," the CIA operator said, "it looks like you might get a good study of your man after all." He pulled the car over to the side of the road and shut off the motor. "Let's just wait to see what direction they're headed."

Skilling leaned back in his seat. He realized how tired he was.

Still, the thought of coming close to Eddie Palmer kept him alert. He decided against trying to nap.

The radio started to speak. "Hello, Audubon, this is bird-watcher on the wing."

Nimz spoke into the walkie-talkie. "Go ahead, birdwatcher on the wing. Audubon here."

"It looks like they're going to land in Panier," said the radio.

"Right," said Nimz. "I'm on my way. Out."

Nimz started the car. "Panier is the native section of Marseilles. It figures they'd head there. The place is full of Corsicans." He wheeled the car in a U and started off down the road.

"The Corsicans pretty much control the drug traffic, right?" asked Skilling.

"They're into it heavily," replied Nimz. "They're a rough group. One of the reasons the French haven't found many leaks in the drug traffic is because of them. Trying to make a Corsican talk is next to impossible. When they're born, they look around to see who's there before they cry."

"Is there much Eastern drug traffic through here?"

"Mostly from Turkey. The drugs are brought here on trucks that are sealed at the Turkish border. A little money there and they can drive across every border with the drugs sealed in. Some stuff comes from Munich, but almost all of it originates in Turkey. The Far East doesn't have to use Marseilles. They have their own factories."

"Thailand and Hong Kong."

"That's what I heard. By the way, how come your boy brought his drugs here?"

"They're hijacked goods. I figure he thought it'd be safer here."

"That's probably true. And they have the routes out of here, too."

Again the radio started speaking. "Hello, Audubon. Our birds have landed."

Nimz picked up the walkie-talkie and spoke into it. "Where?"

145

"The Café Ajaccio."

"I know it. Out."

Nimz stepped down on the accelerator. "It's a bar right in the middle of Panier."

"Can we go in?"

"I can't. Somebody'd sure as hell recognize me. You might. Can you speak French?"

"No."

"Then, I wouldn't chance it."

Skilling nodded. He knew Nimz was right, but he wanted a good hard look at Eddie Palmer.

The Café Ajaccio had once been painted red. Now, it sat in the middle of a block, peeling paint. There was a small window to the street and a door. Nimz stopped the car a few doors away. "We can sit here and wait. He's bound to come out soon."

Skilling squirmed in his seat. "Yeah. If he turns this way, I'll get a glimpse of him."

Nimz turned in his seat. "Look, Skilling. You're gonna bust a gut if you don't see your man, I can see that. All right." Nimz tore a piece of paper from a pad in his pocket and wrote an address on it. "You go in the bar as an American tourist and ask directions to this place. Just play it straight. If you're lucky, you can eye your man."

Skilling smiled. "Is this a legit address?"

"Sure." Nimz smiled. "It's a whorehouse about a block from here. They may get a few laughs from it, but it gets you in the place without suspicion."

Skilling took the piece of paper and folded it. He rubbed it between his hands and then unfolded it again. "Thanks," he said and stepped out of car. He walked along the street slowly, looking up at addresses, gazing about, lost. When he came to the Café Ajaccio, he stopped. He looked up at the building, then down at the paper. Then he looked inside. And in he walked.

Inside were a dozen or so tables. Stale air sat heavily in the room. Skilling's eyes had trouble with the semidarkness, but he made out men at a table near the back. One of them was black. He walked back toward a small bar where an old man in a dirty striped apron waited, watching him. The men had been talking. They stopped when Skilling walked in.

Skilling smiled and nodded his head. He held out his piece of paper to the bartender. "I'm trying to find this place," he said too loudly. "I seem to be lost."

The old man shook his head. Skilling offered the paper, and the man held it at arm's length to read it. He smiled, showing dark teeth. He spoke in French to the table, and they laughed. Skilling now turned to look at the table. And now he could see. There was Eddie Palmer, his eyes on Skilling.

Skilling swallowed. He smiled self-consciously. Then he dropped his gaze. He wanted desperately to kill Palmer right here.

The men spoke some more in French. Skilling turned to the bartender. Then he heard a voice. "Hey, man, you stay on this street about a block. You got it?"

Skilling turned again to the table crowded with men. Palmer was speaking. There was a Vietnamese and Palmer and one other man, probably a local.

"A block?" asked Skilling.

"Yeah. A block." Palmer pointed. "That way."

"Thanks. Thanks very much." He turned to the bartender. "Thanks very much."

He knew he couldn't stay any longer. He took the piece of paper from the bartender, turned, and walked out into the street. Ahead of him, he saw Nimz waiting.

"Okay," said Eddie Palmer. "The excitement's over. Let's get back to business, okay?"

The Corsican spoke with a heavy accent. "We cannot do business. I don't know what you talk about."

Eddie turned to Lieutenant Tri. "You tell him once more,

man. And this time, you tell him if we don't do business with him, we'll find somebody else."

Tri nodded and spoke to the Corsican in French. Eddie leaned back and looked toward the door. Something about that tourist had bothered Eddie, and then it struck him. When he said hello to the bartender, he had nodded his head like a gook. It's a habit everyone picks up in the East. He could be a tourist who just came from Japan. Or he could be something else.

Eddie tried to recall his face. Average. But Eddie filed it in his head. If he ever saw the face again, he'd remember it.

He got up and walked quickly to the door. He couldn't see the tourist on the street, but a Renault was just pulling away from the curb a few doors down.

"Tri," Eddie spoke loudly. "Ask him how far down the block that whorehouse is. The one the tourist wanted to find."

Tri nodded and spoke. The Corsican spoke back. Tri turned. "Just over a block."

Eddie nodded. Whoever that tourist was, he'd gotten into a car. Tourist, shit, thought Eddie. Somebody's onto us.

He walked back to the table. "How you doin'?" he asked Tri.

"He said for us to come back here tonight. He will try and talk to some people, he said."

"Okay. Tell him we'll be here."

Tri spoke once again to the Corsican. Then he stood up. The two men walked out onto the street.

Back in the villa now, Colonel Linh rubbed his hands. "But how could anyone know of us?"

"Man, I don't know how. All I'm sayin' is that I know they do. Now we got to take some precautions, you dig?"

"We must leave immediately."

"Nobody's leavin'. Those dudes are probably lettin' us play our hand. They don't know we got them spotted."

"What do you suggest?" asked Linh.

"Somebody's gotta be watchin' us. I'd guess they're up on the road. They got a clean look at us from there. It's hard to tell, but I think someone followed us back here. If he did, he's good. A professional."

"The police?"

"Police, MPs, U.S. agents—who cares. It ain't some no-account group, that's for sure. I just can't figure why they exposed themselves today with that whorehouse trick."

"Perhaps it was innocent after all."

"There's one way of findin' out, Colonel. You send your boys out. They're used to workin' this kind of terrain. Tell 'em to scout around. If they're keepin' us under their thumb, we'll find 'em. Then we can decide what to do."

"Yes," said Linh. "I'll do that."

When Eddie and Tri and his man returned to the Café Ajaccio that night, he knew they were being followed. He saw the headlights trailing them, turning at every corner. But he didn't mention it to Tri.

Claude Marceau was a part-time dock worker, part-time thief, part-time assassin. At thirty-eight, he felt bitterness and anger. The big score continued to elude him. His apartment needed paint and new furniture. His wife always waited too long between blonde rinses, allowing the black roots of her hair to grow to over an inch. Then she would shout at Claude that she couldn't afford to have her hair done.

Claude was a Corsican. He was acquainted with nearly everyone in the Corsican underworld, and they knew him. But he had no solid base of operation, no gang membership.

Then it all changed in a bar. A black American and an Asian told him they had 100 kilos of morphine base. Claude stood on the threshold of the big time. All he must do now is process the drugs. There were many drug factories in Marseilles. Claude did not know the location of one, but he knew someone who did.

"I have a business proposition," said Claude. He was seated

in a small room in the back of a dock warehouse.

"Yes, Claude," said the man, "what is it?"

"I have one hundred kilos."

The man stared steadily at the Corsican. "You have one hundred kilos? Why do you come to me?"

"Hey, I come to you because you can process it. You are talking to Claude Marceau."

The man lit a cigarette and shook out the match. "All right, Claude. Tell me about it."

"I met these men," said Claude. "They have brought in one hundred kilos from Indochina. It needs processing. You do it; we split. It is that simple."

"We split? You talk as though they are your drugs."

"Before this is over, they will be."

The man pulled at the corners of his mouth in what might have been a smile. "You are not biting off too big a bite, eh, Claude?"

Claude struck his chest with his pointed finger. "Hey, that is my problem, yes?"

The man nodded. "That is true. So, you speak of a split. What split, Claude?"

"Seventy percent for me. Thirty percent for you for the processing."

The man cackled. "Claude." He coughed. "Claude. I process the drugs. Then you want them back, eh? Sure. I give them back. Or I get them to America where there is money. Claude, I get eighty percent."

Rage welled up in Claude, but he held it in check. He could not insult this man before him. He was too important. "I deserve a bigger share."

"Perhaps. But you do not show me anything, Claude. Only words. You tell me about one hundred kilos. You can have all of one hundred kilos of words."

"Thirty percent."

"When you bring the base, we will talk."

"Thirty percent."

"Claude." The man sighed. "All right. You insist on doing business with words. Twenty-five percent."

"Done," said Claude. "Where?"

"Here in the warehouse. There is always someone here."

Claude rose. "All right."

The man snubbed out his cigarette. "Don't look so glum, Claude. You're a rich man."

Claude left the warehouse and moved swiftly along the noisy streets. He considered the possibilities and, in the end, decided to continue on alone. This was his big chance, and he was determined to see it through. He would, indeed, be a rich man.

He arrived at his apartment. He called for his wife, but the apartment was empty. He was glad of that. He kept his Beretta wrapped in plastic and hidden inside the toilet tank. He figured the police would find it if ever he was arrested. But this hid it from his wife. If she ever found it, he knew she'd sell it.

He unwrapped the gun, checked it out, and then shoved it into place under his shirt. The cold made his stomach contract.

He wrote a note for his wife telling her not to expect him until late that night. Then he headed for the Café Ajaccio to wait and drink the dark red wine.

By the end of the third glass, Claude had worked out his plan. It was simplicity itself. Step one: When the Asian and the American delivered the drugs, he would check it. They would probably bring it in suitcases. The exchange would have to be in an out-of-the-way place. Once he had established that the drugs were there, he would kill them both on the spot. Step two: He would then deliver the drugs, return and take the bodies out into the harbor, and toss them over tied to a weight. Neat and clean. One and two.

He worried briefly that the men might be part of a larger gang, but he eventually decided they weren't. And even if they were, he was safe in Marseilles, a Corsican among Corsicans.

One worry. His Beretta. Suppose the gun jammed before he

could kill them both? He felt they must have guns. One did not carry around 100 kilos without protection. So he had to kill them both quickly. The Beretta was reliable. But if something went wrong, it would mean his death. So he must wait for the exact moment. A time when one man was turned away, perhaps.

A friend came to his table and sat down. "Business," said Claude, motioning him away. The friend moved to the bar. Claude resumed his thoughts.

Twenty-five kilos. His. Money for the rest of his life. And Philippe's daughter had bumped against him last Sunday in church and then smiled at him. Claude turned to wave for another wine. The black American blocked his view. He was leaning against the bar, watching him. How long had he been there? It startled Claude. He blinked. He had drunk too much wine.

Claude looked for the Vietnamese. He saw him by the door and motioned them both to his table. He held up his glass. The black American shook his head. The Vietnamese said, "No."

Claude felt disgusted with himself. He swore to be more watchful. He didn't want to spoil this job. This job was too big, his way out. He tensed his stomach muscles and felt his Beretta, hard against his flesh.

"It is all set," he said to the Vietnamese. The Vietnamese turned to the black and nodded.

"When?" asked the Asian in French.

"Whenever you are ready," said Claude. "I will take the merchandise. When the processing is complete, I will notify you. It will then be taken to the United States, where you can pick it up. It is all very simple."

The two spoke for a moment in English. Then the Vietnamese turned and said, "How much?"

Claude's mind went blank. He took a sip of wine. He had not even thought about a price, since he had never considered going through with the deal. Then he said, "Twenty percent."

When the black American was told, he moved his gaze from the Vietnamese to Claude. Claude felt panic in this throat, but the black broke into a smile and Claude relaxed. The black held out his hand, and Claude took it. They shook hands warmly.

The black then pointed at Claude's glass, and Claude smiled. He waved for two more glasses of wine. When the wine arrived, the black clinked his glass against Claude's and smiled again. Then they drank.

Then Claude asked, "When will you bring the merchandise?"

The two spoke. Then the Vietnamese said, "Tomorrow night. We will meet you here. Same time."

"You won't bring it in here?" The Vietnamese shook his head. Claude smiled and nodded. Excellent, he thought. "I will be waiting," he said.

The two men stood and smiled at Claude and left the café. Claude felt good, the best he had felt in a long time. He waved for another glass of wine.

When Eddie and Tri pulled into the drive to the villa, they saw someone waiting for them. It was Colonel Linh, leaning against the building. He stepped back out of the lights while they parked, then waved them over as they emerged from the car.

He confirmed Eddie's suspicions. "There are two men on the road at the crest of the hill," said the colonel. "My man has only just come back. They have a radio."

"Whatta you plan to do?" asked Eddie.

"I have sent another man up there to watch them. If I flick the light off and on quickly, he will kill them."

"Hey, man, hold on," said Eddie. "Let's figure out what's up first."

"It is only an emergency measure, Ong Eddie. We have no way to contact my man in case of trouble."

"Tomorrow we better get some radio equipment. Did your man hear 'em talk?"

"Yes," said Linh. "They spoke English."

Eddie nodded. "Americans. Damn, how did they get onto us? Man, it's got to be somebody with manpower. Two followed us into town in another car."

"So," said Linh, "we must consider our next step carefully."

153

"You think they got the house wired for sound?" asked Eddie.

"I do not know," said Linh. "That is why I waited for you out here. Tomorrow we must scout their location."

Tri spoke. "I will go there now," he said. "In the morning, I can see if they are listening with earphones."

"Look for a way for us to slip out of the house without bein' seen," said Eddie.

Tri nodded. He started off into the woods.

"Ngo will be expecting you," called Linh softly. Tri nodded as he disappeared into the black of the night.

"You figured he'd spend the night up there?" asked Eddie.

"Yes," said Linh. "He is very dedicated."

Eddie stared into the darkness. "I say we go ahead. We get nabbed anyway if we try to run. They want to make a big score, or they woulda moved in before now. They want us, the drugs, the factory."

"Yes," said Linh, "I agree there is no point in trying to run. Not yet, at any rate. And it could be to our advantage to know we're being watched."

"Yeah. But it's gonna be hard. That Frenchman we're dealin' with is fixin' to double-cross us for sure. He's not too bright, but I figure he's mean and he's got a lot of friends. But he just knows he's gonna end up with the whole hundred kilos himself."

"What will you do?"

"Play him along. He's already figured out how he's gonna dump us. So we gotta be careful. Everybody's on our tail. It's a mess, Ong Linh." Eddie smiled.

"You do not seem worried. Nor am I. We are still in control."

"The Frenchman is dealin' with someone else for a cut. So we got to let him deliver the goods. Then he's dead."

"And our friends on the road seem content to observe for the time being. So we proceed as planned."

"But I'm keepin' my safety off, Ong Linh. It's gettin' crowded."

154

The following morning, everyone was gathered in the kitchen, waiting for Tri to make it back to the house. It had been agreed that they would wait until 9:00. If he didn't show by then, Linh was to send another of his soldiers to search him out.

Tri arrived before 8:00. He came in from the woods behind the house. Eddie saw him walking, keeping low.

"It's Tri," he said.

A window was opened, and Tri was helped inside. "Report," said Linh.

"All is well," said Tri. "I came in a blind spot. We can also leave that way. From where they stand, it would be impossible for them to see."

Tri walked to a table and took a piece of paper from his pocket. He'd drawn a rough map of the area. "This is where we are. The drive. They are here. Behind them, it rises for another fifty meters; then it drops off sharply. I left Ngo here." He put the point of his pencil on a spot behind the men watching the villa.

"I will send someone to relieve Ngo," said Linh. He signaled another Vietnamese. The man bowed his head and went to the window.

"Keep heading straight for that large tree," said the lieutenant. "Go about twenty meters in the woods, and then turn right and cut up toward the road. Be careful of going too far. There is another villa to our right."

The man nodded and crawled out the window and dropped to the ground. He ran to the tree and was lost in the woods almost immediately.

"They watch with binoculars," said Tri. "They are not cautious."

"They think they got us cold," said Eddie.

"I will go to Marseilles," said Tri. "We must have contact with our outpost."

"I will go," said Linh.

"Why don't we all go," Mau Mau said. "I could use a little fun."

"Not yet, man," said Eddie. "Let's get set up first; then we have some fun. They'll be expectin' it. Right now, we gotta protect our flank."

"You always protectin' your flank, man," said Mau Mau.

"Dig," said Eddie.

Linh and one of his soldiers were back from Marseilles about 4:00 in the afternoon. By 5:00, they had set up radio contact with their man on the hill.

Just after dark, the yard lights were turned on. Eddie, Tri, Mau Mau, Turk, and Apache Joe walked in full view of their observers to the car. Four suitcases of morphine were put in the trunk.

Just after they turned on the main road, Tri heard from his lookout that two men were following in a car. "That's right, you bastards," said Eddie. "Come on along. Come on."

Tri and Eddie dropped their companions off in the Panier a few blocks from the café. They made a show of joviality, and Eddie noticed the car following them barely slowed down. The two men had obviously been ordered to follow the drugs.

Claude stood when Eddie and Tri walked into the Café Ajaccio. "He's ready for us tonight," said Eddie. "Must be sober."

Claude waved to them and held his wine glass aloft. Both nodded at the suggestion of wine. Eddie could see the greed showing on the Corsican's face.

Tri jangled the car keys in his pocket. "The merchandise is in the trunk, my friend," he said to Claude.

"Are we ready?" asked Claude in French.

"My friend has other plans," said Tri. Eddie smiled when they both looked at him. He rubbed his groin. Smiled more.

Claude wondered if he should kill the Vietnamese at the car but thought better of it. Instead, he drove away, watching in the rearview mirror as the man turned and went back into the café.

He failed to notice the car trailing him. One CIA man drove the car; the other waited across the street from the café. Eddie had slipped quickly out the back of the café, where Mau Mau was waiting with a motor scooter. He completed the parade, staying nearly a block behind the CIA car.

The drive to the waterfront was quick and direct. Eddie felt neither man knew he was being followed. Claude stopped at a warehouse near the water. He honked, and the warehouse door opened and he drove in. The CIA man slumped in the car seat, lit a cigarette, and waited. Eddie drove his Vespa around the block to survey the rear of the building. He knew that if drug operations worked the way his old hijacking system did, there'd be a rear exit, and they wouldn't keep the drugs in the warehouse long.

He waited in the shadows. In under two minutes, he saw the Corsican drive his car around the corner a block away. The other car took up the pursuit. Eddie waited. Then the door opened in the rear of the warehouse. A small Fiat truck pulled out, battered and nondescript. Eddie smiled. He pulled back into the shadows and watched the truck turn away from town and head toward the hills. A man who had opened the warehouse door gave one more look around and then pulled a chain to slide the heavy door down. When it hit bottom, Eddie moved.

He had no difficulty in picking up the truck, but he kept well back and tried to hide behind what traffic he could find. He knew he was dealing now with careful men. Once they were in the hill country, he closed in and shut off his headlight, using the truck's taillight to guide him. He had no idea where he was. He concentrated only on the pursuit.

They had been driving for nearly thirty minutes when the taillight disappeared. Eddie pulled the Vespa to the side of the road, shut it off, and listened. He could hear the truck laboring up a hill ahead of him and to his right. He fired up the scooter again and drove a short distance ahead for a better view. He saw the headlights of the truck pulling into a villa. Then the lights on the truck went out. A single light in the villa went on. Eddie had found the factory.

Eddie pushed the scooter to the side of the road and looked around in the black night. He could see the glow of Marseilles to his right, and he knew he'd have no difficulty finding his way back to the Panier. He searched for a large stone on the ground, found it, and then placed it in the fork of a tree as a marker. Then he started the Vespa and headed toward Marseilles, stopping on occasion to leave a broken branch or a rock as a marker.

Linh was waiting for them at the villa. Eddie made a quick report. Then he said, "We're stirrin' up the pot, Ong Linh. Somethin's gonna happen."

"We tread a narrow path, Ong Eddie," said Linh. "Perhaps we could approach the men running the factory, deal with them directly."

"We may have to later," replied Eddie, "but right now, we're a step ahead of everybody. If we can keep it that way, we come out good."

"How long did the Corsican say the processing would take?" asked Linh.

"A week," replied Tri.

"Then we can assume it will be four or five days at the most," Linh said.

"I reckon," said Eddie. "I'll check the place out in the daylight. Anything been happenin' here?"

"They continue to watch from the crest," said Linh.

"I just can't figure how they picked us up," said Eddie.

"It could have been an informer on the ship," said Tri.

"Yeah," replied Eddie. "Maybe."

"Whoever they are, they want everyone in their net," Linh said. "That would indicate a large organization at work. When your unit is large, it is necessary to have large victories."

Eddie smiled. "Dig," he said. "What they're doin', though, is makin' it hell to get the skag outa here. You know they'll be watchin' every damn route to the States."

"There is one escape route they won't suspect," said Linh.

"Back to Nam," said Eddie.

"Exactly, Ong Eddie."

"How?"

"The ship leaves again in four days."

"Four days it is, Ong Linh, even if we have to leave a few kilos."

Tri spoke. "As long as we're careful of the possibility of an informer on the ship."

Eddie nodded. "How big's the crew?"

"Seven or eight," replied Tri.

"Then, once we get close enough to Nam, the ship is gonna have one of those mysterious accidents." .

Linh stared at Eddie. He felt tired. "Yes," he said quietly.

"Hey," said Eddie, suddenly full of life. "How 'bout some dinner?"

"No, thank you. I think I will retire."

"Listen, Colonel. You're all tight. I can see it in your face. If you're gettin' nervous now, what's gonna happen when we start blowin' up the United States of America?"

Linh met Eddie's gaze. "Dinner, Ong Eddie. An excellent idea."

"Some of that French food, Ong Linh. Just what you need." Eddie turned and yelled, "Hey, who's for a night on the town?"

Lieutenant Skilling dropped the phone on the hook. It had taken him nearly seven hours to get through to Sergeant Logen in Saigon. And then he didn't have that much to say. Logen had tried to calm his worries about being away. But Skilling knew he'd be in trouble if he didn't go back soon. His was too small an outfit. He was too exposed.

He decided to give it two more days at the most. Then he'd have to return to Saigon. It didn't help any to spend one entire day just waiting in his hotel room for a telephone call. He didn't sleep well that night.

The next morning, the telephone awoke him. He answered it

after the first ring. It was Russ Nimz. "Good morning," said Nimz.

"Hi," said Skilling. "What'd they do last night?"

"Went to dinner again. Christ, you'd think they were tourists."

"How much longer you figure?"

"Well, it's been four days since they gave the stuff to the Corsican. I would have figured another two or three days, but I got a report there's a lot of activity at their villa."

Skilling sat up in bed. "What?"

"I thought we'd take a run out there. It looks like something is about to happen."

"How soon?"

"I'll pick you up in thirty minutes, okay?"

"I'll be in front," said Skilling.

Skilling hurried to bathe and dress. At last, some action. Frustration had weighed heavily on him as he watched, unable to move against his enemy. He understood Nimz wanting to wait, to bring all the fish into the net. But he hated seeing Eddie Palmer walking free. He told himself that Eddie was caught, arrested, executed. Late at night, however, he didn't believe it.

Eddie and his friends moved around Marseilles with an arrogance that showed their complete confidence. They were headed for a big fall, thought Skilling. And I want to be there, to be one of the king's men to put Eddie back together again.

In all the days Skilling had been in Marseilles, he'd been unable to come up with an identification for the Vietnamese. Nimz had taken telephoto shots of the men and had sent the pictures back to Saigon. But, so far, not a glimmer. Eddie Palmer and friends unknown.

Nimz was a few minutes late. Skilling paced the sidewalk. He spotted the Fiat and stepped out into traffic. Nimz honked and forced his way to Skilling, who jumped in at a trot.

"Anything new?" he asked the CIA man.

"Yeah," said Nimz. "They just booked passage on Air France

for New York for the day after tomorrow."

"And?"

"And what?"

"Are you going to let them leave?"

"Sure," said Nimz. "That way we get the New York contact."

"A bird in the hand," said Skilling.

"You got a bird in the hand. But it's a small bird, Lieutenant. I want a big bird."

Skilling was silent for a moment. Then he said, "Just what's going on this morning at the villa?"

"They're packing. Big flurry of activity. But they won't be leaving for two days."

"Eddie is always one to be prepared."

"Just like a Boy Scout."

Eddie and Mau Mau approached the factory villa from the uphill side. They sat for nearly an hour in the woods, watching. Eddie made out three men inside. "Three," he said quietly to Mau Mau.

"Yeah," said Mau Mau. "The dude in the kitchen is makin' breakfast."

Eddie nodded. "He keeps lookin' down the driveway. You think they're expectin' somebody, or is he just watchin'?"

"I figure he's just watchin'. He don't bother lookin' our way. Dumb."

The house was low-slung, on the small side, and probably not much more than ten years old. It sat on the slope of a heavily wooded hill. There were other villas both to the right and left and downhill, but they were all obscured by the foliage. There was a garage under the house.

"I suppose the factory's in the basement," said Eddie. "So we figure there's the stairs and a door from the garage. The one dude is on guard, and the other two must be workin' the skag."

"Right."

"Okay, I'm goin' in. You stay here and cover me. I'm comin'

161

in from over there at the far end of the house. If you see the man in the kitchen do anythin' funny, pop him."

"Right."

Eddie stepped back into the cover of the woods and worked his way along the clearing until he was on the opposite side from the garage. He checked his M-16, then put it behind his back, and casually stepped out onto the open lawn and began walking toward the house. He kept his eyes on the window. There were white, lacy curtains, and he watched them for any sign of movement.

He saw nothing, and then he was against the house, under the window, and safe. He moved to the corner and waved to Mau Mau that he was okay. Then he crept around the house toward the garage. He passed two basement windows, but they were both painted over. When he arrived at the garage door, he slowly raised his head to look inside through a pane of glass. He could feel the sun on his neck, and a bead of sweat rolled down off his forehead and onto his cheek. He wiped the sweat away with his shoulder.

The truck he had seen the other night sat in the garage. The door to the basement was ajar. A panel in the side of the truck was propped open, revealing a space where the drugs would be put for transport.

Eddie ducked back down and returned to the far end of the house. He signaled to Mau Mau that he was going inside. Mau Mau nodded. Eddie moved to what he figured would be a bedroom window. He tried to see inside, but a curtain cut off most of his vision. The window didn't budge when he tried it. He moved around onto the uphill side, where a small patio extended from a glass door. It exposed him to view from the inside, but Eddie took a chance. He looked in. The living room was empty. He could see one corner of the kitchen, but the man inside wasn't visible. He tried the door. It was locked. He put his left shoulder to the door, keeping the M-16 leveled in his right hand. He pushed. It opened with a small cracking noise, and Eddie stepped into the living room. Eddie walked quickly toward the kitchen. He was nearly there before the man in the kitchen went to investigate the noise he'd heard. Eddie pulled the trigger twice, still walking. The *pfft-pfft* of his gun was the only sound until the man made a half cough, half gurgle and started to fall. Eddie moved quickly to him and grabbed his shirt and lowered him to the floor. The man's blood ran over his hand, and Eddie wiped it as best he could on the dead man's trousers.

A door was open in the kitchen, and Eddie could see the top of the stairs leading to the basement. He heard noises in the basement, but the sounds were soft, unhurried. They hadn't been alarmed.

Eddie waved Mau Mau in. He waited as his companion worked his way around and through the glass door. Mau Mau came up silently.

Eddie pointed toward the basement and then to himself. Mau Mau nodded. He then pointed to Mau Mau and moved his finger outside. Quietly, he said, "Cover the garage. I don't want 'em makin' a run. If they do, shoot careful, man. That truck is worth a million dollars."

Mau Mau nodded and moved back into the living room and on outside.

He gave Mau Mau the count of ten and then walked to the basement door. He saw the stairs led straight down against the wall. He quickly moved down. The acid fumes made him wrinkle his face as he moved into the basement. When he was halfway down, he crouched, looking straight out into the laboratory.

The entire basement was covered with a powdery white substance. Two men leaned over a table, face masks hiding their features. They both turned toward Eddie, expecting their companion.

For an instant, Eddie and the men stared at one another. Then Eddie fired. One started to move for a cabinet. But he took only half a step. They were dead in seconds.

Eddie pulled his shirt up over his mouth and moved down to the basement floor and quickly checked the bodies to satisfy himself they were dead. Then he hurried to the garage and opened the door.

"Careful, man," said Eddie. "The air is full of poison."

Mau Mau moved cautiously up. "Look at this place. Weird."

Eddie handed Mau Mau his M-16. Keeping his shirt over his face, he walked quickly to the men and pulled off their face masks. He slipped one on and then tossed the other to Mau Mau.

"They finish the junk?" asked Mau Mau, his voice muffled by the mask.

"I don't know," said Eddie. "I'll see. First, though, you check out the house. Maybe there's somebody asleep upstairs."

Mau Mau nodded and turned and climbed the stairs out of sight. Eddie began to check the laboratory.

A centrifuge was spinning, and Eddie unplugged it. Inside, powder was clinging around the rim of a container. Beside the centrifuge, a plastic bag lay empty and waiting. Eddie poured the powder into the bag and folded the top. He then looked around.

Behind him, piled in neat stacks of plastic bags, was the heroin. Eddie heard a noise and turned. It was Mau Mau returning.

Eddie pointed. He heard Mau Mau mutter something. The two of them grinned through their masks. "Lookee that," said Mau Mau. "I never seen so much horse. Hey, man, shit."

"They musta just been finishin' up," said Eddie. "Come on."

They carried the drugs to the truck, gently placing the bags in a compartment behind the opened panel. In ten minutes, they were finished.

"I'll drive," said Eddie. "You follow on the scooter."

"Protect your flank?"

"You got it son."

In twenty minutes, Eddie was back in the villa. He left Mau Mau guarding the drugs.

"What's goin' on?" Eddie asked Linh.

"It was as you predicted. All of our activity has brought six men out. They are all up there and have been for over an hour." Linh hesitated. "You had no difficulty?"

Eddie smiled. "No sweat. The drugs are in a truck down the road. Mau Mau is there with 'em. You're gonna have to transfer the drugs to your car. The truck belonged to the gang, and somebody might spot it. Better take some empty suitcases."

"Had they processed it all?"

"Looks like it. One hell of a load of white powder, Ong Linh. How soon does our ship leave?"

Linh looked at his watch. "Three hours."

"Then I reckon I better start movin'. How many men you got up on top?"

"One."

"Tell him I'm comin' up."

"The ship must leave on time. And I need you, Ong Eddie."

"Relax, Ong Linh. You take care of blowin' up the United States. I'll handle the details." Eddie smiled.

"Then you had better get started," said Linh.

"Yeah." Eddie took four fresh clips of ammunition and stuck them inside his shirt. "Apache, Turk." Eddie called to his companions. They came out of a room in the back.

"Yeah, man," said Turk.

"Turk, you get a car ready down here. Soon as I give the signal, haul ass on up to the road, dig?"

"I hear and obey, oh master," said Turk.

"Apache, you come on with me, man. Grab your piece."

Apache Joe returned to the back room and came out carrying his M-16. "I'm loaded for bear, big daddy."

Eddie and Apache Joe left the house in back and worked their way around and up to cross the road about 200 yards away from the CIA outpost. They then made a semicircle and ended up above and behind the men on the road. Linh's soldier was waiting.

Eddie gestured for the Vietnamese to notify Linh he'd ar-

165

rived. The soldier nodded and spoke softly into the walkie-talkie. He then signaled that the message had gone through.

Skilling felt his nerves tingling. This waiting made him want to grab a gun and charge down the hill, firing as he ran. He had spent some time watching the movement below. There seemed to be a great deal of activity of some kind, but Skilling didn't really see that much accomplished. He lost interest when he realized Eddie Palmer was not one of the men involved in the work.

As he'd watched, he'd imagined the binoculars to be a telescopic sight on a high-powered rifle. He'd judged the distance at about 300 yards. He'd felt a slight breeze on his right cheek and compensated for it. Then he'd pulled the trigger in his mind.

Now he stood, wondering about himself. Skilling had never killed a man before being assigned to Saigon. Now he relished the thought of it. He decided execution was the only answer for Eddie Palmer. Death by a firing squad—and he was the firing squad. Society needed to rid itself of Eddie. And Skilling could do it. Permanently.

The more he saw of the CIA operation, the more he felt bound in and held in check. In Saigon, his unit moved swiftly. The CIA reminded Skilling of one of Scrooge's ghosts, a form dragging behind it chains tied to ledger books, filing cabinets, and time clocks. And he knew the CIA moved with speed compared with most government agencies. He remembered his days in the Pentagon and how he took channels for granted. His whole life had been one of channels and ruts to be negotiated with determination.

I should have brought a gun, he thought, and waited outside that Corsican café and eliminated Eddie myself. One short pull and channels level out.

Next time, he thought. He heard Nimz grunt beside him. Skilling turned to have Nimz's blood spurted in his face as the

CIA agent's heart gave its last dying spasm. Skilling tasted the warm, salty liquid in his mouth. Out of the corner of his eye, Skilling saw another man kick up his legs and fall backward over the embankment. Nimz now fell against him and continued to bleed.

Fire exploded in his neck, and he heard himself cough. A force struck Nimz, and it knocked Skilling backward a step. Now he became aware of a burning pressure in his chest. I'm being killed, he thought. We're all being killed.

Nimz slid off of him, and Skilling stumbled forward into a parked Fiat. He felt the steel hit his head, and it seemed to set his brain in motion. Thoughts raced. Hit the head. First you get his attention. Dead. I'm dying. Cough. Nimz has hold of my feet. He's lying on my feet. Cast this body into the sea. Amen.

He reached up and opened the door. His eyes were level with the seat. The top of another bleeding head lay a few inches away. The keys? There. Where they're supposed to be.

Why was there no noise? Eddie Palmer is doing this. No channels for him. He moved in across the body and turned the key. The car caught and was moving. Skilling held the wheel, crouched half on the seat, half off, sitting on a dead man's arm.

Something tapped him on the arm, and he looked down to see a piece of his own arm bone lying exposed. Glass splinters flew about in the car like angry hornets. He felt them bury in his face. Then he could no longer see, and the car was still moving.

He took his good hand off the wheel and wiped his eyes. He could see again. His hand was now slippery with his own blood. He tried to scream and heard only a rush of air. Pain hunched his body. His mouth filled, and he let the liquid spill down over his chin.

I'm dead, he thought. Everybody is dead. And there was no noise. No sound except the impact of the bullets and the death rattles of five men. He coughed. His death rattle? Let it happen.

Eddie Palmer has won. Eddie Palmer, winner and still champion. Damn Eddie Palmer. Goddamn Eddie goddamn Palmer.

Skilling shut his lips, spit, and stopped dying. He stepped on the accelerator, and the car leaped along the road, around a corner, and away from the silent bullets.

"Hey, man," said Apache Joe. "That son of a bitch is hard to kill."

Eddie stood over the bodies on the road. More in frustration than anger, he pumped another bullet into each of the corpses. "Tell Turk to get his ass up here with the car, man. We got to catch that boy."

Skilling knew it was over. His head fell against the wheel as he stopped the car. Then, nothing. Blackness.

Pain woke him. He still sat behind the wheel of the car, half on a dead man, half off. The motor was still running. He opened the door and stepped out and caught himself as unconsciousness nearly took hold of his mind. Then he stared at the car. Eddie Palmer would be coming for him. He took a Zippo lighter out of his coat pocket. He lit it and tossed it in the back seat. Then he flicked the car into drive and watched it careen off down the road away from him. He watched the car go over the road and heard it smash into an embankment. He waited. Nothing. He could wait no longer. He walked to the side of the road, his arm dangling. There was a broken tree branch. He fell to his knees and crawled under it. As he fainted, he heard the explosion, saw the flash.

Turk stopped the car a little distance away. "Hey, I can see him in there. Look at that. See his arm?"

"There was somebody else in the car," said Eddie.

"Come on, man. Hey, everybody in there is burnt, you dig. We got to haul ass outa here," said Apache Joe.

"Yeah. Somebody's gonna see this fire. But I don't like not knowin', man," said Eddie.

"Hey, Eddie. He's dead," Turk said.

Eddie nodded, and Turk turned the car around and headed back toward their villa. By the time they arrived, the Vietnamese soldier had pulled the bodies into the woods. The drugs were unloaded from the truck. Eddie waved them on, and Linh headed his car for the waterfront. Turk stopped to pick up Mau Mau and then headed the car toward the Panier.

"This ain't gonna take long," said Eddie as Turk pulled up in front of the Café Ajaccio.

"You keep your pieces ready, and if you hear me yell, come a-runnin'. But I ain't gonna yell."

Eddie tucked his M-16 inside a folded newspaper and held it in his left hand. He stepped out of the car and into the café. The café was dark, and he stood a moment until his eyes became accustomed to it.

Then he saw Claude seated with two other men at a back table. They were looking at him, quietly. The old bartender leaned against the wall behind the bar, watching.

Eddie broke into a grin and waved to Claude. Claude smiled and held his glass aloft. The Corsican started to stand and turn, and Eddie's bullet hit him square in the chest, knocking him backward into the lap of one of the men at the table. Eddie kept firing. *Pfft. Pfft.* The two men at the table fell to the floor. The old bartender, holding a long, thin knife, came around the bar for Eddie. Eddie fired three times. The old man stopped and fell dead.

Eddie walked to each man and put another bullet in each of their heads. He looked around. There wasn't even a glass broken. He picked up the bottle of wine from Claude's table and took a swallow. His throat was dry. It had been a busy day.

Skilling regained consciousness two days later in a Marseilles hospital. As his mind cleared, he became aware of his body. He lay at the bottom of a gauze pit, encased in the white stuff. He could see the edges of bandages both above and below his eyes.

He moved various portions of himself and met resistance everywhere. Suddenly, a face moved into his line of vision. Skilling stared. It was Sergeant Logen.

"Lieutenant?" Sergeant Logen smiled. "Can you hear me? Don't try and talk. You're going to be all right."

Two more faces appeared. Skilling tried to speak, but he was aware no sound came forth.

"Sir, you may have some difficulty speaking. A bullet hit you in the throat. Do you hear me?" Skilling nodded his head slightly. "You damn near didn't make it, sir. But you're okay now. All you need is some time to mend. Do you understand, sir?"

Again, Skilling nodded his head. "He hears you, Sergeant," said one of the other men.

"Sir," said Logen, "I know it's tough, but these men want to ask some questions. It's important."

"I'm Paul Picket," said one of the faces, "CIA. Eddie Palmer did this?"

Skilling swallowed. Then he forced himself to speak. "Plane," he said in a whisper.

"Plane?" said Picket. "Yes, we know about the plane reservations. Is that what you mean?" Skilling nodded. "I'm afraid they didn't show up for the plane, Lieutenant. It was obviously a diversion."

Skilling began to shake his head. Sergeant Logen spoke. "Don't get excited, Lieutenant. The reservations were for today. You've been out for two days."

Skilling closed his eyes. Two days. "Lieutenant." Skilling opened his eyes. It was the third man. "I'm Emil Hobert, representing the French government. Can you tell us anything about where these men are hiding out?"

"Gone," said Skilling.

"We think not," said Hobert. "All of the usual drug channels are sealed tight."

Skilling felt a tear form in his eye. "Underestimate," he said. Then the room went dark. He heard and saw nothing for another sixteen hours. It was morning when he awoke again. And this time the pain was startling. There was agony in every part of his body, and his throat was aflame. He tried to raise his head, but the movement sent pulsing shocks of torment into his head. The hurt was nearly unbearable, but he wanted to bear it. He relaxed, cleared his mind, took hold of the pain.

Then he began to run over his days in France, the days he'd spent watching Eddie Palmer. He searched for his mistake. It was obvious he had made one. It must have been the meeting at the Corsican café, he decided. It was the only time they'd ever met face to face. Skilling ran over the meeting time and again in his head, but he could not find his mistake. Finally, he took some satisfaction in knowing that Eddie Palmer, too, had made a mistake. Lieutenant Gerald Skilling was alive.

Then there was a face in his line of vision. A doctor. Next Sergeant Logen stood over him. "Good morning, sir. What I can see of you looks better," he said, smiling.

Skilling nodded his head. "Give me a few moments," said the doctor. The doctor took thirty minutes. With practiced skill, he worked on Skilling's body. Bandages were replaced, needles removed. When he was through, Skilling hurt but somehow felt better.

"Thanks," he mumbled to the doctor.

"We have to take good care," replied the doctor. "You are important. Government, you understand?"

Skilling nodded. "How long be here?"

"Three weeks, perhaps. Good-bye. I see you tomorrow."

"Uh," said the lieutenant as the doctor turned and stepped out of his room. The doctor had cranked the bed up a few degrees, and for the first time, Skilling was able to see his room. It was a hospital room, barren, cold, a trifle hostile. Skilling turned his head slightly to see Sergeant Logen and the two men from the day before.

"Ah, you look alive again, Lieutenant," said the Frenchman. "I hope your government appreciates the fine care France has given you."

Skilling looked at Logen. There was obviously some ill feeling. "I do," said Skilling hoarsely.

"Save your voice, sir," said Logen. "These gentlemen would

like to know everything if you're up to it."

Skilling nodded. "No warning," he said. Picket held up his hand.

"I want to get this on tape, Lieutenant," said the CIA man. "Just hold on." He brought a small recorder out of his pocket and set it alongside the bed near Skilling's head. Then he crossed and closed the door. He came back and turned on the machine, satisfied himself it was working, and then pointed to Skilling. "You said you had no warning, Lieutenant," he said.

"Yes," said Skilling. "Watching villa. I turn; Nimz falls dead. All dead?"

"All dead," said Picket.

"Five of those men," said Hobert, "four men in a bar in the Panier, and three others at another villa, which held a drug-processing factory. Twelve men in all, Lieutenant. And seven of them were Frenchmen."

"Eddie?" asked Skilling.

"Yes," said Hobert. "According to ballistics, the seven Frenchmen were killed with the same gun. Three of the five men with you also were killed with that gun. We assume it belongs to that mad dog you have been watching and who you failed to have the courtesy to notify the French authorities about."

"We've been all through that, sir," said Picket. "It was a serious breach of courtesy, and again I apologize."

Hobert waved his hand. "Seven Frenchmen are dead. Apologize to their widows."

Picket turned. "Oh, come on, Hobert. Every one of them was a drug pusher, thief, murderer, what have you. If your government did more to stop the flow of drugs into the United States, maybe we wouldn't have to have men like Russell Nimz breaking a few rules."

"A few rules?" Hobert was shouting now.

It was Sergeant Logen who jumped in. "Listen. I personally am going to toss you both out of here unless you calm down. The lieutenant tried to get Nimz to move against Palmer. I got

172

it all in a report he sent me. The lieutenant did everything he could to wipe that bastard off the face of the earth, but the CIA had to play big shot. Now you two get on with your questions quietly or get out."

Picket and Hobert, both their faces flushed, turned toward Skilling. "Do you have any idea where Palmer might go?" asked Hobert.

"Not here. Sure of that," said Skilling.

"And we're equally sure he is," said Picket. "He didn't land in the U.S. Not with the drugs, at any rate."

"Ahead of you," said Skilling. "Always ahead. Not like normal." Skilling paused, his throat raw and sore. "Do anything. Kill twelve. Doesn't mind. Kill anybody. Not normal. Always ahead. Hate him."

"Yes," said Hobert. "Perhaps we'd better come back later. The lieutenant doesn't seem to be in any shape to tell us much."

"Don't be hard on Nimz. Tried to get everybody," said Skilling.

"He should have notified the authorities," said Hobert.

"Going to," said Skilling. "Afraid not let drugs out. Wanted New York contact."

"I see," said Hobert.

"Want to talk. Warehouse?" asked Skilling. "Know warehouse?"

For the next hour, Skilling talked to Picket and Hobert. At the end of that time, his throat gave out. But he filled them in on nearly every detail he knew. He was totally exhausted and showed it.

Hobert, by this time, had calmed himself. He said to Skilling, "Lieutenant, I thank you for your cooperation. I hope you feel better."

"Tomorrow?" asked Skilling.

"Yes," said Hobert. "Twelve men are dead."

Skilling nodded. "Tired," he said.

The following morning, Skilling sat up in bed for a short time.

Drugs had lessened the pain, and he felt ready to talk. He drank a full glass of orange juice. Shortly after, Hobert and Picket came into the room. Another man was with them, fifty, his clothes rumpled, and his hairline cutting straight across the top of his head from ear to ear.

"Lieutenant Skilling," said Hobert, "this is Inspector DePaepe." They both nodded.

"You are a lucky man, Lieutenant," said DePaepe.

"Yes," said Skilling. His throat was raw. "I was so pompous. And all the time—" Skilling raised his good arm in a gesture of defeat.

"He must have known of you from the start," said DePaepe.

"Yes," said Skilling. "I made mistake. Don't know what."

"Lieutenant Skilling," said DePaepe, "I have listened to your conversation yesterday. Your sergeant has filled out a lengthy and quite good report on this Eddie Palmer from the very beginning. It is my job now to track him down if he is in France."

"I know where he is," said Skilling. "I know."

Picket spoke. "How?"

"It came to me. All clear," said the lieutenant. "So simple. Every door but back door closed. He is back in Vietnam."

"So," said DePaepe. "Yes. It makes sense. As a policeman, I know one thing. From what you and your sergeant tell me of this man, he had some way out before he pulled the trigger."

"Yes," said Skilling.

"I will see if I can find his escape route, Lieutenant," said the inspector. "We will see if he did as you suspect." The inspector walked to Skilling's window and looked out. "What is it that makes this man do what he does? He is missing something here." He tapped his heart. "But nothing here." He tapped his head.

"I'll get him," said Skilling. "One day."

DePaepe turned to Hobert. "So. I believe the lieutenant is right. I will investigate, of course. But I think I will find nothing. I will find no killer, no mad man with a silent weapon. We are too late, too late."

"Very well," said Hobert. "I want the entire matter sewn up in a tight police package. From there, I will proceed on an official level." Hobert turned to Skilling. "Mister Picket turned over the files kept by Mister Nimz. It is as your sergeant had said. Mister Nimz mentions more than once of your objections to his procedure. I am sorry for everyone he did not listen to your advice. I wish you well."

Picket came over to Skilling. "If you want anything, just let me know."

Skilling nodded. "Thanks," he said.

DePaepe turned to Skilling. "Take care, young man."

"Thank you," said Skilling. "I will. I learned that lesson the hard way."

DePaepe shrugged. "In such matters, there is no easy way."

19

Eddie followed her from her father's shop. He waited until her tea arrived. Across the street, Mau Mau kept watching the street and Eddie. Eddie checked Mau Mau, nodded for him to stay on watch, then casually walked over to the Vietnamese girl. "Hello, Co Mai," said Eddie.

She looked up, stared for a moment, then her left hand flew up to her mouth. "Ong Eddie?" Her eyes swept the sidewalk café and then came back to Eddie. "We thought you were dead."

"Yeah," said Eddie. "Me, too. Can I sit down?"

"Please," she said. "I am sorry. It is such a surprise."

Eddie slipped into a chair facing Duong Thi Mai. "How is your father?"

"He is well, Ong Eddie."

"I'd like to see him, Co Mai."

"You may come back with me," she said.

"Is it safe?"

"Safe?"

"I don't have any papers, Co Mai. I don't wanna have to cause any trouble."

She swirled the green tea around in her cup. "It is safe. When you disappeared, he had people searching for you. He could find no trace."

"I don't suppose he could."

"Why did you not notify him?"

Eddie smiled. "Have a rice cake, Co Mai."

She smiled back. "I am sorry, Ong Eddie. I know you would have if it had been possible. But he was so worried for so long. He thought you were indestructible, a good luck charm. Then suddenly you were gone. Disappeared."

"But I *am* indestructible, Co Mai. Here I am again."

She stood. "Come, Ong Eddie. I will take you to my father."

Eddie pushed back his chair quickly and stood beside her. She walked quickly out onto the street. Eddie checked to see that Mau Mau was behind him and then followed her at a leisurely pace. As they neared her father's shop, she stopped. "I will go in, Ong Eddie," she said.

"Okay," said Eddie.

She entered the shop. In a few minutes, she stepped back through the door and bowed her head slightly to Eddie. Eddie crossed over and entered the shop. He stepped quickly into the back room.

The old merchant Duong Van Minh sat at his desk, his hands folded. Eddie bowed his head. It was as though no time had passed, as though Eddie's months in the jungle and in Marseilles were only hazy episodes from years before.

"So," said Minh. "You indeed are alive."

"Yes," said Eddie, "I'm alive."

"You look well, Ong Eddie."

"And you, Ong Minh. You look good, too."

"I am well, Ong Eddie. Sit down, please. We shall have tea."

Minh gestured for Eddie to sit in a small chair facing the desk. Tea was brought, and they drank it mostly in silence. When they finished, Minh spoke. "I will tell you what I know," he said. "The day you disappeared, the house you were in was raided by military police. Because you were not arrested, I assumed you had fled and would surface later."

"Raided?" asked Eddie.

"Yes."

"Who?"

"A special military police unit, Ong Eddie. I was questioned by them extensively. But the most they could do was accuse me of owning the house. Since you and your men were not in the house, nothing more happened. They found some money there, some other things. But there was no danger for me. I halted operations for a time and waited them out."

The news had upset Eddie. He'd had no idea he had come that close to being arrested. Eddie had never quite forgiven himself for allowing Linh to capture him and his men. Now to discover another unit had moved in on him without his knowing unnerved him. "Damn," said Eddie.

"Then you did not know."

Eddie shook his head. "First I heard of it."

"During the questioning, they said you shot one of their men. One of the men from their unit."

Eddie blinked. His mind raced backward. Then, suddenly, he fit it all together, from the dead MP to a burning car in the hills outside Marseilles. "Man, am I dumb."

"I do not understand, Ong Eddie."

"It's nothin', Ong Minh. Just me. I thought I had everybody hangin' cool, and all the time they were doggin' my trail. You got to be careful all the time. Real careful."

"This is not a profession where one can afford overconfidence."

Eddie smiled. "I reckon. So, they raided the place, and they got my money."

"Some of it," said the old man. "You do have several hundred thousand piasters coming to you which are in my possession, Ong Eddie."

Eddie bowed his head. "Thank you, Ong Minh. I appreciate that."

"Now, Ong Eddie, what can you tell me of these past months?"

"I'll tell you anythin' you want to know, Ong Minh," said

Eddie. "But I don't really think you'll want to know much. I was up north."

"North?" Minh was surprised. "So, it is true. I do not want to know, Ong Eddie. It does explain why I could find no trace of you. Can you answer me this. Have you come back to work?"

"That's up to you, Ong Minh. I need a safe house and papers. Good papers. If I have to work to get it, I'll do it. If I have enough money to cover for a while, take the money."

Minh nodded. "Very well, we shall see. Yes, I have a safe house. Safe for both of us. I do not own it, but it is available to me. It is yours. Papers are no problem, as you know."

"I need U.S. passports," said Eddie.

"Expensive but available."

"Thank you, Ong Minh."

The door opened behind Minh, and a young man stepped into the room. The two spoke in Vietnamese for a moment. Then Minh said, "He will guide you to the house." He bowed. "I am happy to know you are not dead, Ong Eddie."

Eddie bowed deeply from the waist. "Thank you, Ong Minh."

After nearly three-quarters of an hour's walk, Eddie and the young man arrived at an industrial area near the perimeter of Cholon. Various warehouses and factories dotted the once residential area. Standing between two large warehouses was an old French colonial frame house, the white paint yellowing now but still bright against the dark drabness of the warehouses. The young man nodded at the house, handed Eddie a set of keys, turned, and walked back toward the center of town. Eddie looked around, slowly and carefully. There was little traffic. Also, there was an absence of refugees. Refugees glutted Saigon, living where they could, any way they could. The large cemetery in Saigon was home for hundreds of them. However, here Eddie could find no evidence of them. Perhaps it was too close to the edge of town, to VC territory.

Eddie turned and called, "Okay, man."

Mau Mau stepped out from between two buildings about fifty yards back. "That it?" shouted Mau Mau.

"Yeah," said Eddie. "Come on in." Eddie waited until his friend walked up. Then they moved toward the house. There was a passageway about three feet wide on both sides of the structure, an alleyway of sorts separating the house and the windowless walls of two warehouses.

Eddie walked back through the one passageway and out into the rear yard. The yard was like a courtyard, blocked on three sides by warehouse walls and on its front side by the house itself. The only way into and out of the yard was through the passageways alongside the house itself.

"No way in, no way out," said Eddie.

Mau Mau pointed. "You could come down from up top," he said.

"So we better have somebody up there, right?"

"Right," said Mau Mau.

"Let's have a look inside," said Eddie. "But be careful."

"Man, I'm always careful."

Eddie opened a side door with one of the keys, and they began inspecting the house. They counted fifteen rooms, each furnished comfortably. There were three doors: front, side, and back. One of the third-floor bedroom windows overlooked the roof of one of the warehouses and was close enough for a man to jump across.

Eddie opened the window, leaned out, and jumped over. Mau Mau followed. They were on a large expanse of warehouse roof leading away from the window. They could walk completely around the house on the roofs of the warehouses. It was like an outer wall to protect the house.

Eddie smiled. "That old man knows his business," Eddie said. "Christ, this is like a fort. Couple of men up here and you could send fire every direction you've a mind to."

"I'm hip. So let's move in."

By nightfall, Eddie had led Colonel Linh and the others back to the house. They had been encamped several miles outside

Saigon. The drugs were locked in a closet in Linh's bedroom, and two men were put on guard, one on the roof of the warehouses and the other on the first floor of the house itself. That night, no one showed a light.

The next morning, Lieutenant Tri scouted the surrounding blocks. Several escape routes were mapped out, and everyone in the company was made familiar with them. Foodstuffs were brought in. By four, the house was secured.

Eddie then told Linh he wanted to speak to him.

"You sound serious, Ong Eddie," said Linh.

"Yeah, maybe I am," said Eddie.

Linh motioned to his aide. "Lieutenant Tri," he said.

Eddie nodded. "Mau Mau," he called.

Linh started to speak but stopped. He nodded to Eddie, and the four men went into a small room set aside as a command post in case of any emergency.

Both Eddie and Mau Mau carried a bottle of Ba Muioi Ba. They sat in chairs facing Linh and Tri. Colonel Linh spoke first. "Well, Ong Eddie. What is it you wished to talk about?"

"I wish to talk about our future, Ong Linh," said Eddie. "I want to get movin'. If you're gonna blow up the United States, let's get on with it, you dig? This place is spookin' me."

"This house?" asked Linh.

"No, man. Nam. I'm pushin' my luck staying in Nam. You said you could get the skag to the States. I want to know how and when."

"Patience, Ong Eddie," said Linh. "Lieutenant Tri will start tomorrow on the arrangements."

"How long that gonna take?" asked Eddie. "One month? Two? Six?"

Lieutenant Tri cut in. "Be careful how you speak to the colonel."

"Hey, man," said Eddie, "pull out."

Tri started to stand, but Colonel Linh grabbed his arm and held him. "Enough," said Linh.

Eddie looked from Linh to Tri and back. "Look, man. I been

181

sloggin' through the jungle for you like I never did for Uncle Sam. I been bitten by leeches and every other goddamn kinda bug. I killed every son of a bitch from here to France. And what have I got, man? I got nothin'. Zero. I want to know about them drugs, or you and your invasion is gonna sink, dig? Eddie Palmer is gonna sink it."

"You will not speak any more to the colonel," said Tri. "There is no—"

Eddie cut in. "Shut your face, man." Eddie felt Mau Mau shift in his chair behind him. He was in a cold fury now. "I ain't no hired help no more, dig? This is my house. My contact. My man is gonna get us papers. My money. No more tellin' Eddie and his boys. From now on, we're gonna do some of the tellin'."

Colonel Linh held up his hand. "Please allow me to speak, Ong Eddie. Please, before it goes too far." Eddie leaned back in his chair, relaxed a bit. Then he took a long swallow of his beer. Linh waited until he was finished.

"You are right," he said. He sighed. "I would not be this far had it not been for you."

Eddie smiled. "Don't gimme the old soldier bit, man. Maybe you would; maybe you wouldn't. Point is, you didn't. So where does that leave us?"

"It leaves us, Ong Eddie," said Linh, "in a different position than a few months ago. We have over one hundred kilos of pure heroin. It is worth much money in the United States. I seek no profit, as you know. All I can offer you, then, is the drug. It is all yours after expenses. All of it. Does that satisfy you?"

"Maybe," said Eddie.

"I can only say further, Ong Eddie, that I know I will need you even more in the future than I did in the past. I have learned to trust your judgment. And I am aware my money is gone and we need yours on which to continue. I thank you for that and hope to repay you a thousandfold."

Eddie turned. "Whatta ya think, man?"

"Things is better'n when we sat down, man," said Mau Mau.

182

"Yeah," said Eddie. "Okay. But I want to know about those drugs, man. They're mine."

"If you will allow me, Ong Eddie," said Linh. "I trust you with my life."

"But not with the drugs?"

"That is my position."

Eddie smiled. "Sensible, man. Hey, Mau Mau?"

"Drugs don't mean nothin' here," said Mau Mau. "Skag's cheap. New York is where we gotta get that junk."

"I will tell you this much," said Linh. "The drugs are going to the United States fifteen kilos at a time, inside the body of a United States civilian who has died here in Vietnam. Eventually, all of the drugs will be buried at various cemeteries in your country. As we need money, I will tell you of the location of a body. When our job is done, I will tell you the locations of all of the bodies. You will only have to dig. Is that agreeable?"

"Son of a bitch," said Eddie. "Hey, I dig it. Fifteen kilos in a dead man's chest." He and Mau Mau started laughing. "Go to it, Colonel," said Eddie.

Tri and Linh sat quietly while Eddie and Mau Mau slapped one another's palms in glee. "I take it, Ong Eddie," said Linh, "that we have a bargain."

"Deal," said Eddie.

"Is there anything else bothering you, Ong Eddie?" Linh asked. "Because if there is, now is the time to speak."

Eddie leaned back. "I got one thing that don't hit me well," he said.

"And that is?"

"The weapons, man."

"They're light mortars," said Linh. "They can easily be disguised with brass fittings."

"That's the rub, man," said Eddie. "They're light. What's the range?"

"Five hundred meters," answered Linh.

"Well, now, see, that's what I'm talkin' about," said Eddie.

"We're not sittin' out in the jungle, man. You got us blowin' up factories, and, man, the parkin' lots are that big."

"We have no alternative," said Tri. "We will strike fast."

"How about a rocket?" asked Eddie.

Linh nodded. "There is a new Chinese rocket," he said. "It's small but difficult to hide. It is fired electrically from a two-tube launch module."

"What size?" asked Eddie.

"It's a 107 millimeter," replied Linh. "Range is 8,300 meters."

"That's what? Damn. It's five miles." Eddie smiled. "That's more like it, man. Tell me more."

"Weight is forty-two pounds," continued Linh. "The shell weighs eighteen and a half pounds, with warhead. The length of the module is thirty-three inches."

"Can you get me some shells back in your brass shipment?"

Linh and Tri looked at one another. "I don't see why not," replied Tri. "It would be the module itself that would be difficult."

"Tri," said Eddie, "you lay your hands on six of 'em. I'll get 'em back to the States."

Linh spoke. "Can you secure some of the 107s for Ong Eddie?"

Tri nodded. "Yes," he said.

"Hey, I dig it," said Eddie. "Five miles."

Eddie bought a lieutenant's uniform from one of Minh's contacts, and he wore it all morning to get the feel of it. He had everyone at the safe house address him as Lieutenant Gibson, the name he had chosen. By lunch, Eddie felt he *was* Lieutenant Gibson, at least enough to pull off what he had to do.

The door was marked Office of Information, United States Army, Vietnam. When he walked in, a lieutenant looked up from his empty desk. "Can I help you?" he asked Eddie.

"I think maybe you can," said Eddie. "My name's Lieutenant Gibson. I'm from the general's staff."

The lieutenant sat up in his chair. "Oh? Who's that?"

"The big man," said Eddie. "General Abrams."

The information officer's brow furrowed. "Right. I'm Lieutenant Peterson. What can I do for you?"

"Well," said Eddie, "it's kinda cockamamie, if you know what I mean. But when a general says something, you know what that means. And down it comes through the ranks, and it ends up with some lieutenant. This time, it's me."

"I know what you mean, Gibson," he said.

"Right," said Eddie. "I figured you would. So, here's the poop. The general wants to send some war souvenirs back to the States."

"War souvenirs?"

"That's right. And I know what you're thinkin', so don't bother to say it. It's wastin' my time, too. Anyway, some unit captured some of those Chinese 107s the VCs been usin'. The army's already tested 'em, so they don't want 'em at Aberdeen. Nobody wants 'em is what it amounts to. So the general decides they'd make nice souvenirs for some of the American Legion posts back in the States. Maybe he's fixin' to run for somethin', I don't know. But that's the story."

"Beautiful," said Peterson. "Actually, Gibson, it's a damn fine idea. From my point of view, it's the kind of thing I wish more of the big boys would do. Makes good copy in a local newspaper. We can use all the friends we can get. Where are the posts?"

"That's exactly what I'm doin' here. The general wants three posts in California and three in New York. Hell, I don't know where to go to find 'em. Maybe you can."

"How much time have I got?"

"How much time do you ever have with a general? I'd like to stick with you today until we get the thing worked out. I'll pass it on tomorrow, and if everything works out, maybe we can both score some points with the old man."

Peterson smiled and pulled his chair in close to his desk. "Okay. Let's see here," he said.

185

By the end of the day, Lieutenant Peterson and Eddie had selected six American Legion posts. Three of them were within hours of New York City. The other three were in southern California. The names and addresses were typed on a sheet and given to Eddie for the general's supposed approval. A memo was then typed and attached indicating the general's assignment was carried out. Eddie insisted they both sign it. Peterson was most appreciative.

The following day, again as Lieutenant Gibson, Eddie checked out procedure at an army dock area. He then arranged for the necessary official papers with a black market contact.

Four days later, an army truck drove up to a dock area. The two soldiers in the truck were Eddie and Mau Mau, both dressed in fatigues. In the back of the truck were six crated 107-millimeter rocket launchers.

A captain with a clipboard waved the truck to one side and signaled Eddie. Eddie hopped out of the truck and approached the captain. He held out a sheaf of papers. "This where this goes, sir?" asked Eddie.

The captain took the papers and studied them. "Yeah," he said. "What is this stuff. I can't make it out here."

"I don't rightly know, sir," said Eddie.

"All right, get it unloaded. Put it right over there against those big crates. I got to open up one and see what we got inside."

"Yes, sir," said Eddie. He waved Mau Mau out of the truck, and the two unloaded the six crates. The captain walked over with a crowbar. He handed it to Eddie.

"Let's have a look inside," he said.

Eddie carefully pried the lid loose from one of the crates to expose the shiny dual barrel of the weapon. He stepped back. "There you go, sir," said Eddie.

The captain bent to look over into the crate. "For Christ sake," he said. "What in hell is it?" He crouched for a closer look. "Jesus, it's a cannon, isn't it? Bring me my clipboard there."

Eddie walked over and picked up the captain's clipboard. The captain took it, still crouched, and started to read. "This sure as hell doesn't say cannon," said the captain.

Eddie pointed with his finger. "That looks like it says 'souvenir,' Captain," Eddie said.

The captain stared. "By God, you're right." He looked again into the crate. "Yeah, here's a brass plate attached." He read, "To Parker-Bale American Legion Post, Ossining, New York. Sincerely, General Creighton Abrams." He looked up at Eddie and smiled.

"A war trophy," said Eddie. "Them dudes is gonna have a new cannon to hang on their walls."

The captain stood, smiling. "All right, nail that lid back on. I'll put this on the first available space."

"Right, sir," said Eddie, grinning. "When I see the general, I'll tell him." Eddie fitted the nails carefully back into the nail holes and hammered them tight. He stood, saluted, and climbed back into the cab of the truck. Mau Mau saluted, too, and grinned at Eddie. Eddie shoved the truck into gear, and Mau Mau hurried to leap in. Eddie moved the truck out of the area quickly. They made fifty yards before they both started to giggle.

Skilling spent three weeks in the Marseilles hospital. On two occasions, the army tried to transfer him to a military hospital, but the move was blocked both times by the French government. France wanted Skilling accessible.

The entire Marseilles incident caused a serious strain between France and the United States. The United States finally persuaded France to label the killings the result of a gang war over drugs from Turkey. The United States, in return, made several concessions, including the replacement of all key CIA personnel in France.

Because of Skilling, the Pentagon was drawn into the squabble, but both the official reports of Nimz and the evidence uncovered by the French police indicated Skilling had acted properly. Officially, Colonel Lancto apologized to the French for having a military man engaged in a covert operation in the country. Privately, however, a few toasts were drunk to Skilling and the way he came out of the incident, as Lancto put it, "smelling like a rose."

Skilling knew none of this. He cooperated as fully as he could with the French. He received a note from Colonel Lancto wishing him a speedy recovery. That was all. His biggest victory was one he didn't know he'd won. His unit was allowed to continue.

Skilling was sent back to Saigon to recuperate. Sergeant Logen waited until the lieutenant had returned before he told him that he'd uncovered Eddie's escape route from Marseilles.

"The same ship?" asked Skilling. "Why in hell don't the French police, the CIA, you, anybody, track it down and shake the captain until he spills everything?"

"The ship went down in the Gulf of Siam," said Logen. "With all hands, as they say."

"Good God."

"Crew of seven and the captain, as nearly as we can determine. No one really knows how big the crew was."

"You figure Eddie did it?"

"No doubt in my mind, sir."

"Nor mine," said Skilling. "Jesus, it always surprises me because I keep thinking of him as a human being."

"It certainly worked for him. We don't know if he's in Saigon or Jersey City, for Christ sake. It's the old story. Dead men tell no tales."

Skilling gingerly felt the scar on his neck and then rubbed it with his index fingernail. The scar itched. At times, it smarted like a sunburn. Now it was itching. Skilling concentrated on relieving the itch. He had studied the scar in a mirror. It was shaped like a red, fleshy fishhook. And now whiskers grew around it because it was still too sensitive to shave. A miracle you didn't lose your voice, the doctor had said.

"I hate him," Skilling mumbled.

"Yes, sir," said Logen.

Skilling brought his mind back to the conversation. "Look, this thing is going to drive me crazy, Logen. I need to forget Eddie Palmer, to relax. I've got to get drunk or something. He's only a man. One day, I'm going to get him. I'll have my hands around his throat, Logen, and he'll die just like anybody else."

"Sir, you need rest, that's all."

"He beat me. He whipped my ass. It's only luck I'm alive today. He's a better man than me."

"No, sir. He just doesn't have any rules."

Skilling nodded. "I remember reading about Al Capone once and thinking what a smart man he was to work his way up in the rackets. Then I read where he killed some men once with a baseball bat. Smashed their heads in. Imagine. That ended it for me. No more backhanded hero worship. I thought to myself, Skilling, you could become president if you could kill people with a baseball bat and then just go on about your business. Take a person with average brains and absolutely no compunction concerning killing, and you have a winner. And it's my idea that Eddie Palmer has better than average brains."

"Yes, sir," said Logen.

Skilling looked up at Logen. The sergeant patiently smiled, ready to listen. "Okay, Logen," said Skilling, "I've had my tantrum for the day."

"Does it help, sir?"

"Hell, no," said Skilling. "There's only one thing that would help."

"We catch Eddie Palmer."

"That's the thing."

"I've been working on our one old lead," said Logen.

"The merchant?"

"Right. Duong Van Minh."

"You think he'd work with Minh again?"

"I don't know. He would if he needs money. Minh may also help him smuggle out the drugs. Minh was his contact before. I'm certain he'll go back to him."

"Have you seen Minh?"

"No. But I'm keeping a man on watch at his shop."

Skilling nodded. "Have there been any reports of hijackings that sound like Eddie?"

"No. It's my guess he's not working. I don't know where he's getting his money. From those Vietnamese he's with, I guess."

"Have you found out anything about them?"

"Dead end. There's absolutely nothing to go on."

"Did you check Minh's properties. Maybe Eddie is using one of his houses again."

"I did. And he isn't."

"So we just wait and see. But we can't wait too long. He'll move those drugs out of here one day soon. We've got to get him before he does."

"Yes, sir," said Logen.

Skilling walked to the door in his office. "You still haven't fixed this damn door," he said.

"No, sir," said Logen.

"Don't," said Skilling. He waved to Logen and walked out on the Rue Pasteur. He studied several faces passing on the street. They were all strange faces, unfamiliar. He ran his finger along the scar on his neck. He went home and slept until the next morning.

Even at 7:00 in the morning, the streets of Saigon were fouled with traffic. Truong Dinh Dzu guided his scooter with care. He wanted to reach the mortuary early, before the other workers came in. Today, Dzu made another shipment for a band of smugglers, and he wanted it all to go smoothly. Today, too, he would tell them of his decision. He must tell them before the next shipment went out.

He thought over the past weeks and of his participation in the smuggling. He had been terrified at first. But it was as he had been told. It had gone without a snag, and he was thousands of piasters richer. With each shipment, he had grown bolder. After all, he told himself, he was taking all the risks. It was he putting the drugs inside the bodies.

He had sent over 100 kilos of drugs back to the United States inside the bodies of seven Americans. He had done the work either before or after hours at the mortuary. He had painstakingly copied the names and addresses to give to the smugglers.

It was after the fifth body that Dzu asked for more money. The smugglers had bowed to his wishes without a whimper. It had surprised Dzu somewhat, but he finally worked it out that he was the indispensable man. After that, it was easy. He discussed enlarging the operation with his contact. He asked for another raise.

Then, when he was preparing for the seventh body, he was told that his plan had been accepted; the smuggling was to continue. And, again, he would get more money, a higher payment.

Dzu thought of all this as he steered his scooter along the Saigon streets. He was to meet his contact at the mortuary at 7:30. Dzu had a new plan. His new decision was he be made a full partner. Dzu knew he must be bold.

He pulled back his shoulders and turned the throttle up a bit. He was prepared to settle for less than a full partnership, of course. A share. He would give in on that point. But he wouldn't give in on the idea of it. Dzu resolved to end this day with a celebration over his becoming a rich man. He set his jaw and imagined life with enormous amounts of money. So intent was he on his thoughts, he failed to notice an army truck driven by a black soldier bearing down on him. Then it was too late, and his last thought was of all the good things he was going to miss now that he was dying.

20

They were leaving Vietnam. Mau Mau stood behind Eddie in line, swearing softly. Each man wore a uniform, carried a small bag filled with male paraphernalia and, in the lining, two hundred $20 bills. Their false papers stated they were flying to Tokyo for rest and relaxation.

"Shit," said Mau Mau, "what if somethin' happens?"

"Nothin's gonna happen," replied Eddie.

Eddie now stood at a table, and he held out his false papers. His newly grown moustache sat like a piece of steel wool on his lip, and he ignored an urge to scratch it. He also wore a pair of round, steel-rimmed glasses. His hair was shorter, too. Enough of a change, he felt, to throw off a curious MP.

Their papers were stamped, and they passed through. Mau Mau took a seat by the window, and Eddie took the middle seat of the three. They both fidgeted in their seats, waiting. But, soon, they were airborne.

Mau Mau pressed his face against the window, looking down at the lights. "I can't believe it man," he said.

"President Nixon said he was gonna bring us boys home," said Eddie.

They destroyed their identities in Tokyo and took up new ones: two students touring. The false passports and immunization cards had been costly for Eddie and all the others. It had taken his last piaster. They'd had to return to hijacking, one large job for his Vietnamese merchant for travel money, and it had been sloppy. No one had been caught, but Eddie hadn't been happy with the entire deal. He felt a tenseness, as though someone was closing in on him.

In San Francisco, they checked through customs quickly. Mau Mau tried to persuade Eddie to lay over there, but Eddie bought them tickets on the first flight to New York. Eddie's only goal, now, was to stand on 125th Street in Harlem. At 8:49 A.M., Thursday, October 7, 1971, he was there.

"Christ, man, we made it," said Eddie. "We're really here."

"And look at them faces, man," replied Mau Mau. "All black."

"Smell. No more dead fish. Hey, this is the smell I grew up with. Garbage." They laughed.

Mau Mau shook. "I'm freezin' my ass. First the jungle and now this freeze-ass weather."

"Come on, man," said Eddie, "we'll go buy some threads."

They bought lined trench coats with high collars. As they walked out of the store, a cold drizzle started.

They then went into the best restaurant in walking distance and ate two greasy hamburgers each.

"This food sucks," said Mau Mau. "It's no different than that damn gook shit we been eatin'."

"I tell you what we can do. We don't have to drink that gook beer no more. Let's go have us a Budweiser."

They walked quickly to a bar on 125th Street and settled into a booth, each ordering a beer. Then they discussed their immediate future.

"My tail is draggin'," said Eddie. "We got to find us a place and settle in."

"I'm hip," said Mau Mau.

"We just take a couple of furnished rooms for the time bein'," said Eddie. "That okay?"

193

"I don't give a shit."

"Hey, man." Eddie shouted to the bartender. "Where can we get us some rooms?"

"You got bread, you go west," said the bartender. "You got no bread, you gonna sleep by the train station."

"We want somethin' good," said Mau Mau.

The bartender shrugged and grinned. "You want somethin' good, what you doin' in Harlem?"

"That dude got a smart mouth," said Mau Mau.

"Hey, man, forget it," said Eddie. "Come on."

They drank their beers and walked out into the cold. The drizzle had turned into a hard rain, the drops chilled with the promise of winter. They moved along 125th Street, heads bent downward against the elements.

The rooms they rented reeked of soot and sweat and age, but the sheets on the beds were clean. And Eddie felt secure, an American among Americans, a black in the dark ghetto of Harlem.

Fatigue plagued them the next day, but Eddie was determined to find a permanent base, and he was out on the street by 11:00. Shortly after lunch, he hit upon the perfect place.

The building was on 121st Street. It had recently been vacated by a storefront church. The front window had been painted from the inside: The Church of Soul and Brotherhood, and there was a larger-than-life-size drawing of a black Jesus.

"The Lord move in mysterious ways," the rental agent said. "That buildin' been empty only a short time. Here you come along wantin' a church. I gots me a church."

"Amen, brother," said Eddie. "How much?"

"You got a flock yet?" asked the man.

"Not yet," replied Eddie.

"Then it's three months in advance." The man smiled. "Not that I don't trust nobody what work for the Lord, but I got to protect myself."

"Three months."

"Plus security, which is one month, plus my fee."

"Which is?"

"One thousand total." He looked up at Eddie, the smile frozen on his face.

"That's two hundred a month, that right, brother?"

"That's it, Reverend."

"I'll take it," said Eddie. "Draw me up a lease."

"Yes, sir, Reverend, sir. You got it. What's the name?"

"Just make it out to Reverend E. Palmer. Praise the Lord."

The man almost feverishly made out a standard printed lease with Eddie's name on it. Eddie signed the lease and counted off fifty $20 bills.

"You'll be givin' me a receipt," said Eddie.

The man filled out a receipt and signed it. "It's nice doin' business with you, Reverend."

"You, too, brother," said Eddie. He nodded to Mau Mau and turned to leave. At the door, he stopped. "By the way, brother. If I wasn't workin' in the service of the Lord, I'd take it unkindly you shuckin' me. You breakin' the law makin' me pay in advance, you know, brother. If you a good landlord, we won't have no trouble. But you stick your nose into my business, brother, the hand of the Lord is gonna tear your nuts out by the roots. Dig?"

Eddie turned and walked out. On the sidewalk, he and Mau Mau laughed.

"Shee-it, man," said Mau Mau, "we got us a home."

"We get some furniture now," said Eddie. "By tonight, we be livin' in style."

Eddie and Mau Mau went to a furniture store on 125th Street. Eddie kept up his preacher role and told the furniture man his needs.

"I'm gonna have some orphan children livin' with me," said Eddie. "I reckon I'll need about a dozen single beds, some places for clothes, some nice sittin' down furniture, and a big refrigerator. We got to keep the little orphans' milk cold, brother."

Turk and Apache Joe arrived the next day. They were to stand at the corner of Lexington and 125th Street after they arrived in New York. Mau Mau checked the corner every hour. It was 8:00 that night when he saw them standing there.

Everyone was tired, but they were also keyed up. The furniture had been delivered, and Eddie had filled out the household needs during various buying trips. The refrigerator was filled nearly to the brim with cold beer.

"A goddamn preacher," said Apache Joe. "Hot damn."

"Drink up, man," said Eddie. "It's the will of the Lord."

"Man, I dig it, Eddie. I dig it," said Turk. "If I wasn't so damn draggin' ass, I'd go out and get us a little of that black stuff walkin' the streets."

"Tomorrow, you can grab anything that's movin', man. We'll just naturally take a little time off for a celebration. I tell you, brothers, we deserve it."

"Right on, Reverend Eddie. Right on," said Mau Mau.

Sunday morning, they began to drink beer. They kept a television set on and laughed all the way through three religious programs, making remarks about Reverend Eddie. Around 2:00 in the afternoon, Turk and Mau Mau went out and returned with five young girls. The party lasted until early Monday morning.

Monday, about 5:00, Eddie and Apache Joe went looking for guns.

They bought four Saturday night specials for $120 and made arrangements with the street dealer to buy better weapons.

"It's the skag we got to get next," said Eddie. "It might take some time to unload it."

"Let's get it," said Turk. "Then we can worry about unloadin' it."

"The old gook gave me the name and the burial town," said Eddie.

Eddie pulled out a map he'd bought and spread it smooth on the plastic-topped table. "I'll show you what we got to do," he said, pointing his finger to a spot near New York. "Here's where the skag is."

Turk bent over. "New Rochelle. It don't look far."

"It's not," said Eddie. "But I never been there."

"We need wheels," Mau Mau said.

"Trouble is, no driver's license," said Eddie.

"I can steal wheels," said Mau Mau.

"No, man," replied Eddie. "We can't crap around and get caught for some dumb-ass reason. Not when we're this close to big bread."

"So what do we do?" asked Mau Mau.

"We go by train, I reckon," said Eddie.

"We gonna take our pieces?" asked Apache Joe.

"You better believe, brother. If things get strained, we start fraggin'. Nobody's gonna get in my way now."

The train ride was short and uneventful. Each man carried a gun concealed in his coat. When they arrived in New Rochelle, Eddie relaxed. The first four faces he saw from the train window were black.

"Cool, so far," said Eddie. "I got to find the newspaper office now and track our body. It'll tell where he was buried."

"We'll wait in a bar," said Mau Mau.

"Hell, no, man. Don't sit and drink. Got to keep the head clear. There's a bunch of movie houses. Go to a movie. I'll pick you up there."

Turk smiled. "I ain't had any popcorn in three years," he said.

Eddie spent only thirty minutes in the office of the *Standard-Star* tracking down the burial place of one Michael Braden Calugia, the late Saigon embassy employee who had a fortune in heroin in his body cavity.

Because it had been so easy, Eddie decided not to pick up his companions just yet. He asked another black man where he might find some soul food, and the man pointed. "Just keep walkin'," he said.

Eddie walked along past various stores, then a car dealer and the courthouse. And then he arrived in what was obviously a black area. He found a cab and gave the name of the cemetery to the driver. It was at the other end of the town, and the driver told him it was an old Catholic cemetery. "You don't know nobody in there, brother," said the driver.

The cemetery was large, facing on a rather highly trafficked street. At one side were the tracks of a railroad; at the other, the town of Pelham. Eddie got out at a small florist shop located in a corner of the cemetery. He paid the driver, went inside the florist's, and bought a small bouquet. He then walked back to the entrance of the cemetery and entered.

The cemetery was originally built near the street. The oldest tombstones sat in plain sight of traffic. The newer graves and smaller tombstones, however, were set in an area that fell away and out of sight of everything except a row of houses that backed up to one side of the cemetery. He began to look for the name Calugia. He knew there might be a family plot near the front, but he decided to play the odds and keep away from the street.

He walked around for the better part of half an hour and didn't find the tombstone. Then he spotted a man in work clothes coming toward him. He wasn't certain how long the man had been watching him, if at all. He took a few more steps and then turned in to a grave enscribed with the name Laitt. He placed the bouquet of flowers on it and stepped back.

From behind him, a voice said, "Found it?"

Eddie turned to face the groundkeeper. "Oh, you surprised me," said Eddie. "Yep. Friend of my mother. She wanted me to put some flowers on the grave."

"Fine," said the man.

"I'll be goin' now."

"Fine," the man said again.

Eddie moved quickly out of the cemetery. He walked under the tracks and cut on back into town. He bought a ticket at the movie theater and went inside. There wasn't much of a crowd, and he found his three companions quickly. He sat down behind them.

"Let's go," said Eddie.

Mau Mau turned around. "Hey, man, I was beginnin' to wonder about you."

They all went outside. A wind had started to blow, and there was a chill in the air. They all turned up their collars.

"This weather is gonna take some gettin' used to," said Turk.

"Did you find the skag?" asked Mau Mau.

"I got the cemetery," said Eddie. "But I didn't find the spot. It's a big place, and we got to move easy."

"So now what?" asked Apache Joe.

"We got to buy some tools," said Eddie. "Then we'll wait for dark." They split up and bought what they needed. They stashed the things near the railroad track.

They ate dinner, then went to another movie. It was nearly 9:30 when they were back at the railroad embankment. They recovered the tools and made their way over an old black iron fence into the cemetery.

They walked quite a distance and put the tools beside a large tombstone with a cement angel on top. The wind had blown away the clouds, and the moon shone with an eerie fall brightness.

"I covered this area over in here," said Eddie. "We're lookin' for the name Calugia." He spelled it. "It's Michael Calugia. I reckon if we keep low, we can cover the tombstones without even flashlights. You can see pretty good. We'll work four rows, one on each row. And keep down. There's houses over there."

Mau Mau spotted the grave after about fifteen minutes. It was in the newer section and was located on a slight downward grade. They were out of sight of everything except the houses.

"Well," said Eddie, "let's shake it. Hand me that mother pick."

A black plastic sheet was spread out next to the grave, and

they put all the dirt on top of it. They worked in shifts, for the most part in silence. They reached the top of the casket a few minutes after 1:00 in the morning.

"This ain't no wooden casket," said Turk, who was in the hole. "It feels like cement."

They boosted Turk out, and Eddie dropped down, brushing away the dirt. He saw it was concrete. "Hand me the pick," said Eddie.

He tried to pry the top off but found he didn't have enough room. Finally, he drove the pick into the concrete, and it cracked. "That's loud, man," said Mau Mau.

"Damn bastards," grunted Eddie. "What they tryin' to *do?*" Eddie stood up in the grave for a moment. "Well, shit, let's take a chance. I'll break through. Keep an eye out."

Eddie hit the concrete casket repeatedly and finally had it sufficiently broken to uncover the wooden casket inside. He had no trouble opening that.

"There's the son of a bitch," said Eddie.

He turned the flashlight beam into the casket, and the dead face stared up at him. "Hi, there," said Eddie.

Eddie set the flashlight down and then grabbed the corpse with two hands. He pulled up, and the body lifted into a sitting position.

"Kee-rist," said Mau Mau softly. "We're not gonna take that mother with us, are we?"

"Just his stuffin's," said Eddie. "Gimme a knife."

Turk handed Eddie a knife, and Eddie made a cut through Calugia's clothes to expose his stomach area. He then made a cut at an angle, slitting the dead flesh from the right rib cage down to the left hipbone. He handed the knife back up to Turk.

"Jesus," said Apache Joe.

Eddie reached inside the body. "Come on, man," said Mau Mau. "Be there."

"Hey," said Eddie. He pulled his hand out and held it aloft. He was holding a plastic bag of white powder.

He pulled thirty bags out before he finished. Then he guardedly turned on a flashlight to sweep around the inside of Calugia's body. "That is all she wrote," said Eddie. "Gimme a hand."

Mau Mau pulled Eddie up out of the grave. The body sat leaning against the back of the grave.

"Now what?" asked Turk.

"We fill it in," said Eddie.

"You wanna put him back?" asked Mau Mau.

"Hell, no," said Eddie. "He's been lying down for a while. Let him sit up." He began to shovel.

Finding a buyer for fifteen kilos of heroin was going to be dangerous. "I reckon the only way is to start at the bottom," said Eddie. "Let's find us a pusher, and we'll go from there."

"Ain't no pusher can buy fifteen kilos," said Mau Mau.

"His boss can," said Eddie. "And if his boss can't, his boss's boss can. We got to start somewhere. But stay cool, hear?"

They were all standing on Broadway, watching a sale take place in a small park off Seventy-second Street. "The skinny one," said Turk.

"Right," said Eddie. "Spread out."

"Hey, man," said Eddie. The pusher, a black man, thin and young, leaned against a signpost.

"Hey," said the thin man.

"I'm just back from Nam," said Eddie.

"So?"

"I wanna discuss some skag," said Eddie.

The youth looked at Eddie. "Skag? Man, I don't know you. What you talkin' about?"

"I don't know you either, slim man," said Eddie, "but I'm gonna take a chance, you hear? I got some first-class stuff for sale. I brought it in from Nam. I'm willin' to sell it reasonable, dig? What you got to say to that?"

"I got to say one thing, man. Move on."

"I guess I didn't have your attention, man." Eddie stepped heavily on the man's foot. The initial shock of pain sent the thin youth hobbling about, cursing. And as the pain subsided, the anger took hold. He started for Eddie, but Eddie briefly unfolded a copy of the *Daily News* he was holding. Inside it, pointed at the youth's stomach, was the Saturday night special.

The young black man stopped. "What'd you go and do that for?" he said.

"I said, man. To get your attention. You're not listenin'."

"I can't buy no stuff, man. I don't have no money."

"You got a source," said Eddie. "You tell your source. If he don't have the money, he can tell his source. Somewhere, somebody's got money. And we're startin' with you."

"Okay, man. I'll see what I can do."

"I'll be back at noon. Right here." Eddie turned and walked to the bus stop. He smiled at the youth, who stood watching him. When the bus arrived, Eddie boarded it, and the young man continued to keep his eye on the bus.

When the youth was certain Eddie was gone, he moved to a phone booth and made a call. Then he waited.

In about fifteen minutes, a black Mercury pulled up near the youth and honked. He went to the car and spoke with another black man sitting inside. None of Eddie's men could hear the conversation, but it was apparent from the gestures and the facial expressions that the man on the street was sustaining a tongue-lashing. Then the car drove off, and the young black man returned to leaning against the post.

At noon, Eddie strode into the park area. He stopped to survey the situation. The black Mercury was parked up the street in a loading zone, the man inside watching. The young pusher was leaning against the signpost, trying to appear casual. Turk and Apache Joe were standing about ten feet behind the Mercury, awaiting Eddie's signal. Mau Mau rested on a bench about fifteen yards away.

Eddie then stepped up to the pusher. "Well?"

"I tell you, man," said the pusher, "I can't do nothin' for you."

Eddie nodded. He made a fist, the signal for Turk to move in on the Mercury. Then Eddie moved quickly and brought his heel down on the pusher's foot once again. This time, the thin young man dropped to the pavement in pain.

Eddie cut across the street to the Mercury. Turk was seated in the front with his gun shoved into the rib cage of the man behind the wheel. Eddie leaned over and spoke.

"I'm gonna tell you once, man," said Eddie. "I got fifteen kilos of good stuff. I wanna sell it for a fair price. And I wanna sell it quick. You wanna buy it?"

"You gonna be dead, man," said the driver of the car. There was a fury in his voice. Eddie took a small knife from his pocket and opened the blade. He reached in and slashed the back of the seat.

"Hey, man," said Eddie, "nobody listens in New York. We gonna do business, you understand?" The black man in the car seemed to shake. His hands started to move. "Keep your hands on the wheel, man," said Eddie, "or your guts is gonna be part of the interior design."

The man froze. Eddie now reached in and took the man's suit lapel. He stuck the knive into the crease in the lapel and cut downward. The lapel fell loose on the man's chest. "Okay, man," said the driver. "We can deal." He spoke softly, almost inaudibly.

"Good," said Eddie.

"There's a candy store on 119th Street between Park and Madison. It's called Lester's. You come there tonight about ten. We talk then."

"Right, brother," said Eddie. "Ten o'clock at Lester's. But don't shuck me, man."

"Be there at ten," said the driver. "That's all you gotta do."

"Right." Turk opened the door and slipped out. "Just keep your hands on the wheel," said Eddie.

The man nodded that he wanted to start the car. Eddie

okayed it. He turned the key and drove quickly out into the traffic. Turk and Eddie watched him disappear around a corner. The pusher was no longer to be seen either. Eddie and Turk then headed for the subway. Mau Mau and Apache Joe kept their distance, following just as a precaution.

"Why'd they tell us where they're set up?" asked Mau Mau. "Don't seem too cool."

"I figure they got a surprise for us when we come," said Eddie. "If they got any brains at all, they got to frag me."

"So whatta we do, man?" asked Turk. "I ain't about to have no war with no buncha dope fiends."

"We ain't gonna have no war, man," said Eddie. "We just gonna convince them that if I die, they die. They'll have some muscle there to burn me. We got to have more. Let's go now so's we can look over the place. They don't know Apache and Mau Mau. You two can look over the candy store."

The four of them traveled to 119th Street. Eddie and Turk went into a bar on Madison, and the other two men walked down the block and around and back. They joined Eddie in the bar in ten minutes.

"It's a stinkin' little place," said Mau Mau. "There's one little door to the front, and that's it. There's probably another one in back. What's across the street is the bad scene. It's a boarded-up buildin'."

"That's not bad, man, that's good. You reckon they gonna put a man there?" asked Eddie.

"Sure as shee-it they are, man," said Mau Mau.

"It'll probably be Mr. Mercury Car," said Eddie. "He's itchin' to burn me."

"So whatta we do?" asked Turk.

"We gets there before that dude," said Apache Joe. "Right?"

"You're a mind reader, man," said Eddie. "And if we get through this, man, they're gonna lay some bread on us. If they don't, there's gonna be a lot of dead dope fiends."

The four worked their way into the abandoned building from

204

118th Street. The building stank of urine and rats. Garbage littered the floors, and large portions of the walls were torn down. But the vantage points from both the first and the second floors were excellent.

"He's gonna stand right here," said Apache Joe. He peered through a piece of plywood covering a first-floor window. "This hole is big enough for a piece, and it's a clear shot to any place in the store."

"Right," said Eddie. "Apache, you set up here."

"All you got to do is drop your hanky, man, and I can spray for pay," said Apache Joe.

"You're my man, big daddy. Turk, you cover Apache's rear."

"Man," said Turk, "his rear is covered."

"Mau Mau," said Eddie, "you can be in the street. I'll take a popgun in with me."

They moved about the entire house, checking it out. They discovered that the front door wasn't locked. "Hey," said Eddie, "this is how the dude will come in. They ain't figurin' we'll be here. You let him get into position and wave or whatever he's gonna do, and then you introduce his head to one of them two-by-fours over there."

"Cool," said Apache Joe.

"Once you stiffed him, man," said Eddie, "you fix him on the inside of the front door. Nail him up there if you have to, dig? When I put up my hand, Turk, you swing open the door."

"Damn, I like that," said Turk.

"Listen, now," said Eddie, "if I put up a fist, you go for the trigger. Somethin's gone wrong, dig?"

"You got it, boss-man," said Apache Joe.

"Okay, then, let's split. We gotta get back here before nine if they're expectin' me at ten."

Turk and Apache Joe were in position at ten minutes before 9:00. Mau Mau waited in the bar on Madison. Eddie stayed on 116th Street.

A little after 9:30, the man from the Mercury walked out of Lester's Candy Store and crossed the street to the abandoned building. He entered through the front door and walked to a window on the first floor. His orders were to wait until the stranger entered the candy store, make certain he was alone, and then cross over the street to block the stranger's escape. If he was not alone, the man from the Mercury car had the drop on anyone on the street. His vantage point was good, and he leaned against the plywood to relax. He was afraid to sit because of the rats. He could hear them scurrying about. Then he heard the sound of rushing air. His eyes shifted. He saw a board coming toward his head. He heard a terrible crunch. Before his mind turned off and his body collapsed, he began to reach for his head to make certain it was still there.

At 9:58, Mau Mau entered 119th Street from Madison, walking casually. Eddie entered from Park almost immediately after and quickly headed for Lester's Candy Store. When he entered the front door, Mau Mau was positioned just out of sight to the east of the store.

Eddie left the door open and stepped in the doorway. There was a middle-aged, heavyset black man behind a dirty counter. The store was jammed with merchandise, dusty and out of date, and the man seemed to be standing in the middle of a cocoon.

"You Lester?" asked Eddie.

"I'm Lester. Who wants to know?"

"We here to do business, man, or get acquainted. I got me some dope to sell. You buyin'?"

"You gotta smart mouth, man."

"Come on, heavy," said Eddie. "Lemme talk to somebody else. Just listenin' to you, I knows you ain't the brains of this group."

Lester started to move toward Eddie, but a voice cut in from behind a heavy curtain hung across a door to the back. "Cool it, Lester," said the voice.

"That's better," said Eddie. "You the money man?"

The curtain pulled back to reveal a figure standing there. But he stayed in the shadows, and Eddie wasn't able to see the features of his face.

"You tryin' to hold up Lester?" asked the man. "If you is, you gonna be shot runnin' from the scene of the crime."

"That your gig, is it?" asked Eddie. "I always thought dope pushers was dumb. Now I know you is." The man in the door shifted his weight. He easily stood over six feet, but he was thin, scrawny even. Eddie could see that even in the shadows. "I got me a backup man outside, stretch. Now, let's stop all the shit and get to business. Christ, I never saw a bunch of folks so cautious 'bout makin' a profit."

"Your backup man is shit," said the man in the shadows. "And I'm gonna burn you myself. I don't take that kinda mouth from nobody."

"First, bones, I am gonna show you my man." Eddie tapped on the window, and Mau Mau stepped around into view. "Now that's my man. And here's yours."

Eddie waved his hand. The front door of the abandoned building swung open. Hanging on the inside of the door was the limp figure of the man from the Mercury car. He dangled from the door as it banged back against the stoop. The door stayed there.

"Look like he got a real bad hang-up," said Eddie.

"You son of a bitch," said the man in the doorway.

"You wanna talk, or you want my dudes to start spraying."

Lester turned toward the man in the doorway. The large man was confused. But he obviously would go for a gun if the man in back ordered it.

"I tell you what," said Eddie. "Suppose I apologize for my bad mouth. But you been shuckin' me, and sometimes my mouth just got a life of its own. So, let's start over. Old Lester, there, is ready to move, I can see that. That's a good man. But if he moves, we got to move. I got me a piece here and there outside. There ain't gonna be nothin' left of this place but the mortgage. Whatta you say. We gonna be business partners or corpses?"

The thin man spoke. "What you got?"

"I got fifteen kilos," said Eddie. "Pure stuff from the East, but

207

its been cooked in Marseilles. I want half a million for it."

"You got a lot of balls," said the man.

"Just two," said Eddie, "but they work good."

"How you know I'm not the Man?"

"I don't care if you is if you give me the half million."

"Too much."

"Bullshit."

"I got to test it."

"I know that."

"Lemme know how I can get in touch with you."

"No. But I'll bring a bag for you tonight. Say in an hour."

"Too dangerous."

"Ain't nothin' gonna happen unless you make it happen."

"I can't test it here."

"Bullshit again. Maybe you don't want to. Good. Test it at the po-leece station if you want. But you and me stay here."

"What's your hurry?"

"I don't like leavin' my boys in this neighborhood. There's a lot of undesirables."

The man grunted. "Get it."

Eddie made a small salute and backed out of the store. He gave the okay sign and hurried toward Madison. An hour later, he came onto 119th Street carrying a bucket of Kentucky Fried Chicken. Mau Mau was leaning against the building.

"Everything cool?" asked Eddie.

"Couple of customers," said Mau Mau. "I checked on Apache Joe and Turk. They're hangin' in there."

"Mr. Mercury Car wake up yet?"

"He's still on the door, last I seen," said Mau Mau. "He's a sound sleeper."

"Dig," said Eddie. He then entered the candy store again. Lester looked up. Then he walked to the doorway and knocked on the frame. The curtain parted again.

"You the folks that ordered a bucket of chicken?" asked Eddie.

Lester ambled over and took the chicken and handed it into

the back room. Eddie moved to the counter. "Got some coffee, Lester?"

Lester poured Eddie a cup. Eddie tasted it. "No wonder you're sellin' dope," he said. "You sure ain't gonna make a livin' sellin' this."

About twenty minutes passed. Then the curtain opened again. Eddie saw the thin man's face for the first time. His face startled Eddie. It was his mouth. It seemed to be a slash across his face. He didn't appear to have any lips. The mouth moved. "That's good stuff," he said.

"I know," said Eddie.

"Then we got us a deal. There's a phone booth at Park and 125th. You be there at noon tomorrow. I'll tell you where to bring the rest of the stuff."

"That's it?"

"That's it."

"I'll be there."

"Is my man across the street dead?"

"Probably," said Eddie.

"He should be. He is too dumb to live."

"No problem. Where's his car?"

"Down the street. He's got the keys on him."

"I'll take him outa the neighborhood."

The thin man nodded and curled his mouth. "It's nice doin' business with ya."

"Business ain't over, yet."

The man signaled to someone behind him. Eddie's bucket of chicken was handed back to him. "There's thirty thousand greasy dollars in there with the drumsticks, brother."

"That's a hair short, man," said Eddie.

"You'll get your half million," said the man.

Eddie looked inside the bucket. It was filled with cash. "Right," said Eddie, "but I'm still out eight bucks for the chicken."

21

Duong Van Minh knew his life had ended. He was seated comfortably in a chair in a two-room office on the Rue Pasteur. An American sergeant sat at a desk opposite him, watching him and working at the same time. A calm setting for a life to end.

Minh felt well. His daughter had called him from Paris. She was safe, and she had enough money to live comfortably the rest of her life. That had been his only stipulation: that he be allowed to speak to his daughter in Paris to be certain she had left Saigon. Now he must talk of Eddie Palmer. That had been the bargain. His daughter's freedom for information.

The American sergeant turned back toward a filing cabinet. Minh leaped to his feet and raced to throw himself out the window in the inner office. He was past the surprised sergeant and running. Then, suddenly, he heard a yelling voice on his right side. Instinctively, he fell away from it, and his left hip slammed against a desk. A sharp pain raced out in both directions from the hip, and he stumbled. As he fell, a hand caught his collar, and he knew his head would not hit the floor. Then the pain again in his hip. Voices. His lower eyelids came up to cover his eyes. Darkness and the end of pain.

When he awoke, he was on a couch in the same room. The pain in his hip was still there but different now, duller. The lieutenant stood over him. Another sergeant sat on the arm of the couch near his feet. "I am an old man," said the merchant.

"I thought we had a bargain," said Lieutenant Skilling. The old man stared at him. "I made sure you got your daughter out, and now you do this to me?"

The black market operator turned his head away from the lieutenant. "My leg is in pain," he said.

"Sergeant Logen," said Skilling. "I want our men in Paris to pick up Duong Thi Mai. Hold her in jail until I can get some papers to bring her back here."

Minh turned. "I will honor my bargain."

Sergeant Logen handed Lieutenant Skilling two cups. Skilling leaned over and put one arm beneath the old man's shoulder and lifted him up. He handed one cup to the old man. "Pain pill," he said.

Minh took the pill and swallowed it with some water from the second cup. Skilling lowered him back down. "Nothing is broken," said the lieutenant. "It's a bad bruise, and it'll hurt for a week. But that pill will ease the pain. You'll probably go to sleep, too. We're taking you to a military hospital. So just relax, and don't try anything like that again."

Minh nodded. "What will you do with my friends?"

"Your friends?" asked Skilling.

"I will inform on my friends. That is our bargain. You will kill them?" asked the merchant.

Skilling leaned over. "I don't care about your friends unless you count Eddie Palmer as one of them. I want Eddie Palmer."

Minh shifted on the couch. There was a knock on the door, and two MPs entered with a stretcher. Skilling stepped aside, and the two men gently lifted Minh off the couch and onto the stretcher. Skilling held up his hand.

"Ong Eddie is gone," said Minh. "American passports."

"Where'd he get them?"

Minh closed his eyes. "Tran Van Hung," he said. "Photographer. He sold Ong Eddie his passport."

"Okay," said Skilling. "I'll see you tomorrow." He nodded to the MPs, and they lifted Minh and went out of the office. Skilling plugged in the hot plate in the outer office and put a pot of water on to heat. Sergeant Logen washed out two cups, and they both stood waiting for the water.

"The bastard is gone," said Skilling.

"Yeah," said Logen.

"Put together a quiet kidnapping. Bring that forger up here, and we'll sweat him. I'll let the old man rest until tomorrow morning. Then we'll sweat him."

"Okay, sir." Logen scooped two teaspoons of instant coffee into the cups and poured the water. He handed a cup to the lieutenant. Then he went to the desk and began to make phone calls. By the time they'd finished their coffee, Logen had located the passport seller and arranged for part of the unit to collect near his shop. "You want to come along, sir?"

"No," said Skilling. "Good hunting."

The photographer was brought back in three hours and kept overnight. He talked freely and even printed the passport photos of all the men connected with Eddie Palmer. For the first time, Skilling had more information than he could handle.

"Why all those people, Logen?" asked Skilling early the following morning. "Our boy Eddie would shoot his own mother for a profit, and yet he shelled out good cash for passports for his gang and eighteen Vietnamese. Why?"

"It's not like him," said Logen.

"There's got to be something on besides the drugs," said Skilling.

"He might be setting up a regular drug network," replied Logen.

"Then why take the Vietnamese to the U.S.?"

Logen shrugged. "I don't know, sir."

Skilling shuffled through the pictures again. "All right, Sergeant. Let's get started. I know everybody's tired, but we've got to check out the names on the fake passports and see if they've passed through."

"I gave a list to Cramer and Fuller. They're on it already, sir," said Logen.

"All right." Skilling leaned back and rubbed his eyes. "We'll need more pictures."

"Do you want that photographer anymore?"

"I don't think so. Unless you want to haul him in and give him to somebody."

Logen shook his head. "What's the point. He's not that big a mark. Let's just let him go back about his business. He might come in more handy loose than locked up."

"Fine," said Skilling. "Let him go, but have him make up a few more copies of these pictures."

Logen nodded. "No problem," he said.

It was the following day before all the names had been traced. Logen and Skilling sat quietly while Corporals Cramer and Fuller went over each name.

"First off, sir," said Cramer, "everybody's in the States. We're certain of that."

"Goddamn," said Skilling. "Okay, go ahead."

"Palmer's been gone over a month. His passport turned up in Tokyo. He went there as a grunt on R and R, then became a tourist on his fake passport. The rest of his gang did the same."

"Were they packing their drugs?" asked Skilling.

"No way of knowing, sir," said Fuller. "They're just a name on a sheet now."

Skilling nodded. Then Cramer spoke again. "The locals all pulled out about ten days ago. They went the other way, via Paris."

"That's it?" asked Logen.

"That's it, Sergeant," said Fuller. "Like I say, they're just names on a sheet now. We went over lists until I thought our eyeballs would pop out."

"Yeah, yeah," said Logen. "I know. Okay. Fine. So they all made it, and here we sit. What now, sir?"

"What now? I talk to the old man again," said Skilling.

Skilling had left Minh confined in the military hospital. Minh was not in need of hospital care, and he had only a slight limp. But it was better than a prison, and Skilling had more access to him.

"You have told us much," said Skilling.

Minh nodded. "Everything," he said.

"Not everything, Ong Minh," said Skilling. "There is a link missing."

"I have told you everything," said Minh.

"Let's go back to when Eddie Palmer reappeared, and you set him up in the house of your friend," said Skilling. "How did he contact you the second time?"

"Through my daughter," said Minh. "He must have followed her, and then he approached her as she was having tea."

"Then she brought him back to your store?"

"Yes."

"Did Eddie mention he had been in France to you?"

"No."

"You didn't ask him where he'd been for the past few months?"

Minh studied his hands. "Yes," he said.

"What did Eddie say? Come on, Ong Minh," said Skilling.

"He said I did not want to know where he'd been," replied the merchant. "He said he'd been north."

"North? You mean North Vietnam?"

"I took him to mean that," said Minh. "And I agreed with him that I did not want to know. And that is all he said."

Skilling rose from the hospital chair. "By God, that may be it. We can't identify those Vietnamese. And the reason is they're North Vietnamese. Christ. No wonder."

214

Skilling sat in a chair facing the street at a sidewalk café in Cholon. He was to wait there, eyes on the street, until he was contacted. He sat nearly an hour. Then a voice spoke behind him. "Continue to look straight ahead," it said.

"I understand," said Skilling.

"You wanted to speak to me?" the voice asked.

"I do if you represent the North," said Skilling. "Do you know of me and my operation?"

"I know," said the voice. "American deserters."

"Yes," said Skilling. "So you know I am no counterintelligence. You are safe with me."

"Perhaps," said the voice.

"All I want to know," said Skilling, "is if you have an operation using some of our deserters." He received no answer. "Did you hear?"

"I hear," replied the man behind Skilling.

"Well?" asked Skilling.

"Why do you ask?"

"I'll tell you all I know," said Skilling. "I'm trying to be honest with you because I'm after a deserter. One specific man. I have reason to believe he's working with some North Vietnamese. If it's some sort of covert operation you've planned, all right. I accept that. I'm still going after my man, of course, and if your people get in the way, then so be it. But if this isn't your operation, maybe there's a way we can help each other."

"Continue," said the voice.

"If this isn't a planned operation," said Skilling, "then the men with my deserter are probably deserters from your army." The man behind Skilling didn't answer. Skilling continued. "I have an envelope. In it are pictures of all the men involved with my deserter. There are also fingerprints from a house they used. We have traced every American. But the Vietnamese are untraceable." Skilling took the envelope from the table and placed it on his shoulder. After a moment, the man lifted it from his hand.

Skilling felt some relief. He had interested the contact enough for him to take the envelope. It meant the operation, the drugs, and the trip to the United States were not initiated by the North. "Take as much time as you want," said Skilling. "If you need any more information, I'll be available to you at any time. All right?"

There was no answer. Skilling slowly turned. The table and chair behind him were empty.

Four days later, Skilling had a telephone call. The man identified himself as the man from the sidewalk café.

"I want to see you again," said the voice.

"When and where?" asked Skilling.

"Same place, same rules, and right now," said the voice.

"I'm on my way," said Skilling.

Skilling couldn't get the same table at the sidewalk café, but he sat in the one next to it. He waited for his contact to come up behind him. He was somewhat surprised when a heavyset man plopped into the chair next to him. His head was clean-shaven, and he dressed in the black clothing of a Vietnamese farmer.

"How do you do, Lieutenant Skilling," said the man. Skilling nodded. "I'll get right to the point, if I may."

"Please do," said Skilling.

"I do not believe your fingerprints or your pictures," said the agent from the North. "I'll have to ask you to prove everything to me."

"Why should I?"

"There are those in my government who think your whole deserter story is a hoax, an attempt to break our intelligence network."

"I'm not concerned with your intelligence network," said Skilling.

"I believe your story," said the man. "As you can see, I have exposed myself. But I need proof. If what you say is true, I can help you."

"What do you want?"

"I want to inspect the house you say these men used."

"I'm ready if you are."

The North Vietnamese agent worked silently and swiftly in the house on the edge of Cholon used by Eddie and his group. He noted the powder smudges used by Skilling's men to lift fingerprints. He studied the smudges and compared them with the prints Skilling had given him.

In just under an hour, he turned to Skilling and said, "All right, Lieutenant. Shall we sit down?"

"You don't want to talk to the photographer?" asked Skilling.

"I did yesterday," said the man.

Skilling sat. "I get the feeling I've stumbled onto something," said the American officer.

"Sometime ago," said the man, "a highly respected colonel in our army presented a plan to his superior. The plan was immediately rejected, and if the colonel had not had an outstanding record, he probably would have been demoted. As it was, his superior merely assumed the strain of twenty years of war had mixed his thinking. The colonel had also lost his wife in an American bombing raid in Hanoi. Then the colonel was killed. Or so we thought."

"And now his fingerprints and picture have turned up," said Skilling.

"Exactly," said the agent. The man reached into a pocket and extracted a sheet of paper. "This is an interview one of our men had with the colonel's superior. I'll read it to you."

"Any names?" asked Skilling.

The man ignored Skilling and began to read. "Interviewer: 'Thank you, General, for cooperating.' General: 'I wish to do all I can, certainly.'

"Interviewer: 'Do you recall the meeting you had with Colonel Linh wherein he mentioned a plan for an invasion of the United States?' "

"What?" Skilling started to smile. The man reading didn't

react. He's really worried, thought Skilling. "Sorry," he said aloud.

The man continued to read from the report. "General: 'Clearly. I only wish now I had spent more time with Colonel Linh. He had his actual battle plan with him. But I dismissed him before seeing it. I regret that now.'

"Interviewer: 'We all regret that, General. Still, you may be able to help us. I want you to recall that day. Take your time, and remember everything you can.'

"General: 'Certainly. I was in my office. The time was morning. Colonel Linh had asked to see me, and I had made an appointment. At the time, Colonel Linh was one of my best commanders and a proven leader.'

"Interviewer: 'I know, General. Continue.'

"General: 'He was exactly on time. I remember thinking, He's always on time. When he came in, he was carrying a folder with him. His plan, of course. We exchanged a few words, and then he asked me if I would study a battle plan he had prepared. I said I would. Then I asked him to summarize the plan for me and to leave it to study at my leisure.'

"Interviewer: 'Did he?'

"General: 'He certainly did. Summarize, I mean. He did not leave the plan. I can still remember him saying, "I want to invade the United States." '

"Interviewer: 'What was your reaction?'

"General: 'Shock. Colonel Linh was not the kind of man to waste time. It flashed through my mind that he might be playing some sort of joke. But I immediately dismissed it from my mind. Not Colonel Linh. Still, I asked him if he was serious. He said he was deadly serious. I asked him if he knew what world opinion did for our cause, and he said he was aware of world opinion. I then asked him if he thought the United States could use an attack such as he mentioned as an excuse to wage an all-out air war on our country, perhaps even invade. He said he was aware of that danger.'

218

"Interviewer: 'Did you see his plan?'

"General: 'I regret I did not.'

"Interviewer: 'Did he mention any names, dates, places?'

"General: 'Nothing. As I said, the meeting was brief.'

"Interviewer: 'How was his manner?'

"General: 'Do you mean, was he nervous?'

"Interviewer: 'Yes.'

"General: 'Most certainly not. He has no nerves.' "

The Vietnamese looked up. Skilling had been listening intently, his face pulled into a frown. Now he consciously relaxed. "Do you believe all of this?" asked Skilling.

"I'm afraid it is necessary," said the North Vietnamese.

"I'd laugh in your face if I didn't know Eddie Palmer," said Skilling. "The damn thing is, your colonel has already pulled off his invasion. Every damn one of them is in the U.S."

"It appears that way," said the agent. "It is unfortunate we didn't talk while they were still in Cholon." The man shrugged. "But how would you know. Now, I'm afraid, I can give you limited help."

"Tell me everything about your colonel," said Skilling. "I'm certain Eddie Palmer will return to New York. With very little effort, he can do a lot of damage there. But let's assume your colonel is still in charge, still calling the shots. What's his plan? How does he think?"

"Both of our men are fanatics, it would appear," said the Vietnamese. "That makes it difficult to know their thoughts."

Skilling nodded. "I've underestimated Eddie Palmer from the very beginning. As much as I hate to keep saying it, he's been ahead of me at every turn." The lieutenant again felt the scar on his neck. "Let's talk about weapons," said Skilling; bringing his mind back to the subject. "Did they ship out weapons from here, or do they plan to get them in New York?"

"It is my thought that Colonel Linh would bring his own weapons. From what I hear of New York, it would be possible to buy certain guns. But Colonel Linh is a soldier, and a soldier plans a campaign on reality, not possiblity."

"Then we might trace them through the weapons."

"My organization is investigating," said the North Vietnamese.

Skilling nodded. He then quickly filled the other man in on what he knew of the drugs and of the Marseilles episode. When he was finished, he smiled. "Quite a pair," said Skilling.

"There is a legend that speaks of the birth of the Vietnamese," said the man. "It tells of a dragon who mated with a goddess. It appears we have two dragons who mated this time."

Skilling spent the remainder of the day writing a full report on the invasion to Colonel Lancto at the Pentagon. Sergeant Logen worked with him because Skilling had difficulty keeping the report laconic.

It was Logen's suggestion that the North Vietnamese agent not be mentioned. "You're opening up a can of worms," he said. "Just call him an informant."

With the two of them working, the report still came to over seven pages, single-spaced. Skilling's recommendations were contained in the final paragraph. He concluded that Colonel Lancto bring every government agency that could help into the hunt.

The following day, Skilling and Logen visited the detention barracks near Tan Son Nhut and talked to the one known member of Eddie Palmer's gang, Mouse. But he couldn't help or wouldn't.

Skilling sent out his men to investigate all known drug smugglers. He also sent inquiries to all units in the area asking about unusual shipments of heavy equipment that might be hiding weapons.

One week went by, and Skilling had no response from either his inquiries or his North Vietnamese contact. He did, however, receive a response from the Pentagon. It was less than one page, single-spaced, and it said that Lieutenant Skilling should get back to business. It was a very impersonal note, as though Colonel Lancto was dealing with a total stranger. But it was clear. Stop wasting time.

After the memo from the Pentagon, Skilling reassigned most of his unit to regular business. Sergeant Logen, for all practical purposes, took over command. The lieutenant continued to dig. He spoke again to the black market merchant. Nothing. He put in a call to Washington to the CIA man he'd met in Paris, Paul Picket. He explained the situation to Picket, outlined Colonel Linh's plan, and asked for Picket's help.

Picket's voice came on a two-second delay over the shaky connection. "What in hell can I do?" asked Picket. "The CIA doesn't have any authority in the United States."

"You know Eddie Palmer," said Skilling. "He can raise hell. And I can't stop him."

"Do you want me to speak to your man at the Pentagon?"

"No. He's told me to forget Eddie Palmer."

"Then forget him. You're in the army. You're not a private detective."

"I can't forget him. You know that. You saw me in Marseilles. I've got to get him. Besides, Picket, I'm telling you, he and this Colonel Linh are going to kill a lot of people."

"Maybe it's just as well, Lieutenant. Then we can invade the North and get it the hell over with."

"You can't unless the public knows it's a force from North Vietnam."

"Listen. I'll ask around. Okay?"

"Thanks. That's all I want. Some help. Any help."

"If I find out anything—and I don't expect to—I'll be in touch."

"Thanks," said Skilling. "Good-bye."

"Good-bye," said Picket.

Skilling spent the following day at the Army Intelligence headquarters looking over files of suspected Communist agents in Saigon. He wasn't able to discover who the man was he'd met at the sidewalk café. But that evening, Skilling had a message slipped under his door at the Rue Pasteur office.

The note asked for another meeting the following day, early, at the same sidewalk café. This time Skilling had Logen set up across the street with a Nikon and a telephoto lense. The lieutenant wanted to be able to put pressure on the North Vietnamese agent, and he could if he had pictures of the man.

But it proved unnecessary. "I have it," said the agent from the North. "An address in the United States."

"I don't understand," said Skilling.

"Lieutenant Tri has been identified as the man who sent off several large crates to New York. The crates contained brass objects—lamps, vases, and the like. I assume that concealed inside the brass pieces were weapons and ammunition."

"Where?"

"One-one-eight-five Tenth Avenue, New York, New York," said the agent. "Shall I repeat it?"

"No," said Skilling. He ran the address through in his head.

"The name of the company is Far East Brass Imports," said the man.

"How long ago did it leave?"

"Twenty-two days."

"Is it there yet?"

"I do not know, Lieutenant. That will be your job."

"Yes," said Skilling. "Did anyone see the shipment uncrated?"

"No."

"Do you have any thoughts on what Linh might have sent?"

"Mortars would be my guess."

"Yes. They're hollow, easy to conceal. And they're damned destructive." Skilling rapped the table. "All right. I'll take it from here."

"I should tell you, Lieutenant, that we are not the only ones involved now."

"How do you mean?"

"The weapons are no doubt either Russian or Chinese. Neither country is anxious to have Colonel Linh's plan be successful under those circumstances."

"Are they going to move in New York?"

"No. Only you know the address. As I suggested, it is now up to you and your people."

Skilling leaned back in his chair. "Then that's it. Thank you. Thank you very much."

"I hope you get your Eddie Palmer," said the North Vietnamese. "And I trust that Colonel Linh will return quietly to his grave."

"I'll do my best."

"Lieutenant Skilling, I mean what I say. Colonel Linh must die."

Skilling stared at his enemy. He nodded. "I understand," he said.

That night, Skilling sat in a window seat of a TWA flight to Honolulu; final destination on his ticket: Kennedy Airport, New York.

22

"Welcome to Fun City, Ong Linh," said Eddie.

The colonel turned. Eddie stood, smiling, dressed in a suit and tie. It was the first time Linh had ever seen him dressed like that. It was, perhaps, why he didn't pick him out in the crowd at the TWA terminal at Kennedy.

"Ong Eddie," said the colonel. "I am happy to see you." He put out his hand.

Eddie took his hand and shook it. "You look a little shook, Colonel."

"I am not unsophisticated, Ong Eddie. I spent many years in Paris. But—this country. It is so vast. And New York. Astonishing."

"It'll be even more astonishing after we blow it up. Where's Lieutenant Tri?"

"He and the others went to collect our baggage."

"We can wait here, then. You look tired, Colonel."

"Tired? Yes, I am tired. But it is like before a battle. I feel alive. We are very near."

"We're movin' along."

Lieutenant Tri and two other men walked up carrying luggage. Tri and Eddie nodded. Then Eddie said, "Come on."

He led them to a parking lot, where he had left the two-year-old Ford station wagon, one of the two vehicles Eddie had purchased with the drug money. The other was a Dodge panel truck.

Eddie had spent over $30,000 of the money he'd received. Some of it went for physical things: the cars, a warehouse on Tenth Avenue, various machine tools for Apache Joe, and M-16s. A portion of the money was used for false identification for him and his men, bogus legal papers to obtain legitimate ones. A fake ID to file for a real Social Security card, to present at the driver's test, to show for insurance for the car. Eddie and his men were now officially real, duly noted in various computers and card files.

The rest of the money was squandered. One night, Eddie and the others went to a top New York restaurant dressed as Africans. Eddie pretended he was the only one who spoke English. The rest of the boys amused themselves by speaking Hollywood gibberish to Eddie.

Their dinner cost over $200, and Eddie paid in cash, tipping lavishly. They then all took suites at the Plaza Hotel for the evening and kept room service busy with drink orders. And with less difficulty than Eddie expected, he obtained four call girls for their pleasure.

Then they all settled into sort of a daily routine of waiting and splurging money. Eddie bought a safe and had it installed on the first floor of his storefront church. They bought clothes: fur coats and flashy suits. Each man bought an expensive watch. They found girls whenever it struck their fancy. But Eddie wouldn't allow them to go with the same girl twice. He kept them circulating, kept them lost in the mass of New York.

Then the first of Linh's men arrived: four soldiers who had some rudimentary knowledge of English. Eddie picked them up at Kennedy Airport, observing them from a distance, waiting to make certain they were not being followed or watched.

At that moment, Eddie had his first twinge of fear. Not fear, perhaps, but a hint of failure. He read terror, complete and total, in the soldiers' faces. He wondered whether to turn and walk away, take the money he now had, and dissolve. But then a moment came back to him—his first day in a Vietnamese jungle—and he understood. He, too, had known their fear of the unfamiliar.

Eddie had then stepped out from behind a row of lockers and approached them. He watched the tightness in their faces melt away as he walked up to them.

Now he drove over the Triboro Bridge with the last of the Vietnamese assault force, heading south on the FDR Drive. "I got you a place at the Plaza Hotel, Colonel," he said. "You get some rest. It's quiet, and you can relax there."

He reached into his shirt pocket and casually pulled out a folded packet of bills. He handed it to Linh. "There's five thousand there," he said.

Linh took the money. "Everything is progressing well?" asked Linh.

"I sold the drugs, your boys are settled in, and we're ready to move as soon as the fire power gets here," said Eddie.

Linh stared out into the water of the East River. The others were silent, watching, feeling that same fear their companions had experienced. "I would prefer to move to headquarters," said Linh suddenly. "Rest is not important."

"Hey, man," said Eddie, "rest is important. Take my word. When that jet lag hits you, you'll be damned glad to have the time. It fogs your brains."

"Perhaps you're right," said Linh. "I must confess to being disoriented."

Eddie turned off the drive at Fifty-ninth Street and headed crosstown. "We got to wait for the field pieces. So there's no hurry. I got you a suite, so you can just take it easy. You're Saigon businessmen, and the Plaza is damned happy to have you. Okay? I also bought you all some coats. They're waitin' for you at the hotel."

"I am chilled to my marrow," said Linh, half to himself. He leaned back, then, and focused on the people in the streets moving to lunch. These were Americans, the people he hated. But he felt no rage well up within him, even when he put his mind on his dead wife.

Linh hesitated as Eddie led him to the desk to sign in. "What name shall I write?" asked Linh.

Eddie stopped. "Your own name's fine," he said.

Linh nodded and stepped up to register.

In his suite, Linh stood and gazed around. "In Paris—" he started, but his voice trailed off.

"Well, it's no Paris, Ong Linh," said Eddie. "But it's a hell of a lot nicer than Harlem."

"It is a fine hotel," said Linh.

"You hungry?"

"No."

"Okay, then I'll be leavin' you. Your boys are in the next rooms, all right in this area. I'll write down the numbers." He took a pad and a pen and scribbled. "You want anything, you just dial for it. They're used to foreigners."

"Yes."

"One last thing before you relax," said Eddie. "I'm gonna put in a call to my place. It'd make your men feel a lot better if you just let 'em know you're here."

Linh stared at Eddie. "Yes," he said. "Yes. Call them. I should be there."

"Don't get in an uproar. Just talk to 'em. That's all." Eddie dialed a number on Linh's phone and waited. Then he said, "Mau Mau? It's me. Yeah, we're cool. I got the colonel right here, and he wants to talk to his men. They there?"

Eddie handed the phone to Linh. Linh took it from him and spoke in Vietnamese. Then he listened, nodding. He spoke again, and Eddie smiled. Even if Eddie didn't understand, a pep talk was a pep talk in any language. Finally, Linh put down the phone.

"Well done, Ong Eddie," said Linh. "They needed to hear from me. You're right. I need rest."

"Your men are cool, Colonel," said Eddie. "They're just a

little tense from being boxed in. They're afraid to leave my place. All they do is watch television, exercise, and eat pizza. Man, do they love pizza."

"They are good men," replied Linh. "They will be ready."

"Right. Now I'm gonna leave you. Remember, if you want anything, just pick up the phone and ask for it. The other room numbers are on that paper, and that phone number at the bottom is the one I just called, my place uptown. Somebody'll be there if you got any questions or problems. Otherwise, we'll talk tomorrow. I got maps and everything for your little war. We can go over 'em whenever you're ready. No sweat. Tomorrow. Next day." Eddie gave a little wave of his hand and left.

Linh realized how tired he really was at that moment. His stomach was distended from travel, the airline food, and fatigue. He moved into his bedroom and kicked off his shoes. On the bed lay a heavy coat. He tossed the coat onto a chair, wondering if he should visit Lieutenant Tri.

He could hear the faint rasping of traffic. He rose and walked back into the sitting room and flicked the lock on his door. Then he returned to the bedroom, stripped, and slid in between the sheets. The crispness of the linen seemed to soothe him. He studied the scrollwork around the ceiling. It faded, and he fell asleep. His last thought was hoping he'd fall asleep before his mind started to work, to plan, to be afraid.

Eddie stared at the brownstone building, his home for six years prior to going into the army. He had decided to look up his mother and give her some Christmas money. He really wanted to help his younger sister, but he knew unless he gave money to both of them, his mother would take it all.

He started up the familiar worn stone steps, and with each step, he seemed to slip backward in time. A small boy sat at the top of the stairs chipping a portion of the building away with a piece of iron.

"Hey, man," said Eddie, "you live here?"

228

"Who wants to know?" asked the boy, probably ten years old.

"Hey, don't get uppity," said Eddie. "I'm lookin' for somebody. My sister."

"Oh, man, you the end. Yo' sister? How you like to meet my sister? She show you a good time." Eddie stared. "Twenty dollah."

Suddenly, he was back on the street. He had nearly half a million dollars in a safe not fifteen blocks away, but he came back to the street. He reached down and lifted the boy up with one hand, grabbing him by the front of his plaid jacket. "Listen, you little bastard," said Eddie, "my name is Eddie Palmer. My old lady and my sister live here or used to. Now don't gimme any of that mouth jive. They still live here?"

The boy didn't flinch, and his eyes looked up defiantly at Eddie. Eddie relaxed his grip, and the boy smoothed his jacket front. "They moved," said the boy. " 'Bout a year ago."

"Where?"

"I dunno. Ask my old lady. She always got her ear to the wall listenin'."

"She inside?"

"Yeah."

"You find out for me, and I'll give you your twenty."

"Don't shuck me, man."

Eddie pulled out his money. He took twenty dollars out and held it, dangling in front of the boy. The boy reached for it. "Hold it, baby. It's payday when the cotton is picked."

The boy studied him for a moment and then ran into the building. He returned almost immediately. "Give, man," said the boy, holding out his hand.

Eddie slapped the twenty into his palm. "There you go, big daddy."

"She live in Mount Vernon. You know where that is?" Eddie nodded. "She live at 821 Third Street. Leastways that where her mail go when she get any. And it nice doin' business with ya."

"You do good work, man." Eddie hurried down the steps,

anxious to leave the brownstone behind him. His breath formed a misty shape in the cold December air. He returned to the storefront church and spoke briefly to Mau Mau. It was now near 6:00, and Mau Mau had had no word from Linh. As Eddie assumed, the colonel and his men were finished until tomorrow.

"I'll be back in a couple of hours," he told his companions.

"You want friends?" asked Mau Mau.

"Not this trip," replied Eddie.

Mau Mau started to speak and then held back. He gripped his fist and gestured, sort of a submissive okay. Eddie left and walked half a block to his panel truck.

It took him just over thirty minutes to reach the town of Mount Vernon. In another ten, he had located 821 Third Street, a large frame house that had been divided and redivided into rooms and apartments. The street was dark, a single light burning on the corner thirty yards away. Eddie shut off his motor and his lights and sat staring at the lighted windows, hoping to see his sister's figure appear in one of them. But he wasn't at all certain he would even know his sister. He would know his mother, though, and he watched the windows for nearly five minutes.

Then he opened the truck door and walked up to the porch, where mailboxes hung. He found his mother's name written on a small piece of yellow paper stuck in the nameplate of one of the boxes. He lifted the lid of the mailbox and looked inside; he didn't know why. It was empty. He entered the rooming house and knocked on the first door. He heard a shuffle inside and waited. An old black man opened the door a crack and looked out.

"Elizabeth Palmer?" asked Eddie.

"Upstairs," said the old man. "Back down the hall." Without another word, he shut the door in Eddie's face. Eddie climbed the stairs, aware of the odors of foods and cleaning compounds and bodies mingling in the hallway. He stood in front of the door, then, marked E. Palmer. He took a deep breath, and a chill quivered his shoulders. He knocked.

The door opened slowly, without a sound from inside. His mother stared out, thin and frail and unchanged.

"Edward?"

"Yeah. How are you?"

She held the door in the same position, only looking out through a crack.

"Tired, Edward, but livin' with Jesus. What you want?"

"I come to say Merry Christmas. Where's Ruthie?"

"South Carolina. She move to South Carolina with some tramp."

"Who? What happened?"

"Why you care?"

"She's my sister, goddamm it."

"Do not take the Lord's name and swear with it, Edward. You just like your father."

Eddie tried to calm himself. "You got her address, Momma?"

"I reckon, somewheres. She run off with this man. He was in the church. He make her pregnant, and she run off with him."

"The address?"

She turned and walked back into her room. Eddie took a step inside. He recognized all the furniture. And prominent in the room was his mother's altar, a candle burning there. She rummaged around on the top of her bureau and finally held up a scrap of paper. "Here," she said. She handed it to Eddie.

Eddie read it. "This is no address," he said. "It's general delivery. Dammit, don't you even care where your own daughter is?"

"What you want, anyways?"

"I came up here to see you, that's all."

"You ain't in the army no more?"

"No."

"You in trouble?"

"No. I'm doin' good. You need any money?"

"What for?"

"For nothin'," said Eddie, his voice rising. "Just 'cause you did so good takin' care of me as a boy."

"That the truth."

"Truth, shit." He dug into his pocket and took out $100. He tossed it on the bed. "Here's a hundred, Momma. That the truth."

"A hundred dollahs?"

"That's right."

She shuffled to the bed and picked up the money and counted it. Then she placed it all under the altar. "Why you givin' me money?"

"I'm rich, that why. Here. Here's another hundred." He reached into his pocket again and counted out another $100. This time, he held it out for her to take. She came to him and took it. Again, she placed it under the altar. "You ain't gonna thank me?"

"The Lord thank you," said his mother.

"The Lord does, does he."

"Reverend John, he need a new piano. I give—"

Eddie cut in. "Don't you go givin' any that money to some phony-ass preacher, Momma. That my money."

"My money now. You got plenty. You said you rich."

"You hopeless, Momma," said Eddie.

"You stayin' for supper?"

"No."

"We could go down to the corner. Some West Indians has got a place. Got good ribs and such."

"I don't want no ribs. I gotta go back to New York."

"What you doin'?"

"I'm 'bout to start a war, Momma. You like that? Gonna blow up West Point."

"You go to church, Edward?"

"Good-bye, Momma."

"Good-bye, Edward."

Eddie stepped back, closing the door. He leaned against the

doorjamb and pressed the palms of his hands into his eyes. She crazy, he thought. She really gone. My mother got no brains workin' in her head. Jesus Christ, goddamn. Nothin' workin' in her head.

He ran down the stairs and to the panel truck. He left Mount Vernon as quickly as he could and drove back to Harlem. He parked the truck, locked it tightly, and went hunting for a bar. He found one within half a block, and he spent the next hour there trying to stupify his mind enough to relax.

The next afternoon, Linh, Tri, and Eddie were all huddled around a coffee table in the Plaza suite. They had eaten lunch there in the room, and the food wagon sat in the middle of the room. Eddie had a map spread out on the coffee table, and the other two were watching his finger move about it.

"This is where we are," said Eddie. "Manhattan. 'Bout here. Fifth Avenue and Fifty-ninth. Headquarters is up here." He moved his finger uptown to Harlem. "The warehouse where the guns is comin' is about here." Again, his finger moved, this time to the West Side.

"Where are the factories?" asked Tri.

"Factories? Shit, there ain't any where we are."

"You seem tired, Ong Eddie," said Linh.

Eddie sighed. "I'm hung over," he said. "Trouble is, for no good reason. I didn't even have a good time. Just got drunk."

"Is something wrong?" asked Linh.

"Nothin's wrong, man. I just wanted to sleep. I'm sorry. I'll be all right. Sorry, Tri."

"That is all right," said the lieutenant.

"Factories are all around. Over here in Jersey. Lots of oil refineries and the like." His finger kept moving. "This here's Long Island. There's lots of factories out there."

Linh bent over. "They do not manufacture the B-52 in Long Island, do they?" he asked.

"Nah," said Eddie, "I don't think so. But what the hell's the difference. There's airplane factories, easy to hit. I don't reckon we could wipe one out, but we could give 'em one hell of a screwin'. It's your gig, man, but I'd be for hittin' the oil refineries in Jersey."

"Why?" asked Linh.

"It don't take much to blow 'em. And it'd hurt. They run outa oil for New York, man, they got big problems. There's a lot of vacant land over there, too. Places we could shoot from."

"Very well," said Linh. "I will study these maps, Ong Eddie. Then we will take some trips to the various areas you have pointed out. Now, to California."

Eddie sighed and unfolded another map, one he'd taken from a gas station. "This is the U.S., just so's you'd know. We're here, right?" He tapped New York. "Here's California. Three thousand miles away."

Tri asked, "How long will it take me to drive it?"

"Christ, man, I don't know," replied Eddie. "Five days, give or take a day."

"There are many war plants in California," said Linh.

"I reckon," said Eddie. "But I don't know shit about California."

"It is obvious you don't think Lieutenant Tri should go to California," said Linh gently.

"Hell, no," said Eddie. "I mean it's all right to sit in Nam and bullshit and pick out targets and say we're gonna do this and gonna do that. But now we're talkin' real stuff. Real. It's three thousand miles. Tri, you ever drive on a goddamed highway?" Eddie didn't wait for an answer. "No, you never did," he said. "You never stayed at a motel; you never did nothin'. How you expect to even drive out there, let alone pick out some goddamned targets to blow up."

Linh pulled the map closer to him and peered at it. "You are absolutely right, Ong Eddie. We forget California."

"I can do it, sir," said Tri.

"Of course you can if you must," replied the colonel.

"He can do it," said Eddie. "I can have him stayin' at motels and drivin' like he was born here. I guess it's nerves."

"I dreamed of the day I would strike back at America," said Linh. "Now I find the sheer size of the country my worst enemy." Tri started to speak but Linh held up his hand.

"But perhaps," he continued, "we can make the size our best ally. There are many targets in this area?" He turned to look at Eddie.

"Christ, man, we could keep busy blowin' up shit for a year." Eddie pulled the map of New York out again from underneath the U.S. map. "We could lob some at the UN building."

He poked a finger on Manhattan. "Jersey is full of targets; so's Long Island. Up in here is all sorts of places." He ran his finger into Westchester County. "Factories like hell in Connecticut. And this here is gonna be a real pleasure." He tapped a place on the Hudson River.

"What is this place?" asked Linh.

"West Point, man. I am gonna get me a few officers. Boom, boom, boom."

Linh leaned over. "West Point?"

"Yeah," Eddie said. "That's where your war started, man. Right there. Some dumb bastard gonna show what a good officer he is, but he need a war. Can't get no medals without no war. Right here, baby. We gonna bring the war right here. We show 'em it ain't all medals when a few of those rockets start flyin' around."

Linh leaned back on the couch. "Yes," he said.

"Yes, what?" asked Eddie.

Linh came forward again. "Yes, you are right, Ong Eddie. We shall stay here. There are many targets, bridges, power plants, docks."

"Now you're talkin'," said Eddie.

"I would like to move to headquarters now," said Linh.

Eddie shrugged. "You got it," he said. "But you're the first dude I ever met that wanted to move to Harlem."

The full invasion force then settled in. Eight of the Vietnamese were billeted at the warehouse, where they kept watch and did exercises to keep fit. The rest called the Church of Soul and Brotherhood home. The Vietnamese caused some stir on the street. Orientals didn't often take up residence in Harlem. Eddie made certain that never more than two or three ventured out together onto the street.

The second floor of the church served as sleeping quarters. The first floor functioned as mess hall, recreation area, meeting place. Eddie installed a washer and dryer for their clothes. A television set dominated the street end of the room.

Linh, by way of keeping his soldiers busy, assigned daily tasks of cleaning and cooking. For the most part, Eddie and his men ate elsewhere. Because the warehouse was not a pleasant place to stay, Linh staggered his men there, leaving them for three days at a time and then moving in a new batch and returning the others to the church.

Linh, Tri, and Eddie made frequent trips out of the city, generally to New Jersey and Long Island. On each trip, Linh would take notes and snap Polaroid pictures. At night, back in the church, he would sit by himself, fleshing out his notes, carefully marking each visit on a map. Then, he would file the day's brief away.

Apache Joe spent most of his time working at the warehouse. He had a machine shop that included threading equipment and a welder. When the M-16s were finally picked up, he began working them into the silent assassination weapons they carried in Vietnam.

The invasion force spent Christmas of 1971 waiting for their weapons. Eddie bought a pool table for Christmas and had it set up on the first floor. He also gave Apache Joe, Turk, and Mau Mau $5,000 cash each. It pleased him to do it. Spending money, he called it.

The day after Christmas, however, Apache Joe took Eddie aside. "Look, man," said Apache Joe, "I been on this gig all the

236

way, you know? Just like I said I'd do; I stayed with it."

"Right on, brother," said Eddie.

"No offense, man," he said, "but when am I gonna be that millionaire. I dig the five thousand. You know that's cool. But there was talk of big bread. Right?"

Eddie felt anger start in him, but he quickly squelched it. Apache Joe was right. "You got a right to ask, man," Eddie said. "And I'll see what I can do. We been sittin' on our ass, and my ass is beginnin' to pain."

"Yeah," said his companion. "There's a lotta bread in that safe, Eddie. It ain't millions, but we could live pretty good, you know?"

"Stay cool, man. Let's give the old gook a little while longer."

"Whatever you want, boss-man," said Apache Joe. "It's the five big ones that started me to thinkin', you know?"

"Yeah. Lemme think on it," said Eddie. Apache Joe had brought his own thoughts to a head. Should he take the money? Should he stick it out? But the next day, it was settled. The mortars arrived.

Everyone but two men who stood guard at the church moved to the warehouse to unpack. Inside the crates were the brass objects, mostly large lamp bases. And concealed in each lamp base was either ammunition or a Chinese mortar.

In two days' time, the brass bases had been stripped away, and an inventory was made. The unit had eight light mortars and four medium ones. The ammunition totaled eighty-five rounds for the light piece and thirty rounds for the bigger mortar. In addition, one crate contained the rockets and electrical systems for Eddie's 107s. All told, Eddie had thirty rockets for the launchers. It was not a large arsenal, but it could prove to be a potent one if used properly.

"So, Ong Eddie," said Linh, "the dragon has teeth."

"I reckon," said Eddie. "We're gettin' close."

"Close," said Linh.

With the arrival of the weapons, a change came over Linh's

men. Suddenly, they seemed to be competing among themselves for positions on the strike teams. They resented guard duty more and more as they jockeyed for Linh's or Tri's favor.

"It's like a damned football team," Eddie told Mau Mau. "Those bastards can't wait to go out and lay their asses on the line for their glorious goddamned leader."

The fervor bristled Eddie, and as the Vietnamese grew more and more anxious, Eddie felt more and more confined, uneasy now that the time grew close.

He and Apache Joe welded a rack into his panel truck and fashioned a metal enclosure around the rack. He then fitted ten rockets and an electrical system for the launcher into the rack. Eddie then made plans to collect one of the 107s.

The Sunday following the arrival of the weapons, Linh called for a briefing. Tri and Eddie and Linh sat at the heavy table used for eating. Linh ordered his soldiers to the second floor, so Eddie sent his men out of the building.

Linh conducted the meeting with some formality. "I have finalized my plan," he began. "The targets are chosen and the dates we will strike." Eddie and Tri both waited.

Linh continued. "I have divided the force into three units," he said. "Each of us here will, of course, lead a unit. We will, therefore, Ong Eddie, need another vehicle."

Eddie nodded. "I'll take care of it."

"A truck like yours seems the most satisfactory," said Linh.

"No problems, man," replied Eddie.

"Very well," Linh said. "Each of us will take five men, four of my soldiers and one man from your group, Ong Eddie. Four of my men will remain behind, two to guard the headquarters and two to guard the warehouse. Ong Eddie, your extra men will be used as a backup in case one of us is unable to fulfill his mission on the day of the strike. I would suggest your second in command."

"Mau Mau," replied Eddie. "You got him."

Linh turned to Tri. "I feel it would be better to have an

American as the standby," he said. Tri nodded. "Because of their familiarity with the area." Tri nodded again.

Linh unrolled a map. "The longer we delay now, the higher the chance for failure," he said. "However, we must assign the men and then make some practice runs. How soon can we have the other truck?"

"I can get it tomorrow," said Eddie.

"Tuesday, then, we shall begin the runs. The following Tuesday, we shall strike."

"Glorious," said Tri.

"Yeah," said Eddie. "Glorious."

Linh went on. "Lieutenant Tri will lead his force to this point." He put his finger on the map in New Jersey. "The large block of oil and gas storage tanks near the Newark Airport will be destroyed. This will disrupt traffic, cause considerable damage to material and supplies, and probably force the authorities to shut down the airport. You will then continue on south and return to our warehouse through the Lincoln Tunnel. Later today, Lieutenant, we will drive to the area, and I will show you your exact targets and a fairly well hidden area from which you can launch your attack."

"I will be ready, sir," said Tri.

"Ong Eddie," said Linh, "you will attack the George Washington Bridge."

"Jesus," said Eddie. "The George Washington Bridge?"

"Yes," replied Linh.

"Man, you can't blow up that thing with those pissy little mortars," Eddie said.

"I am aware of that," said Linh. "I am striking at the bridge in order to cripple it. It is a civilian target, as Hanoi has become a target for your bombers. There will be death and panic. You will strike this area."

He placed his finger on the New York side of the bridge. "Several highways interconnect here," he said. "Traffic will be stopped up for miles in every direction. If you get a lucky hit, perhaps you can crack one of the bridge ramps."

Eddie shook his head. "And where you gonna be, Ong Linh?"

"I will be here," said Linh, moving his finger to Long Island. "I will attack and destroy what I can of the Grumman aircraft factory." He leaned backward from the table. "Three targets, all some distance apart. Three targets, all vital to the enemy."

"And our weapons?" asked Tri.

"Each unit will carry two light mortars with six rounds for each piece. In addition, one of the longer-range mortars will be used at the same time. Since each target is a large one, the mortars can be fired from the same spot but will damage different areas of the target. Everyone in the unit will be used in the firing of the weapons. We will not use spotters or guards. The advantage of this will be the rapid fire, the short time each team will be exposed to discovery. Once the rounds are fired, each team will pack up and leave the area at once."

No one spoke. So Linh continued. "Once we have all safely and successfully returned to headquarters, I will post a letter to the *New York Times*. In it, I will detail the raids and reveal the presence of an enemy force in the United States. Is there any discussion?"

"Yeah, there is," said Eddie. "You're sendin' me to one of the big traffic places in the world, man. I mean the fuckin' world. And you're expectin' me to shoot off mortars and then just drive away like it's a Sunday afternoon drive. Well, bullshit."

"Shall we then trade targets, Ong Eddie?" asked Linh. "Or is it perhaps that you're not as anxious as you once were to wage war on your country."

Eddie spoke in almost a whisper. "I'd like to set fire to the whole shitty country," he said. "I hate it. Burn it. Blow it up. I don't give a fuck."

"Is it the money, then?" asked Linh.

"Listen, Ong Linh," said Eddie. "I'm holdin' back payin' my boys, you know. A little here, a little there. They don't want for nothin', but they don't have the big loot, you dig? But if they

240

are gonna blow up the goddamned George Washington Bridge, man, I mean they are gonna want a lot of bread. And if they get it, I don't know if they'll stick."

"Will you stick, Ong Eddie?" asked Linh.

Eddie rubbed his palms on his pants. "I don't know, man. I really don't know."

"I will make a bargain," said Linh. "If you will help me with this raid, then all of the drugs are yours. I will reveal the locations of all the bodies. I will need the money you have collected so far. But the rest can be yours. You and your men will be free to leave."

"Why?" asked Eddie.

"The one raid is more than I ever hoped to accomplish. It will spread fear everywhere," said Linh. "Once the mission is made known, every future explosion, every power failure, every fire will be thought to be of our making. Your city will be gripped with fear, as Hanoi is now."

"I reckon," said Eddie.

"We will move on out of New York after the raids," said Linh. "You must help me set up a new headquarters. Then we will wait for a time and strike again. I will continue to hurt the enemy as long as I can."

Eddie stood and faced Linh. He looked away then and walked toward the front of the room. Suddenly, he turned. "You got yourself a deal, Ong Linh," he said. "I'll blow up whatever the fuck you want. Then I'll help you get set up somewhere else. After that, we dig up the skag, and I'll give my boys their bread."

"And you, Ong Eddie?" asked Linh.

"I don't know, Ong Linh," said Eddie. "I want to hurt those bastards. But I don't know."

"That's good enough for now," said Linh. "Good enough."

"Well, shit, if I'm gonna blow up that fuckin' bridge, I might as well do it right," said Eddie. "Tri, I'm goin' out and get me a rocket if I can. Tell me everything you know about it."

Tri glanced at Linh. Linh nodded. Tri then took a blank piece of paper and began to sketch the launching module and to explain the operation of it and the rockets.

Late that evening, after Tri and Linh had returned from their trip to New Jersey, Eddie and Mau Mau headed north to Ossining, New York, to find the Parker-Bale American Legion Post. This was the nearest post to New York where Eddie had sent one of the souvenir rocket launchers. If all went well, Eddie hoped to return that night ready to fire at the George Washington Bridge from a safe distance.

After the two men arrived in Ossining, Eddie located the post quickly. When he drove by, it was bright with lights.

"Look at the cars," said Mau Mau. "Those dudes are havin' a party. Now what?"

Eddie hit the steering wheel in annoyance. "I'll try and look inside."

"Don't get caught, big daddy."

"You just stay in the car and keep those wheels ready. If anything happens, I'm gonna split, and you hit the gas."

"Do your thing."

Eddie parked the van. He studied the parking lot for a moment, then slipped out the door and circled on the dark side of the building, moving away from the street. When he reached the far corner, he paused, allowing his eyes to adjust to the darkness, trying to pick out any movement outside.

Laughter and loud talk drifted out of the building. He walked to the nearest window and looked inside. His angle of vision was upward, and he could only see a covey of about fifteen people drinking, huddled together talking. He ducked down and moved along the building, keeping under the spilled light.

At another window, he stood and looked in. And there it was, almost directly across from him, over a fireplace, the Chinese rocket launcher mounted on a lacquered board. Eddie blinked once, smiled, and ducked his head.

He came up on the van. "What's up, man?" asked Mau Mau.

"Stay cool," said Eddie. "It's there, man, hangin' up like one of them dudes killed a dink for it."

"So you wanna wait it out?"

"No tellin' how long them folks is gonna drink. Nah, hell, it's there. That's all I wanted to know. Let's haul ass outa here." He flipped the shift into drive and moved on down the street.

"So when you wanna come back?"

"Soon, man. It's gettin' close."

Mau Mau turned toward Eddie in the darkness. "We really goin' ahead with this bullshit?"

"Yeah. There's a lot of skag out there buried somewhere. We gonna be rich."

"Hey, man, we rich now."

"I'm talkin' about rich. Shit rich."

"How much bread can you spend, man?"

"It's not just the bread, man. I want my pay, you dig? I want a thousand dollars, man, for every time I had to say 'sir' to one of them fuckin' officers."

Mau Mau laughed. "Yeah."

"Dig? I want ten thousand dollars, man, for every one of them damned leeches sucked my blood in Nam."

"Ten thousand. That's two million right there."

"Dig."

"I want a thousand for every plate of that gook food I had to eat."

"You got it, daddy. Now you got it."

They drove in silence for a moment. Then Eddie spoke again, softly. "Bread is fine, man. I dig it. And we gonna have it. But it's not all my pay. Not all."

"You are really gonna shoot up the Big Apple."

"Yeah. You and me and Turk and Apache, we are gonna get us a piece of this place. We are gonna hurt us some folks. And that's my pay, too, you know? I'm gonna hurt me some folks bad."

243

The following morning a TWA red-eye flight from Los Angeles landed at Kennedy. The touchdown jolted Skilling out of a half sleep. He'd dozed in spurts across the country, falling off and then snapping awake as though a hand had shaken his shoulder. But his arrival at Kennedy seemed to give him his second wind. He felt almost refreshed. When he stepped out of the terminal, the near-freezing wind caught his lungs unaware, and he gasped. Cold air. It shocked him, and he accepted the fact, for the first time, that he was in the United States, New York.

He caught an airport bus to midtown and walked to the nearest hotel. He checked into the least expensive room. It was small; the furniture and rug, in a state of fatigue. Alone in the room, his energy dissolved, and the pressure of the trip suddenly gripped him. A throb began at the base of his skull, and he squeezed the back of his neck with his hand. He sat on the bed and felt sleep approaching. He stood, then, and stripped and walked into the bathroom, where he turned the shower on full force. Once under the stinging pressure of the water, he felt his muscles relaxing.

After nearly ten minutes, he dried himself off and unpacked. He put on a civilian suit and an old topcoat he hadn't worn since he'd left Washington. Then he went down to the lobby, bought a bottle of aspirin, and took three.

He walked west on Forty-second Street and turned in to Grand Central Station. In the first phone booth, he put in a call to Picket in Washington.

"Skilling? Where are you?" asked Picket.

"New York," replied Skilling.

"You're in New York?"

"Yeah. I'm at the airport."

"What in hell are you doing in New York?"

"They're here."

"What's your colonel say?"

"He doesn't know I'm here yet."

"Why don't you catch a plane for Washington. We'll talk about it."

"Don't play dumb, Picket," said Skilling. "I'm going to kill that bastard."

"You're not using your head, Skilling. You can't go around like some damned avenging angel. Get a grip on yourself."

"I let a CIA man talk me out of killing Eddie once before. Not this time."

Picket didn't speak for a moment. Then he said, "Listen, Skilling. All right. We know about you and your little talk in Saigon. The talk with a friend from up north, you understand?"

"I understand."

"He brought some Oriental friends of his in on this matter."

"I know. He told me. But they can't move here."

"To a point, Skilling. But we don't know what point. Now listen to me. Listen. I'll come to New York and meet you. Out in the open, no tricks. Tonight for dinner. Okay?"

"Why?"

"I think I can square things with your colonel. You may never go higher than a lieutenant, but I can keep you out of Leavenworth."

"Will you help?"

"Yes."

"All right. I'll have dinner with you."

"And I'd like to bring Colonel Lancto with me. It'd make things easier on both of us."

"Do what you want. When and where?"

"The Hotel Algonquin. Seven o'clock."

"I'll be there," said Skilling. "But I can't promise I won't kill that son of a bitch if I see him." Skilling slammed down the phone and leaned back against the glass wall of the booth. His headache was nearly gone, but he still couldn't seem to think clearly.

He walked outside and hailed a cab. "Where to?" asked the driver.

"Which way does Tenth Avenue run?" asked Skilling.

"Uptown," said the driver.

"I want you to go over to Tenth Avenue and drive slowly uptown. Okay?"

The man shrugged. "It's your money," he said and turned out into traffic.

Skilling hadn't known what to expect at 1185 Tenth Avenue. But the feeling he felt was disappointment. The cab drove slowly past the building. The blank front revealed nothing. There were only two people in the entire block, one a woman shuffling along with her head down and the other a man picking his teeth in front of a cheap diner.

"All right," said Skilling. "Just keep going on uptown, but you can pick it up a little."

"Where to uptown?"

"Take me to One Hundred Twenty-fifth Street."

The man shook his head. "Hey, I'm not supposed to go that far north. I—"

Skilling spoke sharply. "Damn you, move," he said.

Perhaps the driver heard the hate and anger in Skilling's voice. Or perhaps he decided to quit for the day and drop Skilling on his way to the cab barn in the Bronx. Whatever the reason, he drove to 125th Street without another word.

Skilling walked to the address Eddie Palmer had said was home on his army papers. Skilling was cold and felt very foreign in the black ghetto. The building's numbers were nearly obscured by wear, and the front of the structure was dotted with aerosol graffiti. He climbed the stairs and stepped inside, past the first door to the street. He studied the line of mailboxes, found no Palmer. One paper nameplate said E. Johnson, Supt. He pushed the buzzer.

There was no answering buzz, instead, the inner door to the hallway opened. A muscular black man moved into the frame. "You want somethin'?" he asked.

"I'm looking for someone," said Skilling. "Mrs. Palmer. Elizabeth Palmer."

"She don't live here."

"Her son, Eddie, is an army buddy of mine," said Skilling. "I'm trying to locate Eddie."

"Mrs. Palmer move 'bout a year ago. She live in Mount Vernon. On Third Street. Eight Twenty-one Third Street."

"Thank you," said Skilling. He turned to leave.

"You just missed seein' Eddie."

Skilling stopped. "He was here?"

"My boy talked to him three or four days ago. He was lookin' for Mrs. Palmer, too. I guess he and his momma don't write much."

"You know how it is, sometimes, in the army," said Skilling. "So, your boy gave Eddie his mother's address?"

"Yep." He nodded his head.

"Thank you very much. Thank you." Skilling wondered suddenly if he should tip the man, give him something. But the door shut, and Skilling was alone in the small entryway.

He hurried out onto the street and made his way to the 125th Street station of the Penn Central. He bought a ticket to Mount Vernon. The train pulled in then, and he boarded it. In twenty-five minutes, he had arrived in Mount Vernon.

He knocked on the door. "Who's there?" asked a female voice.

"I'd like to see you, Mrs. Palmer," called Skilling.

"What about?"

"Can I talk to you?"

The door opened a crack. One eye viewed Skilling. "What you want?"

"Is your son Eddie here?" asked Skilling in a low voice.

"Edward? No, he not here. He live in New York."

"I'd like to find Eddie. It's important. Could I have his address?"

"You the police, ain't you?"

"No," said Skilling. "We were in Nam together. Just a personal thing. I owe him some money."

247

She opened the door fully now. "You the police. Don't surprise me none. Always a big shot. He come in here few days ago throwin' money around and sayin' he rich. Only reason I took it was for Jesus. But you ain't gettin' the money back. No. I give it to the Lord."

"I don't want the money back, Mrs. Palmer. And I'm not the police." But he knew he'd never convince her. "Just tell me where Eddie lives, please, and I'll be on my way."

"He livin' in New York. Didn't say where. He ask about his sister. He toss me the money. He say he gonna start a war, gonna blow up West Point. He throw me some more money like it was dirty. The spirit of the Devil is in that boy. If he let Jesus in his heart, he be a good man. I try to beat Jesus into him when he was a boy, but it never take. He bad."

"Did he say he'd be coming back to visit you?"

"He not comin' back. He can't face me and the Lord. The Devil and Jesus don't get along. He not comin' back."

"He didn't say anything about where he might be staying."

"No."

"Thank you, Mrs. Palmer."

She closed the door. It was 1:35 P.M. when Skilling arrived back at his hotel. He undressed, flicked the night lock, and put in a wake-up call for 6:00 that evening. He fell asleep listening to the cold wind rattle his window.

He awoke knowing something was amiss. His watch said it was 6:52. He leaped out of bed. The desk hadn't called him at 6:00.

"Jesus," he said aloud. "Dammit." He moved to the bathroom but decided not to shower. He quickly dressed and hurried out of the hotel.

The cold air surprised him again, shocked him out of any sleep hangover. He lowered his head and pulled his coat collar up, shifting his shoulders to raise the collar up to cover his ears. He hurried west toward the Hotel Algonquin.

At 7:35, he stepped into the lobby, his face red now with the night cold. He wondered, briefly, if he was walking into a trap,

248

if the room was salted with MPs, waiting to lead him out to a court-martial and prison. He was greeted, however, by a wave of friendly chatter of people, unaware of cold nights, of an invasion force somewhere in the city.

He moved past the desk and stepped into the cocktail area of the Algonquin. Near the back, he saw a man stand up. Picket. He moved toward him. Colonel Lancto was seated, waiting.

"My God," said Picket, holding out his hand, "I was afraid you were dead somewhere."

Skilling shook his hand. "Sorry I'm late," said Skilling. "Nothing important. Just overslept." He turned to Lancto. "Hello, sir," he said.

"Skilling," said the colonel.

The lieutenant sat and ordered a Canadian Club and soda. The other two men waited until his drink had been served. Then his superior said, "All right, Skilling. What in hell is going on?"

Skilling leaned back and took a sip of his drink. Then another. For the first time since he'd come to New York, he was beginning to feel warm. "Yes, sir," he said.

He talked for nearly twenty minutes. Picket and Lancto interrupted only occasionally, to check a point, to straighten out a name. The only piece of information he held back was the address of the warehouse. He admitted to being told only that a warehouse on Tenth Avenue was rented. But he gave them so much information they didn't make a point of it. When he was finished, he was just emptying his second drink.

"A can of worms, for damn sure," began Lancto.

"It's one hell of a story," Picket said.

"You say 'story' like it's a something I invented," said Skilling.

"I just mean it's a little difficult to believe," replied Picket. "But, hell, I believe it. I have to. I've got other evidence to back it up."

Lancto waved his hand for another round of drinks. "I'll be straight with you, Lieutenant," he said. "I came here at Picket's insistence, and I was ready to burn your ass. At the very least, you were going to leave the place a private. But I'll tell you, I'm not so sure you haven't acted right. I don't hold with your personal manhunt, but under the circumstances, you got a good argument for everything you did."

"Thank you, sir," said Skilling.

"You're still going to have to answer for all of this, though," said the colonel.

"I'm prepared to do that, sir," said Skilling. "I understand what I did was, well, unorthodox? But it seemed like my only course of action, given all the facts."

"So," said Picket, "where does that leave us? Somewhere in the city are some fanatics."

"Killers," said Lancto. "Imagine what a handful of trained soldiers could do in New York. Why, Christ, they could hit and run until they damned near shut the place down. Shut it down."

The waiter came up with the new round of drinks, and they all sat back, silent for a moment. Then Skilling said, "So, now what?"

"We've got to stop those people," said Lancto.

"How?" asked Picket.

"I think it's an army matter," said Lancto. "Military Intelligence should be notified tonight."

"How about the FBI?" asked Skilling.

Picket shook his head. "We need court orders and Christ knows what else for them. It'd take time, and even then, they might pull out if things began to look sloppy. I think you're right, Colonel. It's a military operation."

"Trouble is," said Lancto, "how do we locate the bastards?"

"If I can locate them, sir," said Skilling, "how soon can you move on them?"

"Can you locate them?" asked Lancto.

"I can," Skilling replied. "I know I can. I know how Eddie Palmer operates. I know his moves, his strengths."

"His weaknesses," picked up Lancto.

"If he has any," said Skilling. "But assuming I can locate them, how soon could you move?"

"Well," said Lancto, "we could put together a strike force. I'm afraid you couldn't be a part of it, Skilling. You might accompany them, sort of an observer, an expert." Skilling nodded. "We'd have to notify the New York City police, clear with Washington."

"How soon?" asked Skilling again, gently pressing.

"Shouldn't take more than a week to assemble the troops, get all the go-aheads," said Lancto.

Skilling lifted his glass and took a long swallow to cover the anger that flooded into his brain. By the time he'd put the glass back on the table, he was in control again. "That seems like a long time, sir," he said. "It seems to me that every minute counts here. It'd be a fine mess if we let that invasion force make a strike while we sat around collecting ourselves."

Lancto looked at Skilling. "A week, Lieutenant. A week if I knew this minute where they were holed up."

"Yes, sir," Skilling said. "I guess it would take that long, considering everything."

"Skilling, what in hell do you have in mind?" asked Picket.

"Mind? Sleep, Picket," said Skilling. "About ten lovely hours of sleep."

"Let's have some dinner," said Picket.

"Would you mind if I pass?" asked Skilling. "I'm bone-tired. I wouldn't want to drop off in the middle of the soup course."

"Go ahead," said Lancto. "Where are you staying?"

"The Commodore Hotel," said Skilling, pulling out his room key. "Room eleven-oh-six."

Picket and Lancto both smiled. "Hell, Lieutenant, go to bed," said Lancto.

Skilling pushed his chair back and stood up. "Thanks for everything, sir," he said. "Picket, thanks for the drinks."

"My pleasure," said Picket.

"I'll be talking to you in the morning," said Lancto. "I'm

headed back for Washington tonight. I think you'd better join me tomorrow."

"Yes, sir," said Skilling. "Is it any warmer there?"

"For you, Lieutenant," said Lancto, "it's hotter'n hell." He laughed.

Skilling smiled and turned and left the Algonquin. He headed directly for the Commodore, went to the front desk, and left word there that he didn't want to be disturbed. He then went back out onto Forty-second Street and caught the crosstown bus to Tenth Avenue.

He walked to the corner across from the warehouse, feeling the chill of the weather and a coldness of fear. It was partly being this close to his enemy and partly being alone at night on a nearly deserted city street. He pushed the fear from his mind, made himself take hold, convincing himself the jet lag and the whiskey were talking their toll.

The warehouse, the entire street, looked deserted. He stood in a doorway, staring at the warehouse. Waiting. Then he moved toward it, crossing the street, moving against the wind racing down the avenue. He stepped up to the door of the warehouse, looking at it, seeking some sign of his enemy.

He wanted to try the door but thought better of it. He knew it would be locked, and he also knew Eddie could be inside, waiting in the dark to finish the job he had bungled in Marseilles. He stepped out and walked around to the side of the building and found another door, a large one used for loading and unloading. There was nearly an inch-high crack under the door, and it showed only darkness inside. He then circled the block, fixing the area in his mind.

He decided then that he'd done all he could. He walked, despite the cold and the darkness, all the way back to the Commodore. It made him feel better, tiring his muscles. His feet felt sore, and his legs ached, but his head was clear.

In his room, he put in a call to the overseas operator, to Sergeant Logen in Saigon. The operator said there'd be a six-hour wait. Skilling stretched out on the bed, turning on the black and white television set in his room. It seemed to him that the only way to pick up Eddie's trail was to keep watch on the warehouse. He decided it was useless to push either Lancto or Picket. They were both locked in a paper prison. Skilling remembered when he'd made every move according to the gospel of the army manual. It seemed a long time ago.

He picked up the phone again and told the operator he wanted a 5:00 wake-up call and to make certain his call to Saigon would be put through.

The operator assured him his call would be put through no matter what time. She then informed him he already had another wake-up call for 6:00. Skilling sighed and told her to move it to 5:00. He lay back. There was a news program on television.

The telephone woke him at 4:37. It was the overseas operator with his call. He turned off the now-blank television screen and waited. In less than five minutes, Logen was on the phone.

"Sir, is that you?" asked Logen, his voice echoing strangely over the wire.

"It's me," said Skilling. "What's up?"

"I've got something. I didn't know what in hell to do. Where are you?"

"I'm at the Commodore Hotel in New York. What is it?"

"Your boy Eddie. He sent six Chinese rocket launchers to the States. I've got a positive ID from a lieutenant in Information."

"I don't understand, Logen."

"He went to Army Information in Saigon posing as a lieutenant from Abrams's staff and said the general wanted to send some war souvenirs back. They helped him, and he sent the damn things off. They're there now."

"I'm a little dense, Sergeant. Where?"

"He sent them to American Legion posts as souvenirs, sir," said Logen. "Three around New York and three in California."

"Jesus Christ," said Skilling. "Do you know the posts?"

"Got a pencil?"

Skilling found a ball-point pen and a small pad. "Go ahead."

Logen read the names and addresses of the posts to Skilling.

He copied them with care, repeating each one. When he was finished, he said, "God, I hate that bastard. Do the American Legion posts know?"

"I only just found out, sir."

"What are the pieces?"

"Chinese, sir. They're 107 millimeters. They were first used by the VC in 1968. Small. Easily fired by one man. But they can blow hell out of whatever they hit."

"Range?"

"Six miles."

"He really is going to start a war."

"Take it easy, sir."

"How'd you find out?"

"The general started to get letters of thanks back from the posts. So they checked it back."

"All right. Anything else?"

"No, sir. We're doing fine. How are you?"

"Okay. Say hello to everyone. I'm off after Eddie now. Wish me luck."

"Good luck, sir."

"Good-bye," said Skilling.

"Good-bye, sir."

Skilling put down the phone. It was nearly 4:45. He decided to get started. He had to move. Now. No looking back. Eddie Palmer was on the verge of declaring war.

He borrowed a map from the night clerk and located the three towns where rocket launchers had been sent. The closest one was in Ossining, New York. Then Skilling remembered what Mrs. Palmer had said. "He say he gonna start a war, gonna blow up West Point." Ossining wasn't within rocket range of West Point, but it was close. Very close.

Skilling stood on Tenth Avenue for nearly three hours, stomping his feet, rubbing his hands. Then a station wagon pulled up and stopped in front of the warehouse. It was driven by a Vietnamese. Out of the passenger side stepped a man Skilling identified as Cleon N. Walker, a known member of

Eddie's gang in Saigon. Apache Joe, he was called.

Walker knocked on the warehouse door, and it was opened by someone inside. Walker entered, and the door closed. The Vietnamese pulled the station wagon around to the loading door. Skilling's hands were shaking, but he was no longer cold.

For thirty minutes, Skilling watched the station wagon being loaded with various crates and boxes. He suddenly realized, as the loading door was being shut, that the Vietnamese was about to drive off. He looked around for a taxi. There were few cars and no cabs. The station wagon pulled around the corner and headed up a block and stopped for the light. Skilling could wait no longer.

A red Pinto waited at the stop light close to him. A woman was alone in the car. He moved quickly to the passenger door. She saw him just as he started to reach for the door handle. Instinctively, she reached to lock the door, but she was too late. Skilling leaped in beside her, one hand in his coat pocket.

She was young. Fear showed on her face. "Police business," said Skilling.

The woman shook her head. "No," she said.

The light turned green. "I have to have this car," Skilling said. "Drive. You'll be all right." He poked his finger at her from his pocket, and she jumped. "Move," said Skilling.

She stepped on the accelerator, and the car leaped forward, about two blocks behind Tri's station wagon. Tri drove north, and the woman followed. She didn't seem aware the station wagon set the course; she only did as she was told.

When Skilling saw Tri stop for a parking space on Second Avenue after crossing on 122d, he told the woman to pull over. Instead, she stopped the car in the middle of her lane. "Dammit, lady," shouted Skilling, "pull over."

She pulled the car close to the curb at a bus stop. Skilling opened the door and stepped out. He leaned over to speak to the woman, but she stomped on the accelerator, and the car careened south on Second Avenue, moving crazily through cross traffic as she ran a red light at 121st. She barely missed

Tri's station wagon, and Skilling cursed the woman. If she only knew how important it was, he thought.

Fortunately, Tri didn't seem alarmed by the woman. He locked the car and tried all the doors. Then he walked toward 121st. Skilling waited until he turned the corner and then hurried after him. He reached the corner as Tri disappeared inside a storefront church.

Skilling walked on across the street and leaned against the building around the corner. A flush washed over him. Eddie Palmer. This time it would be different. He pushed off the building and walked, head down, toward Lexington Avenue and a subway entrance. No mistakes this time.

He found a phone booth. "Picket. This is Skilling."

"Lancto has been trying to reach you at the hotel, Lieutenant," said Picket. "Better check in with him. He's getting nervous."

"I've located them," said Skilling.

"You have? Wonderful. Get up here, and we'll start making plans."

"The time for bullshit is over, Picket," said Skilling. "You and Lancto or whoever you want get a force together. You hit their place tonight. That's it."

"Wait a minute, there, Lieutenant," said Picket. "You don't—"

"I'm taking care of the warehouse," interrupted Skilling.

"How?"

"Oriental help."

"Damn you, are you crazy? Yes. You are."

"Maybe. But that's it. I need you to take their other place. I can't do it alone."

"Out of the question. But we can talk. I'll meet you. Where are you?"

"If you don't move, Picket, I won't wait. I'll start shooting myself. I can get a gun somewhere. Somehow. And I'll start shooting. There'll be a lot of fire. There'll be even more explaining to do. But it's tonight. And that's it."

"You'll get twenty years for this, you bastard," yelled Picket.

"The house is on One Hundred Twenty-first Street between First and Second Avenues. It's the fourth one from the corner of First Avenue. It's a storefront church. I'll be in the area to make sure nobody slips out early. If they do, I'll let you know. If they don't, good hunting."

Picket was calmer now. "Skilling, listen to reason."

"Tonight."

"Skilling, I can't. Good God."

Skilling cut off the connection.

A woman answered the second call.

Skilling spoke slowly. "I would like to speak to the person in charge of your security. My name is Lieutenant Gerald Skilling, and I've recently arrived from Saigon."

"I'm sorry, sir," said the woman, "but we have no one in security."

"Suppose I told you I'd planted a bomb in your building," said Skilling.

"One moment, sir," she said. The line went dormant as she put Skilling on hold. In a few seconds, a man's voice said, "May I help you?"

"My name is Lieutenant Skilling. I am calling you about Colonel Linh. Do you understand me?"

"Colonel Linh?"

"Of North Vietnam."

"Hold on, please." Again the line went off. The wait was longer this time.

Then another voice. "Hello."

"My name is Lieutenant Skilling."

"Who is your sergeant?"

"Sergeant Logen."

"You had a meeting the other day. Describe it."

"It was in a sidewalk café. The man I spoke to had no hair and wore—"

"Very well," interrupted the voice. "What is it you want?"

"I need help," said Skilling. "My people are moving too slowly. Colonel Linh is about to hit."

"How can I help? We are new to your country, and we want no problems."

"There'll be problems if I tell the authorities that Linh is working out of your place, with your 107s."

The man was silent. Then he said, "What help do you need?"

"There is a warehouse. The address is eleven eighty-five Tenth Avenue. It is guarded. It must be taken care of."

"When?"

"Tonight."

"Tonight," said the voice. "Do not call again." The connection clicked off.

Eddie Palmer lay with his hands clasped behind his head. Things were going sour. He could smell it. He had checked into Linh's Long Island target and had found that the Grumman factory the colonel picked for destruction manufactured, not military airplanes, but motor homes. His damn war would be laughed out of the country. And the George Washington Bridge. Jesus Christ, he thought.

So he'd been promised all the skag. All right. He could get rid of it, sure. Slowly would be best. But you never did know with those dope dudes. He pushed 'em pretty good the first time, and they wouldn't forget it.

Linh was like an old boxer he thought. He been hit in the head so much he's punchy. It was punchy to even start this gig, but, what the hell, it got him back to the States.

Eddie sat up. Light from the street filtered in the window, and he looked at his watch. Just about 1:00 in the morning. He could hear the heavy breathing of the men around him in the room. He got up and walked to the window and looked out on 121st Street. What he saw made his eyelids blink and blink again.

There were two men moving across the street, keeping to the shadows. But it was unmistakable. They were carrying guns.

Eddie slipped on his clothes. He hurried down the stairs to the first floor. A Vietnamese was on guard near the door, and Eddie smiled and waved to him and turned back toward the back of

258

the building. He opened the cabinet containing some weapons, took out an M-16 with a silencer, and moved back toward the front of the building. His angle allowed him to see over to First Avenue, and he saw other men moving into position. He'd have to hurry, or they'd cover the back. He aimed at the Vietnamese standing guard and pulled off a shot. The Vietnamese's mouth opened, and he then slipped to the floor with barely a sound.

Eddie then moved quickly to the safe and opened it. He stuffed money in his pockets, all they could hold. He then opened a rear window and dropped out to the backyard. He stayed in the one spot, listening. Nothing. He moved across to a wooden fence and flipped over it into another backyard. He had seen all the yards from the second-floor vantage point, and he knew where he was moving. The next fence was smaller. Then through a yard littered with garbage, and he kicked a can. The noise echoed about, but he couldn't wait. He kept moving.

In this yard, there was an exit alongside the building. He hurried down it and out onto 120th Street. He nearly started out onto the street when he spotted the flare of a match in a car parked near his panel truck. Two men were outlined in the flame. He ducked down and kept cars between himself and their point of view. He worked around behind them and cut across the street. Now he was at his panel truck. He kept moving. Eddie could see them now. One of the men, a nonsmoker, had rolled down his window a crack. It was through this crack that Eddie put the barrel of his M-16. He pulled four shots, *pfft, pfft, pfft, pfft.* One never even turned his head.

Eddie then walked back to his truck, unlocked it, and slipped in. He put the M-16 on his lap and started the motor.

Then he heard gunfire. He pulled out of his spot and turned north on First Avenue.

Skilling watched the attack from a vantage point across the street. He hid in the doorway of an apartment building, and he'd been there for nearly two hours. He'd begun to think Picket wouldn't attack, but at 1:00, he saw some men move into the street carrying guns. He leaned back in the shadows and waited, conscious of the noise of his breath.

The men worked efficiently, and there seemed to be no noise from them. Eddie's building was dark. It took ten minutes for the men to get into place. Then they moved in.

They were in the building before anyone inside seemed to know. Skilling couldn't believe their good fortune. There had been no guard on the door.

There began a series of shots. He listened. Light shots. A heavy one. Riot gun, perhaps. Rapid fire. M-16 or AK-47. Sounds too light for an AK-47. Now a barking type. A .45.

Then all was still. He peeked out. Several people were on the street. Police sirens could be heard in the distance, but there were already two police cars at either end of the street. The New York cops had evidently been in on the raid.

Then he heard his name. "Skilling." It was Picket, calling. "Skilling, can you hear me? Give yourself up, Skilling. It's all over. They're all dead. They're all dead at the warehouse. It's all over."

His voice vibrated through the street. Windows opened at various spots, but no heads came out. Those people knew better.

Skilling stepped out onto the steps. "Here I am," he said. He saw several men turn toward him, their guns at ready.

"Come on in," said Picket. "You better put up your hands."

"Come on, Picket," said Skilling.

"Do it," replied Picket.

Skilling raised his hands and started down the stairs. A man came toward him and signaled for him to lean against a car, feet back. He quickly moved his hands over Skilling's body.

Picket stood waiting.

"It's clean," the man said.

Then Skilling said, "Picket, for Christ sake, I'm not going to give you any trouble. Just let me see Eddie." He stood, facing Picket.

Picket turned his back. "He got away," he said quietly.

Skilling moved with animal instinct. No one expected him to

260

move quickly or even move at all. He grabbed a rifle from a man about three feet away from him, and he spun the man around, putting the rifle at the back of his head.

The man shouted, and Picket turned at the sound.

"I'm walking out of here, Picket," said Skilling. "Now let me out, or I kill this man. I don't want to, but you know I will. Dammit, don't make me."

Picket called out. "Let this man through."

Skilling began to move. "Did you get the weapons?"

"Yes," said Picket.

"Any Chinese rocket launchers? One-oh-sevens?" Picket didn't answer. "Dammit, Picket. Answer."

"No. Why?"

"I know where that bastard is going," said Skilling. "How'd he get away?"

"Through the back," said Picket. "He killed two men back there. Skilling, tell me where he's going. We'll get him. Don't make it harder on yourself, for Christ sake."

"I can't, Picket. If I'm wrong and I tell you, I lose forever. If I don't tell you, I'll just keep hunting the bastard."

"You need help, Skilling. You're just as bad as he is. Give it up."

"I need a car. A car, Picket."

Picket shouted. "Murphy. Give him your car." Ahead of Skilling, a man opened his car door and stepped out and away. Skilling headed toward the car, keeping the rifle on his hostage. Once there, Skilling slipped in first and then motioned the other man in. "You drive," he told him. "And don't worry. This isn't your fight. Move."

Skilling leaned back as the car started to move. "Swing out onto—" Skilling stopped. A red light was glowing on the dash. The man had left the radio on. Skilling switched it off. Then he said, "Just head north."

Eddie held his rage in check. Who? How? It all went down the fuckin' toilet, and he was left holdin' shit. He cursed aloud. But he kept his speed down and moved along the less traveled highway, northward through various towns in Westchester County.

All gone. The skag, the raids, the life of luxury. How much money? He must have left $200,000 in the safe. He had a little gettin' even to do.

He arrived at his destination at 3:15 A.M. and parked the truck in the lot at the Parker-Bale American Legion Post in Ossining. He had ten rockets in his truck, and he figured on firing all of them. Then what? He didn't know.

There was a single streetlight back where he moved to enter the building. He aimed carefully at it with the M-16, and it popped out, leaving a welcome darkness. He took his gun barrel and hit a window with it. The crash sounded loud. He didn't care. He reached in and unlatched the window and pushed it open. He boosted himself inside.

The Chinese weapon was bolted to the studs in the wall, and Eddie hunted around in the darkness for something to pry the piece loose. He found a hammer in the kitchen, and he began to pry away at the plaster and wood.

He worked feverishly, banging and prying. He got one end loose and then grabbed it and wrenched the other end from the wall. The broken window in the post faced south. He'd fire five shells south and five north, toward his own target, West Point. He was not certain how far away the place was, but he knew the general direction. Tomorrow he could read the papers to see where the shells landed.

He moved back to his panel truck and unloaded the rockets and the electrical system. It was nearly 4:00 when he was ready to fire.

He primed one of the rockets. He slipped it into the barrel and propped the barrel against the windowsill.

Skilling spotted the panel truck. "Stop," he told the man. The man stopped the car. "Now listen," said Skilling, "you get to Picket and tell him where we are. You got a gun?"

"No," said the man.

Skilling patted his armpits. He felt a lump. "Crap," said Skilling. "Gimme. Come on, up." The man raised his arm, and Skilling reached in and took out a small revolver. "I'll put it over there. That'll give me time to get into place. But for Christ sake, don't come in. Just get to Picket. But if you see Eddie Palmer come out of there, kill him. Do you understand. Kill him."

The man nodded, and Skilling opened the car door and slipped out. He didn't close it for fear the noise would be heard. He ran across the street, working toward the American Legion post. Once across the street, he turned back toward the car and held the gun aloft to show the man where he was putting it. Then he moved on around the building, silently.

He saw the rocket barrel being pushed out of a window. He didn't hesitate. With the rifle in his right hand, he grabbed the rocket barrel with his left as flame spewed out of it. The rocket fired nearly straight out.

Inside, Eddie's hand moved toward his M-16. He heard a voice. "Eddie Palmer. It's me. Skilling. You son of a bitch. You didn't kill me in Marseilles."

Eddie remembered, and a chill passed through him. He started to move away from the window, but Skilling had already pulled the trigger. A bullet passed through the wooden frame and slammed into Eddie. He stumbled backward. Another shell hit into the ceiling.

Eddie's vision blurred. He yelled, "You bastard." He stepped to the window and closed his finger on the trigger of the M-16. He felt another bullet from Skilling's rifle cave in his chest. He saw Skilling's face, then, saw it explode, disintegrate from the force of an M-16 shell. Then Eddie Palmer died.

Skilling triumphed. As he died, he knew.